THE KLAATU TERMINUS

THE KLAATU TERMINUS

PETE HAUTMAN

CANDLEWICK PRESS

Copyright © 2014 by Pete Hautman

The epigraph on page vii appears courtesy of The Stanley Kubrick Trust

First paperback edition 2015

Library of Congress Catalog Card Number 2013944132
ISBN 978-0-7636-5405-4 (hardcover)
ISBN 978-0-7636-7675-9 (paperback)

15 16 17 18 19 20 BVG 10 9 8 7 6 5 4 3 2 1

Printed in Berryville, VA, U.S.A.

This book was typeset in Adobe Garamond.

Candlewick Press
99 Dover Street
Somerville, Massachusetts 02144

visit us at www.candlewick.com

For Jennifer, Jen, and Jenny

The most terrifying fact about the universe is not that it is hostile but that it is indifferent.

—STANLEY KUBRICK

PART ONE

CITY
OF
TREES

After the fall of Romelas, the Klaatu artist Iyl Rayn contacted the Boggsian technician Netzah Whorsch-Boggs and asked him to construct a device capable of transmitting Klaatu through time.

Whorsch-Boggs, a slender man with a wispy beard, listened to her proposal, then shook his head.

"You already have the capacity to travel through time. Simply wait for the future to arrive."

"I am more interested in viewing past events," said Iyl Rayn.

"Consult your memories and your histories."

"I wish to witness events of which I have no direct knowledge."

"Feh," said Whorsch-Boggs, rolling his eyes. "If in the future we provide you with a means for traveling back in time, then it follows that you have already succeeded in doing so. Therefore—I repeat myself—you do not need us."

"If you help me, I will compensate you."

Whorsch-Boggs stroked his thin beard. "With what?" he asked.

"Information."

"Unanswered questions sustain us."

"Unanswered questions may destroy you."

Whorsch-Boggs shrugged. "Traveling into the past might destroy us as well. In any case, it is impossible. I cannot help you."

— E³

 1 ON THE FRUSTUM

ROMELAS, *ca.* 3000 CE

"WHAT HAPPENED HERE?" TUCKER ASKED.

He felt Lahlia's shoulders move beneath his arm, a faint shrug.

They were sitting on the edge of the frustum, pressed together, looking out over the ruins of the city. The partial moon had broken free of the clouds, risen high, and now cast a ladder of shadows down the sides of the stepped pyramid. Below, a carpet of treetops tufted through the pale shapes of low stone buildings, spreading in all directions to a dark horizon.

"This was Romelas, the city where I was born as Lah Lia. Later, I returned and became the Yar Lia. Now I am simply Lia."

Tucker tasted the name with his mind. *Lia.* It seemed too short, too small, too slight for this hard-faced girl in her shiny black vest and thick-soled boots. He thought of the last time he had seen her, striding confidently into the tent in Hopewell

Park, where his father and Master Gheen had planned to sacrifice him on their makeshift altar.

"The Romelas I knew is gone." Lia broke a chunk of limestone from the edge of the frustum with her fingers. "This stone is crumbling. The streets have become forests. How long does it take for a tree to grow taller than a building?"

Tucker did not know.

"I've seen no lights," she said, tossing the broken stone down the steps of the pyramid. "No people."

"How long have you been here?"

"Not long. The sun was low when I arrived. For me, it's been only a few hours since I last saw you. In Hopewell." She turned her face toward him. "I knew you would come."

In the light of the half moon, he could see the faint scar inscribing her cheek from the corner of her eye to her jaw. Tentatively, he reached out. She flinched slightly, then held still as he traced the scar with his forefinger. "How did this happen?" he asked.

She touched his chest. "It was the same blade that left that scar over your heart."

"The priest?"

Lia nodded.

Tucker looked into her dark eyes. He wanted to kiss her, but he was afraid she would pull back. He did not want to risk driving her away. She was all he had.

"I jumped into the maggot right after you," he said. "But I ended up back in Hopewell, before I was born. I saw my dad.

And Kosh. When they were younger. Tom Krause was there, too. Then these Boggsians came after us and sent us through another disko. I don't know where Tom ended up. I landed at the Terminus, and I saw Awn, and she said you'd just been there."

Lia frowned. "That was *before* I returned to Hopewell to save you."

"Yeah, that's what I finally figured out. She told me you walked to Harmony to see the Boggsians. I went after you."

"It's good you didn't catch up with me," Lia said. "If you had, I might not have stopped your father from killing you."

Tucker sat with his mouth open for a few seconds, trying to wrap his head around that.

"How did you get here?" Lia asked.

"Well, it's kind of a long story. For a while I was stuck at the North Pole, but eventually I made it to Harmony. The Boggsians were gone, but there was a disko. A Klaatu sent me into it, and I came out here."

Lia nodded slowly. "A Klaatu sent me through a disko as well. There was a Boggsian in Harmony. He had a device for communicating with the Klaatu."

"I wonder what the Boggsians have to do with the Klaatu."

"The Boggsians *made* the Klaatu. They call it *transcendence.* They once tried to make *me* into a Klaatu."

Tucker did not speak for a few moments. He was thinking about how little he really knew about Lahlia. *Lia.* He had once

5

thought her a young girl with a small but mysterious past. Now both she and her past seemed larger.

"The Klaatu knew I was looking for you," Lia said.

"I bet it was the same one. But why did we end up *here*?"

Before Lia could answer, an animal sound rippled up the tiers — something between a snarl and a roar — raising the hairs on the back of Tucker's neck.

"What was *that*?"

"That," said Lia, "was a jaguar."

"There are jaguars here?"

"When I lived in Romelas, there were jaguars in the forests south and east of the city. They ate wild pigs, and sometimes people. The woodcutters would venture into the forests only in pairs."

"But aren't jaguars from South America? I thought this place, Romelas, was the same as Hopewell. In Minnesota. Just a different time."

"In Romelas we grew limes and mangos. I never saw snow until I came to Hopewell in your time. Everything changes. The jaguars migrated north."

She turned again to face him. "As for why the Klaatu sent us here, I don't know. I expect we will find out."

The cry of the jaguar came again. It sounded closer.

"I suppose we should stay up here until it gets light," Tucker said.

"I think that would be a good idea."

They listened to the night sounds drifting up from below.

Lia leaned her head on his shoulder. "In this time, everybody we ever knew is dead."

Tucker thought for a moment, then said, "Kosh was alive when I left him. He's alive in Hopewell."

"I liked Kosh."

"I have to go back," Tucker said. "He's the only family I have left."

Lia gestured to where the disko had been, now an empty place in the air. "The Gate is gone."

"There must be others."

Lia searched his face. Her eyes were enormous.

"I will go with you," she said.

A shadow detached itself from the wooded margin of the zocalo. A mottled silhouette, stealing from shadow to shadow, wove its way across the sapling-studded cobblestones. The jaguar paused at the base of the pyramid and looked up. Tucker could see glints of moonlight reflected in its eyes.

"It knows we are here," Lia whispered.

Tucker exhaled — he had been holding his breath.

"Can jaguars climb pyramids?" he asked.

"They climb trees."

"Oh."

 **2 KOSH**

"DESTINY? MY *DESTINY* IS WHAT *I* MAKE OF IT!" WITH those words, Tucker Feye stepped into the maggot and disappeared in an orange flash. Kosh Feye, holding a Lah Sept *arma* in one hand and a shock baton in the other, blinked back greenish afterimages.

Father September let out a despairing moan. "You have destroyed us all," he said.

"Shut up," Kosh said. He needed time to think. Too much had happened in the past few minutes — the fight with the priests, Tucker blowing off Ronnie Becker's leg at the knee, the shock of seeing Adrian, his brother, transformed into an old man calling himself Father September, the girl Lia jumping into the maggot, and Tucker, who had grown half a foot since Kosh had last seen him a month ago, following her. He looked at what remained of the maggot, a sagging band of pink flesh surrounding the crackling disko.

"Curtis, you don't realize what you've done," Father September said in a shaky voice.

Master Gheen, unconscious on the floor of the tent, groaned and shifted. Kosh jabbed the baton against his neck. Gheen convulsed, then lay still. Kosh walked to the doorway and looked out of the tent at the sea of people gathered in the park waiting for the revival to begin. Some of them were seated on folding chairs; others were sitting on the grass. All of them were undoubtedly wondering what all the commotion in the tent was about. On the steps of the pyramid, the man whom Kosh had knocked senseless was stirring. Kosh closed the tent flap and looked back at his brother.

"Is it true?"

"Is *what* true?" Father September said.

"What Tucker said. That Emily is here."

"That is none of your concern, Curtis."

"If you call me *Curtis* one more time—"

"It is your God-given name!"

"God gave me nothing. My name is Kosh. Where is she?"

Father September's shoulders sagged; he seemed to grow smaller. "What does it matter? We are all lost."

"You might be lost." Kosh pointed the baton at his brother. "I know exactly where I am. What I want to know is, *where is Emily?*"

Father September scowled petulantly. "The woman Tucker saw is at the house where you grew up. It is where she belongs. But she is not the Emily you seek."

Without another word, Kosh turned and triggered the *arma*. A jet of blue flame ripped through the back of the tent. Kosh strode through the smoking gash. A moment later the roar of his motorcycle shivered the tent fabric. Father September groaned and sank to his knees beside the unconscious Master Gheen.

"What have we done?" he asked, but there was no one to answer him.

Kosh hit the park exit at sixty miles per hour. The bike's tires chattered on the washboard surface of the dirt road as a black cyclone of memories, hopes, and fears raged inside his head. Tucker had said that his mother, Emily, was alive, brainwashed by those strange priests. As unlikely as that sounded, Kosh believed him—it was no more insane than everything else that had happened that day, beginning with the sudden appearance of the girl on the roof of his barn that morning. The crazies in the park. Tucker, looking and acting years older. And Adrian— what had *happened* to him? Images flickered and whirled through Kosh's brain: Ronnie Becker's leg, the futuristic weapons now in his saddlebags, the disko, maggot, whatever . . . He had let Tucker follow the girl into that thing. What had he been thinking?

He downshifted as the dirt-surfaced park road curved toward the highway; his back tire skidded and he nearly lost control. *Too fast.* He slowed and turned onto the paved highway, then brought the bike up to a relatively sedate seventy miles per hour. As he came around the bend just north of downtown Hopewell he saw a swirling, twisting gray cloud dancing just off the highway over a field of recently harvested wheat.

Kosh backed off the accelerator. For a moment, he thought it might be smoke, but there was a deliberateness to the cloud, a sense of intelligence and purpose. As he drew nearer, the cloud resolved itself into tiny specks. Kosh laughed at himself. Birds! He was so paranoid from all that had happened, he'd let himself get freaked out by a bunch of birds!

The flock settled onto the field. What were they? Crows? They didn't look like crows—too pale, and there was something odd about the way they flew. He slowed as he came abreast of the field. They looked like big doves, or pigeons . . .

Pigeons! Suddenly he knew what he was seeing. Passenger pigeons. He pulled to the side of the road and stopped.

Kosh had seen a recent news headline about the passenger pigeons, but he'd dismissed it as another unconfirmed sighting. There had been sporadic reports of passenger-pigeon sightings in the Hopewell area ever since Lorna Gingrass had killed those two birds with her car, back in ninety-eight. All the subsequent sightings had remained unconfirmed and, as far as Kosh was concerned, pure fantasy.

This, however, was real. The nearest bird was about fifty feet away from him—a large, blue-gray, rose-breasted creature.

"Hello there," Kosh said.

The bird regarded him suspiciously with one red eye.

"Aren't you supposed to be extinct?" Kosh asked, half

expecting an answer. With all the other weird stuff he'd seen, a talking bird seemed perfectly reasonable.

The pigeon took flight. The rest of the flock followed as if they were all connected by invisible elastic strings. Kosh sat back and watched as the birds twisted and flowed into a bullet-shaped mass and shot off to the east. There had to be thousands of them.

Just one more impossibility piled atop all the others. Kosh wondered if the pigeons had arrived in Hopewell through the diskos. If so, what next? Dodos? Dinosaurs? He shook his head at his own foolishness and dropped the bike in gear. Maybe he was strapped to a hospital bed in some asylum and this was all happening in his head. It seemed as likely as anything. But if what Tucker had told him was true — that Emily was here — he had to see her.

Kosh pulled back onto the highway and headed for his childhood home, thinking about the last time he had seen Emily, almost fifteen years ago. The house came into view. It seemed so small now. As he approached the driveway he saw a young woman with long coppery hair and pale skin standing in the garden. Emily? Kosh's heart filled his chest. As he slowed and began his turn, he sensed another presence and glanced at his rearview. The chrome grille of a truck filled his mirror. Time slowed. With a screech of tearing metal, his bike exploded from beneath him and he was airborne, hurtling toward a spinning sky.

I'm flying, he thought, and then all went to black.

3 THE DEPARTURE

JUNE, 1997 CE

THREE DAYS AFTER KOSH FEYE'S SEVENTEENTH BIRTH-day, he hugged his brother for the last time. Adrian, older by ten years, was an awkward hugger. Kosh wasn't much better. They held each other for about two uncomfortable seconds, then let go and stepped back. Adrian, the taller and leaner brother, nodded to Kosh, acknowledging the relief they both felt at having gotten past that awkward ritual, and the unbreakable bond that remained between them. Kosh faked a punch at Adrian's right shoulder, but Adrian did not respond by fake-punching back. He had become so serious over the past several years. Kosh couldn't remember the last time he had heard Adrian laugh.

"You two are ridiculous," said Emily Ryan, a half smile on her face, tears welling in her eyes.

They were standing on the train station platform in Winona. The Amtrak Empire Builder, bound for Chicago, was about to depart. In Chicago, Adrian would be joining a group of Bible scholars on a seven-month pilgrimage to the Holy Land.

Adrian turned his head toward Emily. "The time will pass quickly," he said, holding out his long arms. "I'll be back by the end of January."

"I know." Emily stepped into his embrace. Adrian Feye's arms came around her like two jointed sticks; his oversize hands flapped against the back of her T-shirt. He kissed her forehead and then, clumsily, her lips. Kosh watched, his mouth curved into a wide smile. He couldn't help it—any emotion other than anger produced a smile on his long, angular features. Kosh hated that about himself. His only family—Adrian—was leaving for the other side of the world, and here he was, grinning like an idiot. He still remembered the time Adrian caught him smiling at their father's funeral. He had only been nine years old then, but still carried the shame of it with him.

Emily, who did not have an awkward atom in her body, squeezed Adrian so hard that Kosh thought he heard ribs cracking. He imagined what it would feel like to be held so tightly by a woman as beautiful as Emily Ryan.

A barely intelligible voice came over the loudspeaker. Time to board. Emily released Adrian.

"God bless you, my love," he said to Emily. "God bless you, too, Curtis," he said to Kosh. "And remember—if you need any help, call the Krauses."

"Or he could call me," said Emily.

"Or call Emily. But do *not*—" His eyes bored into Kosh. "Do not even *think* about driving my Mustang."

"Don't worry," Kosh said. He hated that Adrian didn't completely trust him, but he was unable to stop his mouth from stretching into a grin.

"I'm not kidding," Adrian said.

"Oh Ade, leave him alone!" Emily said. "Kosh has the pickup and his motorcycle. He doesn't need your old Mustang."

Adrian gave a sharp nod, satisfied. Kosh grabbed Adrian's bag, an oversize backpack stuffed to bursting.

"Come on," he said. "You're going to miss the train."

The two brothers crossed the platform.

Adrian stepped up into the train. Kosh handed him the backpack.

Adrian said, "Take care of her, okay? Take her to a movie or something now and then."

"Sure," said Kosh, straining to keep a sober expression on his face.

"Take her shopping. Bring her flowers for her birthday. Tell her they're from me."

Kosh nodded.

"Take care of yourself, too. And the house."

"Don't worry," Kosh said. "I got it."

Adrian held his eyes for a moment, gave another of his sharp nods, then disappeared into the train car.

Kosh walked back to where Emily was waiting.

"I guess that's that," he said.

Emily was staring up at something, a puzzled expression on her face.

"What are you looking at?" Kosh asked.

Emily shook her head and smiled quizzically. "I thought I saw something, like a funny cloud."

Kosh looked up at the cloudless sky.

"I see things when I'm riding sometimes," Kosh said. "Especially at night. But it usually turns out to be something ordinary, like a puff of smoke, or a wisp of fog."

"Greta says I was born with an overactive imagination."

"I think, to Greta, any imagination at all is overactive."

Emily laughed again, a deeper, more natural sound, and gave Kosh a loose-knuckled punch to the shoulder. "I suppose Adrian told you to look out for me," she said. "Make sure I don't get in trouble."

"He said I should take you to a movie sometime." They started toward the parking lot. "Or shopping. We could drive to the Mall of America, up in the cities."

"Hmph. While he's gallivanting all over Israel looking for Noah's Ark or whatever, I get to go to the megamall with a teenager."

"It's better than staying in Hopewell twenty-four–seven. Besides, you're a teenager yourself."

"I'll be twenty soon."

"You're nineteen today."

Emily grinned and bumped him with her shoulder. "I suppose you think I'm too young to be engaged."

"I don't think anything like that," said Kosh.

"Yeah, right."

When they reached Kosh's pickup truck, an aging Ford F-150, Kosh opened the door for her. Being charged by his brother to care for Emily during his absence had stirred up a courtly impulse. Emily gave him a quizzical smile. Kosh grinned and shrugged.

"Thank you, kind sir," said Emily.

As Kosh walked around the truck, Emily reached over and unlocked his door. He climbed in, started the engine, and pulled out of the parking lot. Emily was staring out the window, lost in her private thoughts.

"Do you think he'll change?" Kosh asked.

Emily blinked and licked her lips. "What?"

"Do you think going to Jerusalem and all that will make him even more religious?"

"Adrian?" She shook her head. "How could he possibly be more religious? Besides, people are who they are. Nobody changes, not really."

"I do," said Kosh. "I change all the time."

Emily once again fell silent. After a few miles had passed, she spoke.

"You know, you don't have to babysit me, Curtis."

"Kosh."

"Kosh . . . why do you want people to call you Kosh?"

"I just like it." Kosh was embarrassed to tell her he had stolen the name from a character on a TV show.

"Well, I think it's silly. I'll call you Koshy-poo."

"Please don't," Kosh growled.

Emily laughed.

"So what about that movie?" Kosh asked, to change the subject.

"I wouldn't mind seeing a movie," Emily said, "but all that's showing nearby is that new Jurassic Park movie. I don't want to watch a show about people killing dinosaurs."

"*Starship Troopers* opens in a couple months," Kosh said.

"What's that about?"

"People killing aliens."

Emily made a face.

"We could drive up to Rochester," Kosh said. "See anything we want at the multiplex."

"I hear they're making a movie about the *Titanic.*"

"That's crazy," Kosh said. "Who'd want to watch a boat sink for two hours?"

4 ARUGULA AND GOAT CHEESE

KOSH DID NOT MISS ADRIAN. NOT AT FIRST. AT FIRST, IT was as if nothing had changed. Kosh spent his days working on his bike, riding it when it didn't need fixing, or working at Red's Roost, flipping burgers and frying potatoes. He also had the garden to tend. That spring he had planted nearly a quarter acre of vegetables, everything from asparagus to zucchini. It was more than he could ever eat himself, but he would sell some to Red, and maybe give the rest to his neighbors. It kept him busy.

He kept meaning to give Emily a call. See how she was doing. But the thought of picking up the phone made him nervous. He was afraid that she would be dismissive, or treat him like a kid, like her fiancé's little brother: *Aww, that's so sweet of you to call, Koshy-poo.* Maybe he'd run into her in town someday.

Ronnie Becker provided other distractions.

Kosh had been getting in trouble with Ronnie ever since they had, at age ten, taken Ronnie's dad's tractor on a joyride through the Jensen's soybean field, with the tiller still attached to the back. Rory Jensen claimed they had destroyed five hundred dollars' worth of crop. Adrian, who had recently become Kosh's legal guardian, had paid Rory two hundred and fifty dollars without arguing. Ronnie's old man thought Rory Jensen's estimate was a bit high, and refused to pay. The Beckers and the Jensens had not gotten along so good after that.

Curtis, as he was then known, was only mildly embarrassed by his misdeed. His father had died only a few months before, and he figured the world could cut him some slack.

Ronnie Becker was his best friend, so Kosh wished he liked him better. It was a small community, however, and there were only a handful of guys his age. He could always count on Ronnie to come to him with some harebrained scheme. It was always interesting, at least.

Most recently, Ronnie had decided to become a drug dealer. He'd found a patch of "ditchweed"—marijuana plants that grew wild in the area, but had no kick—and was drying a few pounds of it in an unused shed behind his parents' barn. His plan was to package the worthless weed and sell it to college students.

As usual, once Ronnie got a bug up his butt, he was unstoppable. One day, as Kosh was mowing the lawn, Ronnie rolled up on his Honda.

"Road trip!" Ronnie yelled.

Kosh turned off the mower. "Road trip to where?"

"Kato."

"Mankato?" Mankato was about a hundred miles west of Hopewell. "Why?"

Ronnie slapped the backpack strapped to the back of his bike. "I got fifty ounces of high-quality weed to move."

"More like *low*-quality *ditch*weed," Kosh said.

Ronnie grinned and shrugged. "As far as those college boys know, it's top-quality bud. They'll probably actually catch a buzz off it. Come on, ride out with me."

If Adrian had been home, he might have stepped out of the house right about then, taken one look at Ronnie, and said, "Don't forget you have to work tonight, Curtis."

"I gotta work tonight," Kosh said, channeling his absent brother.

"Come on! We'll be back by four. Tell you what, I'll buy you a burger in Kato."

Kosh thought about the thousands of burgers he'd flipped over the past year at Red's Roost.

"No burgers for me," he said.

"A steak then. Whatever. Come on, it'll be fun!"

Fun, coming from Ronnie Becker, was a rather dubious proposition.

"I got a lot of stuff to do," Kosh said.

"Like what? Hoe the garden? Gimme a break, dude. Break out the wheels and let's go. This is a riding day if ever I saw one."

Ronnie was right. Clear blue sky, gentle breeze, seventy degrees. Kosh imagined himself on the road. He had just tuned his bike. He had a full tank. And if they didn't spend too long in Mankato, he could be back before his five o'clock shift at the Roost.

"Let me get my jacket," he said.

They took the back roads to Mankato, through rolling farmland dimpled with lakes and tufted with patches of woodland. Kosh quickly forgot his qualms and enjoyed the feel of wind sliding over his gloved knuckles, inflating the sleeves of his leather jacket, scouring his cheeks. Usually, Kosh and Ronnie pushed their bikes hard, thriving on the speed and danger, but Ronnie's backpack full of weed made them uncharacteristically cautious.

Ten miles east of Mankato, Ronnie pulled into a roadside rest area. Kosh followed. Ronnie got off his bike and pulled two cans of Leinenkugel's out of his pack. "Beer break," he said, and tossed a can to Kosh.

The last thing Kosh wanted was a beer. It wasn't even noon yet, and they had a long ride home ahead of them. But he didn't want to look like a wuss. He thumbed the pop-top open. A jet of foam shot out, soaking his sleeve.

Ronnie laughed and carefully opened his own can.

"Sorry about that," he said.

Kosh tasted the beer. Warm. Bitter. He wished he had a Coke.

"How are you planning to find customers for your stuff?" Kosh asked, gesturing at the backpack.

"I got this guy says he's got connections with all the frats. Piece of cake." Ronnie poured half his beer down his throat and belched. "Course, it's gonna have to be a one-time deal. Once they smoke a few bowls of my product, they won't be giving me any repeat business."

"So when do I get that steak?"

"Anytime you want, bro."

Kosh sipped his beer, grateful that most of it had foamed out when he opened it.

"How about we eat as soon as we get to Kato. That way if you get busted, I still get lunch."

"Deal." Ronnie drained the rest of his beer, crumpled the can, and threw it in the direction of a trash bin. Kosh took another sip of warm beer, walked over to the can Ronnie had tossed, picked it up, and deposited both cans in the trash.

Ronnie was already pulling out of the rest stop. Kosh hopped on his bike, wondering as he did why he would follow Ronnie Becker anywhere.

On the outskirts of Mankato, they pulled into a crowded parking lot.

"Still hungry?" Ronnie asked, taking off his helmet.

Kosh looked skeptically at the sign above the small building: BURGER BOB'S.

"What about that steak?" he said.

"I heard this place is good. Maybe they have a steakburger."

Inside, Burger Bob's was similar to Red's Roost: a long bar along one wall, a row of vinyl-upholstered booths on the opposite wall, and a scattering of tables between. There was no pool table, though, and it was busier than the Roost—nearly every seat was filled.

Kosh and Ronnie took an empty booth back by the restrooms. A chalkboard menu mounted on the wall listed about thirty burger variations, from the "Plain Burger," to "Bob's Favorite." The more exotic toppings offered included prosciutto, pickled asparagus, and smoked eel. There were a dozen different types of cheese, including Limburger, the stinkiest of the stinky cheeses.

A waitress appeared at their table and cocked one formidable eyebrow. She reminded Kosh of his third-grade teacher.

Ronnie said, "You sell a lot of smoked eel?"

"Every day," the waitress deadpanned.

"How about Limburger cheese?"

"That's for take-out only. What can I get for you?"

"Cheeseburger basket," Ronnie said. "And a Budweiser."

The waitress's left eyebrow climbed another half inch. "Got an ID?"

Ronnie produced a driver's license. The waitress lifted a pair of reading glasses from the chain around her neck, perched them on her beak, examined the license, and handed it back.

"How about a soda," she suggested.

Ronnie grinned and pocketed the phony ID. The waitress turned to Kosh.

"I'll have the goat-cheese-and-arugula burger," Kosh said. "And a Coke."

The waitress scribbled on her pad and whooshed off.

Ronnie said, "Goat cheese and arugula?"

Kosh shrugged. He'd never had arugula or goat cheese before, and he was curious.

"I was wondering about something," Kosh said. "That stuff you got, it's ditchweed, but it's still technically marijuana, right? What happens if you get busted?"

"We're not gonna get busted."

"Just say you did. They can throw you in jail for lousy pot the same as for the good stuff, right?"

"What's your point?"

"Why didn't you just dry some nettles, or alfalfa, or something legal?"

Ronnie looked offended. "That would be dishonest!"

Kosh wasn't sure if he was kidding.

The goat-cheese-and-arugula burger was like nothing Kosh had ever tasted before. The flavors were on the skunky, funky side, but they were fascinating. He took another bite.

"Well?" Ronnie said.

"I like it," Kosh said.

"I can smell it from here. Almost as bad as Limburger."

"I like Limburger," Kosh said.

"You would. Speaking of reeking, how you liking life without Adrian?"

"I like it all right." Kosh was trying to figure out which part of what he was tasting was the cheese, and which was the arugula.

"Hard to believe he's leaving Emily for so long. I bet she hooks up with somebody else. She's a hottie."

"They're *engaged*," Kosh said, irritated.

"Good-looking girl like that, man, if it was me leaving town I'd worry. You think she'd go out with me? A little summer romance before she shackles herself to Adrian?"

"I don't think you're up to her standards."

"Why do you say that?"

"Well, for one thing, you're kind of a jerk."

Ronnie put down his burger and stared at Kosh, then broke out laughing.

"You got a point," he said.

They finished their meal quickly. After the waitress brought their check, Ronnie asked Kosh if he had any money.

"I thought you were buying," Kosh said.

"I am! As soon as we move that weed, I'm golden. I'm just a little short right now."

"How much do you have?"

"Okay, I'm a *lot* short. I'll pay you back as soon as I score some cash."

Resignedly, Kosh paid the bill. He'd half expected that things would go that way. They always did, with Ronnie.

It took them an hour to find Ronnie's guy's apartment, a beat-up fourplex a mile off campus. They parked their bikes under a tree across the street. Ronnie unstrapped his backpack from the bike and threw it over his shoulder.

"Let's do it," he said.

"How about I just wait here," Kosh said.

"What, you want me to go in alone?"

"You get cracked, you're on your own."

For once, Ronnie couldn't convince him otherwise.

"Okay then, but you don't get a cut."

"When was I ever going to get a cut?" Kosh said.

Kosh waited by the bikes as Ronnie entered the building. Half an hour later, he was still waiting. He checked his pocket watch. Two thirty. He had to be at work by five, and it would take him a couple of hours to get back to Hopewell. *Another ten minutes,* he thought, *then I'm out of here.*

Ten more minutes passed. Kosh straddled his bike and put on his helmet. Ronnie was probably sitting in the guy's living room, drinking beer and talking. But if he was in some kind of trouble . . . "Aw, crap," Kosh muttered. He got off his bike and started across the street.

He was halfway there when a cop car rounded the corner. Kosh turned and walked back to his bike, trying to act casual. A second squad car appeared from the opposite direction. Four policemen, two from each car, ran into the building. Kosh started his bike. He rode halfway down the block, then pulled over and watched. Five minutes later, the police emerged with Ronnie and another guy, in handcuffs.

Kosh dropped his bike into gear and took off for Hopewell. Apparently, lunch was on him.

5   THE BIG WHITE DRESS

Emily Ryan feared she was going mad.

Seated on the edge of her bed, she stared fiercely at the big white dress hanging on her closet door. Greta had extracted it from a trunk in the attic three days ago. It still smelled faintly of mothballs. Emily had not yet summoned the courage to try it on.

She shifted her gaze and watched a purplish afterimage form on the white wall. Like a ghost.

Emily did not want to believe in ghosts.

But she kept seeing them. She had been seeing them ever since she could remember.

She looked back at the wedding dress, at the intricate beadwork and lace on the upper bodice and at the ends of the long sleeves. How many hours of a seamstress's time did that represent? She tried to imagine Greta—her small, round, buxom mother—fitting into it. Of course, that had been fifty years ago.

The dress was in extraordinary condition. It had only been worn once. The taffeta skirt was crisp yet pliable, the beads still had their original sheen, and there was no yellowing whatsoever. Greta had stored it carefully in tissue paper in its original box from Dayton's downtown store in Minneapolis. The only flaw was a wine stain above the left breast.

"A perfect place for a lovely corsage," Greta had said when Emily pointed out the stain. Greta had been pestering Emily to try it on ever since. "I know it will fit you, dear. I was just your size when Hamm and I got married."

Emily's only thought at that moment had been that she would never let herself go like Greta.

She stood up and ran her fingers across the beaded bodice. The slick hardness of the beads made her think of chain mail, as if the dress could deflect a bullet. She turned the dress to look at the back. Getting into it would not be easy. She would need help with the loop fasteners—again, like donning a suit of armor. Getting it off would be just as difficult. The thought of being trapped inside it made her shiver.

Emily thought she knew what love was. Hamm and Greta loved each other. But theirs was a gentle, daily, practical love. They loved her, as well, with the tender, protective love that parents have for their children. And she loved them back.

But what of Adrian? She had seen the sudden, melodramatic love that swept away many of her school friends—almost a parody of the burning, all-consuming love depicted in movies and on television—but she had never experienced it for herself. Did she *love* Adrian? She cared for him, certainly. She was attracted by his self-confidence, his masculinity, his harsh good looks, and most of all by his desire for her. Sometimes she could feel it coming off him, that hunger. But did she *love* him?

When they walked through town arm in arm, she felt proud.

When he fixed his eyes upon her, she felt beautiful.

When he spoke of his dreams and plans, she felt inspired.

If that was love, then, yes, she loved him.

Still, the thought that there might be something more, something missing, something she had never experienced . . . gnawed at her.

A few days after Adrian left, Emily had tried talking about it with Karen Jonas, her best friend from high school. Karen, who had gone out with more boys than Emily could count, had laughed at her.

"You want something that doesn't exist," Karen had said. "Look at me. I'm going out with Stan Elkin. Chances are I'll marry him. Do I love him? Eh. But I know I can make him into a lovable guy if I work at it. He's going to college up in Saint Paul next year. I'm moving in with him."

"You're going to *live* with him?" Emily feigned shock though in truth she was not at all surprised.

Karen shrugged. "Think of it as a test run."

"I don't think Adrian would go for that."

"Probably not," Karen agreed. "Anyway, you two are officially engaged. That's way better than being in love."

Now, staring at the big white dress, Emily wasn't so sure.

The three weeks since Adrian left had been the emptiest weeks of her life. Nothing but long days of working at the Economart, evenings of doing nothing at all, and endless nights of lying awake and thinking about what life would be like for her once she got married. She no longer hung out with Karen or any of her other girlfriends. Their lives revolved around their boyfriends or ex-boyfriends. Now that Emily was engaged to Adrian, she had entered another phase.

In part, she knew, it had to do with the fact that Adrian was almost a decade older than her. And that he wanted to be a preacher. Once they'd become engaged, her girlfriends had stopped talking about sex—or anything remotely sinful or interesting—in Emily's presence. It was as if Emily had suddenly become older, alien, part of the adult world. The future wife of a future preacher. Excluded. And she was only nineteen.

A prickling sensation at the back of her neck made her turn to the window. Hovering just outside the glass was another person-shaped cloud. She squeezed her eyes closed, counted to ten, then looked again. The cloud was gone. She stepped to the window and lowered the blind. She certainly wasn't going to change clothes with a ghost watching her. Even an imaginary ghost.

She had once mentioned seeing them to Adrian. He had suggested prayer, or an eye doctor, in that order.

That didn't make the ghosts any less real. She had thought about talking to her doctor, but she didn't feel sick or crazy, and she didn't want any pills. These days, she kept what she saw to herself. Mostly. But at the train station in Winona, when she had seen another one of the strange, cloudy figures, she had mentioned it to Kosh and he had taken her seriously. He was the only one who listened.

She wished he would call. He'd said he would. She would love the distraction of a movie or a trip up to the cities for some shopping. And she *liked* Kosh. He talked to her like a regular person, and he was funny. In some ways he reminded her of Adrian, but in most ways he was so different that it was hard to believe they were brothers.

She should just call him. Emily regarded the phone on her bedside table. It would be the same phone number as Adrian, but Kosh, not Adrian, would answer. She wondered how he was doing, taking care of things on his own. He's only seventeen, she reminded herself. Not even out of high school. But he seemed older, more mature than she was in many ways. As far as she knew, he'd never had a long-term girlfriend, but girls liked him. Even Karen had once confessed to having a crush on him. He was the closest thing Hopewell had to a bad boy rebel biker. Except for Ronnie Becker, who was just a pathetic delinquent and not nearly as good-looking as Kosh.

She'd heard a rumor that Ronnie had been arrested in Mankato a week ago. Kosh would know. She would have to ask him. She looked again at the phone, then laughed at herself for being so tentative. He was just a teenage boy. Her future brother-in-law. What was she fretting about?

* * *

Kosh was working in his garden when Emily pulled into the driveway. He looked up and waved as she got out of her car.

"Hey!" He stood up and wiped his hands on his hips.

Emily smiled, feeling self-conscious in her red and white Economart smock, complete with name badge.

"I was just on my way to work," she said. "Thought I'd stop by and see how you're doing all on your own here."

"Doing fine. What's up?"

"Nothing." Emily looked at the newly seeded row. "What are you planting?"

"Arugula," Kosh said. "I'm growing it for the Roost."

"You're kidding. Red Grauber is serving *salads?*"

"Actually, it's for a new burger. Arugula and goat cheese."

"Now I *know* you're kidding!"

"Seriously, I had one in Mankato. Amazing."

Shaking her head, Emily walked down the rows, checking out his tomatoes, Swiss chard, lettuce, and summer squash. She stopped at the herb bed.

"Lavender!" She bent down and ran her fingers through the frondlike leaves. "What do you do with it?"

"I just like the way it looks."

Emily smelled her hand. "Mmm. You could make potpourri."

Kosh crossed his arms. "I don't *think* so."

Emily laughed. Kosh looked embarrassed.

"Have you heard from Adrian?" he said abruptly.

"Just a couple of postcards. He's in Jerusalem. He sent me a picture of the Wailing Wall."

"That sounds like Adrian."

Emily straightened up. "I have to get going. But I was wondering . . . do you still want to see a movie?"

"Really?"

"I'm not doing anything next Friday. *Men in Black* is opening in Rochester. It's about aliens. You like aliens, right?"

"I do," said Kosh.

6 MEN IN BLACK

THIS IS NOT A DATE, EMILY REMINDED HERSELF.

She was just going to a movie with her fiancé's little brother. But it was the first time she'd been out on a Friday night since Adrian had left. Actually, since a long time before that. Adrian was not big on going to movies and so forth. He would be more likely to take her to some church-related event — a Bible discussion group, or if he was feeling adventuresome, charity bingo at the church in Ghentburg.

She checked herself in the mirror. Jeans and a plain pink T-shirt. Was the T-shirt too tight? She took it off and replaced it with a sleeveless white blouse. It was hot and humid outside, but the theater might be cool, so she draped a cotton sweater over her shoulders.

In the kitchen, Greta was kneading a ball of sourdough, as she did every other night. Emily would wake up in the morning to the aroma of fresh-baked bread. Greta looked up at Emily, askance. "What are you all dressed up for at this time of night?"

"Night?" Emily laughed. "It's six o'clock!"

"Hmph!" Greta lifted the ball of dough and slapped it back on the butcher-block table. She and Hamm were usually in bed by eight.

"I'm going to a movie," Emily said.

Greta pursed her lips, which caused the entire bottom half of her face to become a whorl of wrinkles. Greta was seventy-five, nearly four times as old as Emily. She'd been sixty when she and Hamm had adopted Emily, who was four then, or maybe five—her exact birthdate was a mystery. Fifteen years ago, Hamm Ryan had found her huddled in the overgrown bushes beside the boarded-up hotel in downtown Hopewell. No one had ever found out who her parents were, or how she had come to Hopewell. After some legal wrangling, Hamm and Greta had formally adopted her. Emily remembered none of that, although she had fragments of memories—or perhaps dreams—from her life before Hopewell.

"With who?" Greta asked.

"Curtis Feye."

Greta gave that a moment, then went back to her kneading. It was her way of communicating disapproval, but not such severe disapproval that she felt the need to say anything.

"Adrian assigned him to take me to a movie now and then," Emily said.

Greta shook her head, indicating that she would say nothing more. Emily went out to the front porch to wait for Kosh. Hamm was sitting on the swing, smoking his pipe. Emily sat down next to him and let the sweet smell of his aromatic tobacco tickle her nose.

"Hey, kid," Hamm said around the stem of his pipe. Decades of smoking had left him with a permanent depression in his lower lip, where the pipe now rested comfortably. Hamm was even older than Greta.

"Hey, Hamm," Emily said. They both lapsed into comfortable silence, as was their custom.

A few minutes later, Emily heard the buzz of a motorcycle approaching. Kosh pulled into the driveway and got off. "I'm sorry," he said. "The clutch burned out on the pickup." He held up a helmet. "I brought an extra helmet."

Greta stepped out onto the porch. "Young lady, you are not getting on the back of that thing."

"I'm not?" Emily said.

Greta, having said her piece, shook her head.

"We could take your car," Kosh said. "Or make it another night."

Emily had ridden on a motorcycle exactly once before, when she was a junior in high school. It had terrified her, but she'd never forgotten the thrill of it. Maybe it was time to try it again.

Emily looked at Hamm.

Hamm took his pipe out of his mouth and pointed the stem at the motorcycle. "Used to have one of them myself," he said. "Took Greta for a ride and she hasn't forgiven me yet."

"Did you crash?" Emily asked.

"Nope. Just went fast as the devil." He set the pipe back in his lip groove and nodded. "Back in the day."

Emily was shaking when she climbed onto the back of the motorcycle, but by the time they hit the third curve on their way out of town, her arms locked in a death grip around Kosh's waist, her fear became exhilaration. Her life was in his hands, and she realized that she trusted him absolutely. As they sped down the rural highway, she had a sense that they were encased in a bubble of invulnerability.

Of course, she knew that a flaw in the roadway, a blowout, a drunk driver, a deer crossing the road—any of these things could send them hurtling into a ditch—but at the same time, she was sure that nothing could happen to them. It made no sense, but it was true. She gave herself up to the wind and the snarl of the engine and the hum of the tires on asphalt, and for a time she did not think about her life, or about Adrian, or of ghosts.

7   MEN IN BLACK 2

THE SUN WAS SETTING AS THEY WALKED OUT OF THE theater.

"That was the silliest thing I've ever seen," Emily said.

"You didn't like it?" Kosh said.

"I loved it!" They crossed the parking lot to Kosh's bike. "Adrian would have hated it," she said. "He doesn't believe in silliness. Or aliens."

"Do you?" Kosh asked as he handed her a helmet.

"Well, I don't know about aliens, but I've seen ghosts."

"Really?" Kosh put his helmet on and swung a leg over the motorcycle.

"Maybe they're just in my imagination, but that doesn't make them less real."

"I guess so. Do you ever think that everything you see is, like, a projection of what's inside your head?"

"Every day," Emily said. "I believe in men in black, too. I've met them. Only they didn't look like the guys in the movie."

Emily had an odd expression on her face. Kosh wasn't sure if she was kidding.

"What *did* they look like?" he asked.

"Like they were Amish."

"Maybe they *were* Amish."

"Maybe . . ." Emily was staring at the helmet in her hands, and showed no inclination to climb on the bike.

"Are you okay?"

Emily smiled, but her brow remained furrowed as she remembered the two men who had attacked her when she was a little girl. She hadn't thought about them in a very long time.

"I was seven, I think," she said to Kosh. "I was riding my bike when I saw something on the road. Like a big fuzzy glass disk. I thought it was really weird, but I didn't know enough to be scared."

Kosh regarded her with a puzzled expression.

"Then these two men stepped out of the disk—it was like a hole in the air—and they started walking toward me. I'd seen Amish people before, but they were always riding in their carts, not coming out of nowhere like that. Anyway, they walked up to me and said something I couldn't understand. Then one of them grabbed me off my bike and wrapped his arms around me really tight, and the other one had this clear plastic rod in his hand. I think I screamed, and he stuck the rod in my mouth. He kind of moved it around a little, then pulled it out. Then they let me go and walked back to the disk and disappeared."

Kosh said, "This is something that really happened?"

"It's what I remember. You don't believe me?"

"I didn't say that. But you got to admit, it's kind of strange."

"Hamm and Greta didn't believe me either. But they took me to Dr. Harmon and he checked me over. You know, to see if I'd been molested or something. It was awful. But all he found was a little scratch on the roof of my mouth. Greta told me I must have dreamed the whole thing, but it didn't seem like a dream to me."

"I wonder what they wanted," Kosh said.

Emily felt a flood of gratitude. "Thank you," she said.

"For what?"

"For pretending to believe me." She put the helmet on her head and climbed onto the bike behind him. Moments later, they were on the highway, riding into the sunset.

8   MEN IN BLACK 3

KOSH TOOK IT EASY ON THE WAY BACK TO HOPEWELL. When he was riding alone, he never thought about having an accident or getting hurt, but with Emily on the back, he found himself driving much slower than usual. That story about the two men made him suddenly see her as a little girl, the same way he sometimes thought of himself as a little kid in a big, clumsy, hairy body. He felt protective. And a little scared.

What had really happened? He believed her — or believed that *something* had happened, something that had scared her badly. She may have seen some Amish men. But Amish men stepping out of a magic disk? Little kids had vivid imaginations. And what was all this stuff about ghosts?

He was hyperaware of her arms wrapped around his belly, and her body pressed against his back — a seven-year-old girl in a woman's body, still frightened by something that had happened so many years ago. He wondered if she'd ever told that story to Adrian.

Lost in thought, he was surprised to see that they were already coming up on Hopewell. He felt Emily's grip loosen slightly as he slowed and rolled onto Main Street. He pulled over in front of Red's Roost.

"You hungry?" he said, looking back at her.

"Grill's closed," Red said, jerking a thumb at the clock behind the bar. Ten o'clock.

"Come on, Red," Kosh said. "I'll clean up. You don't have to do a thing."

Red Grauber's features contorted into a scowl. He looked at Emily. "What are you doing hanging out with this reprobate?"

"You mean my future brother-in-law?" Emily said with a grin.

Red snorted, then shook his head. "How is Adrian, anyways? You heard from him?"

"He sent a postcard," Emily said. "He's says he's fine."

"How are your folks? They know you're frequenting my little den of iniquity?"

Emily looked around. Henry Hall was slumped at the end of the bar, a dead, forgotten cigar wedged between his fingers, staring into a flat schooner of beer. Henry was only thirty-five or so, but he looked as if he'd been drinking since the dawn of time. Jake and Ivy Anderson were filling the back booth—spilling out of it, almost—eating French fries and drinking orange sodas. A lean man with a long nose and a cigarette in

43

his mouth was shooting pool by himself. One of the Petersen brothers. Otherwise, the bar was empty.

"Is this what iniquity looks like?" she asked.

"Iniquity, Hopewell style," Red grumbled.

Kosh was behind the bar, scraping the grill clean.

"I suppose he's gonna make you one of his goat burgers," Red said. "Four days I've had that thing on the menu. You know how many I've sold? Five. Four of them to Henry."

"Your best customer," Emily said.

"Oh yeah? You know how long he's been nursing that beer?"

Emily laughed and managed to get a rare smile out of Red. She hiked up onto a stool and leaned her elbows on the bar.

"Can I get you something?" Red asked.

"What do you have that goes with arugula and goat cheese?"

"You twenty-one yet, honey?"

"You know I'm not, Red."

"How about a lemon soda? It'll cut goatiness."

While Red searched under the bar for a soda, Emily watched Kosh cooking, fascinated by the way he moved. Normally, Kosh was tentative and awkward—unless he was on his motorcycle. Now his movements were efficient, precise, almost graceful. His long fingers formed the meat patties and skipped them onto the hot grill. As the meat sizzled, he sliced disks from a log of soft white cheese using a thin knife. He used the same knife to cut open two buns, then fetched a bag of greens from the cooler.

Red set a bottle of Sprite on the bar in front of Emily. "I

gotta say, for a shiftless reprobate, the kid knows his way around a grill."

"I heard that," Kosh said as he picked through the arugula.

"Has good ears, too," Red said.

Kosh put the split buns facedown on the hot grill. He salted and peppered the burgers, flipped them, then placed a thick disk of cheese atop each patty. He watched the burgers sizzle for half a minute, then grabbed a handful of arugula and arranged it on the grill in two hissing piles. He was moving quickly now—it seemed everything was happening at once.

"How about you grab me a couple baskets, Red?" Kosh said.

"What, am I your galley slave?" Red grumbled, but he took two red plastic serving baskets from a shelf. He laid a square of parchment over each one and set the baskets on the prep table next to the grill. Kosh piled the slightly wilted arugula leaves on top of the cheese and turned off the grill. Seconds later, Emily was looking at a perfectly prepared hamburger, skewered with a jaunty cellophane-tipped wooden pick.

"Voilà," said Kosh.

"Thinks he's French now," Red said sourly. But Emily could hear the pride in his voice.

"Thank you," Emily said. "That was delicious."

"I sort of have Ronnie Becker to thank for it."

"Ronnie?"

"Yeah. He took me to this burger joint in Mankato. I stole the idea from them."

"What happened to Ronnie, anyway?"

"Oh, he's back home now. He has a court date next month. He got caught selling weed. Or trying to sell it. Funny thing was, it was just ditchweed. About as likely to get you high as corn silk."

"You were with him?"

"I was along for the ride."

"Told you he was a reprobate," Red said. There were only the three of them still in the bar. Henry had stumbled out after Red refused to refill his beer. The pool player and the Andersons had left as well.

"I told him it was a dumb idea," Kosh said. "Not that Ronnie ever listens." He stood up. "I suppose I should get you home."

Outside, the temperature had dropped several degrees. Main Street was dead quiet. Red's Roost was the only nightlife in downtown Hopewell, and Red usually closed up by eleven. Kosh and Emily stood on the sidewalk, enjoying the feeling that they had the town to themselves. Across the street, the shuttered Hopewell House loomed.

"Sad that the old hotel isn't open anymore," Emily said.

"The freeway bypass killed it," Kosh said. "It closed the year I was born. I suppose they'll tear it down eventually."

"Such a nice building. I wonder if—what was *that*?"

A thumping sound echoed across the empty street.

"Sounds like it's coming from the hotel," Kosh said. "Maybe a bird or something got trapped in there."

46

The thumping came again, followed by what sounded like muffled curses.

"That doesn't sound like a bird," Emily said.

Kosh started across the street. Emily followed.

The front entrance to the hotel had been boarded up with sheets of painted plywood. The sound seemed to be coming from there. They stopped a few yards away. Someone inside the hotel was hammering on the door and shouting. It didn't sound like English. Kosh could see the plywood flexing, chips of paint flying from its surface.

"Sounds like somebody's stuck in there." Kosh raised his voice. "Hello?"

The banging stopped for a moment, then resumed at a more frantic tempo. Kosh tried to think where he could find a crowbar at that time of night.

"Why doesn't whoever it is come out the same way he got in?" Emily said.

"I don't know." He moved closer to the door and yelled, "Just hang on. I'll get a crowbar or something!"

The response from inside was a guttural roar of unfamiliar words and more banging. After a moment, it stopped.

"Maybe you should go back inside the Roost," Kosh said. "Tell Red to call the sheriff, just in case."

"You come too," Emily said, grabbing his arm.

Before they could move there was a tremendous crash. The plywood split and a man wearing a long black coat blasted through the opening and tumbled face-first onto the sidewalk.

His black hat flew off and landed in the gutter. The man lay still for a few seconds, then groaned and pushed himself up. He crawled over to his hat, put it on his head, and stood.

The man was normal height, but he looked bigger with the black coat hanging off his wide shoulders, the black, wide-brimmed hat perched upon his head, and the long black beard reaching halfway down his chest. He shook himself like a wet dog. His dark eyes cast about wildly, then locked onto Kosh and Emily. He flung his arms wide and shouted, *"Vaht shtot? Vaht jahr?"*

Kosh said, "Are you okay?"

The man tipped his head. His brow furrowed. *"Vaht?"*

Kosh took a cautious step toward the man and said, "What?"

"Da! Vaht!" the man said, stamping his right foot.

Kosh looked back at Emily. "Can you understand him?"

Emily's face had gone dead pale. Her mouth was working, but no sound was coming out.

The man stamped his foot again and tugged at his beard. *"Vaht jahr! Vaht jahr?"*

Kosh shrugged and turned his hands palms up. "I don't know what you're saying!"

The man shook his head in frustration and started toward them.

Emily, backing away, looked utterly terrified. Kosh put himself directly between them. If he had to hit the guy, he would.

The man stopped a few paces short of Kosh. He looked at Kosh's balled fists.

"Ach!" He threw up his hands, turned his back, and went running off down the street. He cut through Friedman's parking lot and headed toward Engleman's soybean field.

"Just some crazy Amish dude," Kosh said, forcing a laugh. He turned back to Emily. She looked as if she was about to collapse. He rushed over and put his arm around her just as her legs failed. Her eyes had rolled up, showing only the whites.

"Emily!" Kosh shouted. She blinked and her eyes regained focus.

"Kosh?" Her legs found the ground. She stood. "I'm okay," she said.

Kosh realized he still had his arms around her and quickly let go.

"Are you sure? You fainted or something."

"I just . . ." She drew a shaky breath. "That man. You know that story I told you, about the men sticking the rod in my mouth?"

Kosh nodded. He knew what she was going to say.

"He was one of them."

9 ON THE FRUSTUM

"THEY ATTACK ONLY PEOPLE WHO ARE ALONE," LIA SAID, gripping Tucker's arm. "At least, that's what the Lait Pike told me."

The jaguar was sitting on a tier halfway up the pyramid, staring at them fixedly.

"Maybe this one can't count," Tucker said. He stood up and waved his arms. "Go away!"

The big cat blinked, but made no move to depart.

"We have you outnumbered!" Tucker yelled.

The jaguar yawned.

Tucker picked up a shard of black stone from the broken altar.

"What are you doing?" Lia asked.

Tucker remembered throwing a rock all the way across Aamold's cornfield back in Hopewell. It had sailed the length of two football fields. The jaguar was a lot closer than that. If he could hit it, he figured it would hurt enough to scare it away. *If* he hit it.

"Don't make him mad," Lia said.

The jaguar's ears perked up. It stood, its tail twitching.

Tucker focused on the cat's center of mass. He drew back his arm and hurled the chunk of obsidian with all his strength. The rock streaked down the side of the pyramid. He could hear the slap of stone on flesh. The jaguar let out a screech and jumped straight up. It twisted in midair, its legs churning, and landed running, descending three tiers with each stride. It reached the plaza and disappeared into the urban forest.

Tucker grinned, pleased with himself. Lia was giving him an uncertain look, as if she didn't know him.

"The Medicants did something to me," he said. "I can throw really hard."

Lia nodded thoughtfully. "I noticed."

Tucker had hoped she would be more impressed. He sat down beside her. "I suppose we can't stay up here forever," he said.

"We should try to sleep. You first. I will keep watch."

"I don't think I can sleep." The way he felt at the moment, he didn't think he would ever sleep again.

"Then I'll rest, and you watch for beasts." She lay back on the hard stone surface and curled on her side, using her forearm as a pillow.

Tucker wrapped his arms around his knees and gazed out

over the lightless city. After a time, he stood and walked around the perimeter of the frustum. Returning to where he had started, he stopped a few feet away and looked down at Lia, a dark comma on the crumbling limestone.

Why do I feel so tied to her? he wondered.

Other than the few days she had stayed with him and his parents—days when she had hardly said a word—they had spent only a few hours in each other's company: that night at the rope swing, the day he had entered the disko on his parents' house, and those few horrific minutes in the green tent at Hopewell County Park.

Lia muttered and shifted. He had an urge to lie down beside her, to nestle his body around her like a spoon and hold her. But he didn't want to wake her, and she might not like it. There was a tension in her, he sensed. A coiled spring of fear and anger. He thought of all the things he did not know about her. Did she have parents? Did she miss being a Pure Girl—whatever that was? Was she homesick for the old Romelas? What had happened to her between the time she first left Hopewell and the time she showed up to save him from Master Gheen and his father? Would she tell him?

Soon his thoughts were circling back on themselves. He had achieved his goals, in a sense. He had found his father, then lost him. He had found his mother, but she was not the mother he knew. He had met his uncle, Kosh, then abandoned him to his fate. And he had found Lahlia. Now they were alone in this strange place, hundreds—or maybe thousands—of years in the future. Images of Hopewell flickered through his mind: his parents, the old hotel, the rope swing, Tom and Will Krause. He wondered if Tom had made it back to Hopewell. But most of all he wondered what had happened to Kosh.

He looked at Lia, at the moonlight reflecting from her scarred cheek, and he thought how beautiful she was; and for a moment none of the rest of it mattered. So far as he knew, they were alone in this world.

No matter what happened, he would not let himself be separated from her again.

PART TWO
FRAGMENTS

*Chayhim, representing the Klaatu faction known
as the Gnomon, noticed a number of disturbing
anomalies in the collective memory of the Cluster.
He brought his concerns to the artist Iyl Rayn.*

*"The timelines are splitting," said Chayhim.
"Hopewell is fragmenting. This is your doing."*

*Iyl Rayn dismissed Chayhim's statement with
a vaporous shrug. "People adapt; the beasts notice
nothing."*

*"Not all are able to adapt. The Lah Sept seek
to alter their own history. Tucker Feye is running
rampant through time. I fear for my own continued existence."*

*"Tucker Feye is the through line," said Iyl Rayn.
"All else will fall into place."*

"This I doubt."

"You must have faith, Chayhim."

— E^3

10 MEMORIES

Tom Krause visited Hardy Lake nearly every day, even if it was cold and raining. He sat by the cottonwood and stared up at the limb where Tucker had tied the rope. There was no rope. He walked the narrow beach, searching in vain for signs of exploded fireworks. He looked out over the lake, and at the empty air above the water.

He remembered. But he could find no evidence to support his memories.

On the few days when he did not visit the lake, he could sense his memories fading, becoming less real. That frightened him. It was like losing part of his life.

The day Tom had returned from . . . from wherever he had been, Father September had vanished from the jail. His empty cell was locked, and according to the police, the door had not been opened.

The other man who had been arrested, the one called Master Gheen, had escaped from his cell within hours of being locked up, but Gheen's escape was not so much of a mystery. One of his associates had entered the county lockup pretending to be his lawyer, disabled the two policemen on duty with some sort of stun gun, and the two had driven off in a black SUV.

There was much talk of Father September being a charlatan magician, a master of stage tricks. That would explain how he had vanished from his cell, and how he had faked stabbing Tom in the heart. The search for him was perfunctory and soon over. Immediately following Tom's reappearance, the district attorney had dropped the charges against Father September, and so there was no compelling reason to pursue him.

Tom sat on the bank above the lake and rubbed his chest. He could still feel a faint ache where the blade had sliced through his rib cage.

He had tried to get Will to remember.

"Don't you remember when you and me and Tucker hauled that rope out to the lake? And Tucker climbed up the tree and tied it?"

"Who is Tucker?" Will had said, giving him a suspicious, nervous look. As if he thought Tom had gone completely insane.

Maybe he *was* insane.

But he *remembered.*

# 11 EMMA

KOSH FEYE THOUGHT HE WAS DEAD.

He had imagined his own death many times—crushed beneath a semi, or flattened against a bridge abutment, or being T-boned by a drunk running a stop sign. There were many ways to die, but he had always assumed that for him, it would be on his bike. There were worse ways to go. Better to die violently at seventy miles per hour than on a bed in a nursing home plugged into a catheter and an oxygen mask.

He remembered the truck that had hit him. The grille in his rearview mirror was the last image he carried in his brain.

It was a very odd feeling, being dead. The main sensation was that of no sensation. He did not seem to have a body. Except for his ears. There was a sound, a sort of frantic, unintelligible chatter coming from far away. Other dead people? As he became more awake, he discovered another sensation. He seemed to be breathing. Dead people breathed?

It occurred to him to open his eyes, just to find out whether he still had them. With that thought, his eyelids popped open and sunlight came crashing in. He was looking up at the branches of a tree, and beyond it blue sky, and he wondered whether it was possible that he was not dead after all. He tried to turn his head, but that didn't work. Except for breathing, hearing, and looking at the tree, he had nothing.

The voices got louder. A woman's voice, and a man's. They were speaking a language that sounded like a mishmash of Spanish and English, with some Asian-sounding words thrown in just to make it more confusing. One thing for sure, they were arguing.

Kosh summoned his will and made another unsuccessful attempt to move. He could not feel his body at all. Was he *paralyzed? Oh my god,* he thought. *I've broken my neck! Severed my spinal cord.* His worst fear. Far worse than death. He'd been ready to embrace being dead, but not this.

Now he could feel his heart pounding.

The woman was yelling at the man. The man was shouting back at her. How could they be arguing when Kosh was laid out on the ground, his life over? What could be more important than that?

"Váyase!" the woman shouted. "Go!"

Seconds later, Kosh heard the roar of an engine and the sound of spinning tires. The leaves on the tree stirred; Kosh felt a cool breeze on his face. A shadow fell across him and his view of the sky was eclipsed by a woman's face. He tried to speak, but he could not.

Emily.

"He is gone," she said.

Kosh would have nodded if he could, though he did not know whom she was talking about. He moved his eyes from her wide mouth to her eyes — that blue-green color was seared into his memory. He remembered Emily smiling, the way her mouth would stretch and her eyes would almost disappear. She was not smiling now.

Her hair was different. Shorter, and maybe a shade lighter. Her brow was furrowed more deeply than he had ever seen it. Still, impossibly, this was Emily.

"I am Emma," she said. "You have been injured."

He wanted to ask her why she was speaking with an accent and why she called herself Emma, but he could only stare back at her, waiting to hear the next thing she said.

"I know you cannot speak. I have applied a pain blocker to your spine. Tamm was very upset with me. He believes the devices we took from the Medicants should be used only by the priests, and only to save Lambs. He would have let you die. He *wanted* you to die."

Why? Kosh asked with his eyes.

She seemed to understand him. "Tamm said you attacked Father September and Master Gheen. Is that true?"

Kosh stared at her helplessly. Her accent and manner of

speaking were nothing like Emily at all. And if she *was* Emily, she had not aged a day in fifteen years.

"Even if it is true, it was wrong of him to hit you with his truck. I do not understand all this violence. Are you a violent man? I sense that you are not, but I do not understand why I think that. I do not understand why the priests killed all those people on the zocalo. I could smell their flesh burning. I do not understand why the Yars fought us on the pyramid. There was a boy here this morning. Tamm attacked him, and the boy became violent, I think because he was afraid. He said this was his house." She looked at Kosh closely. "The boy looked like you. I do not understand any of this, but I could not let Tamm kill you."

She seemed to be talking more to herself than to him. Kosh figured the boy she mentioned must have been Tucker.

"You were unconscious," she said. "You flew so far and landed so hard. I'm sure Tamm intended to kill you. I convinced him to leave, but I know his anger will grow, and he will be back. You cannot stay here. I am going to turn the pain blocker off now." She stared into his eyes and put her hand behind his neck. "I do not know how badly you are hurt. Brace yourself."

Kosh heard a soft click. Emma sat back, watching him as sensation flooded his body. For a moment, it was a tremendous relief to feel again, then every nerve in his body lit up. The pain rocketed from his spine to every extremity. He gasped.

Emma, alarmed by his reaction, reached to turn the device back on.

"Don't," Kosh croaked. The worst of the pain was on his right side—a hot, stabbing pain that could only mean broken ribs. He'd broken ribs before, when he'd fallen off his barn. The ribs would heal. The pain would pass. He moved his legs. That hurt too, but knowing that he could move them made up for the agony.

Slowly, carefully, he sat up. His lower back felt as if it had been pounded with a sledgehammer. He looked at his hand. His ring finger was bent back at an impossible angle, dislocated. Kosh knew if he thought about it he'd chicken out, so he quickly grabbed the finger with his other hand, pulled it straight, and popped it back in place. He almost passed out. Or maybe he did pass out, because the next thing he knew he was on his back looking up at the tree. Emma was leaning over him.

"I'm okay," he said. His voice cracked. He held up his hand. The finger was swollen like a boiled sausage, but it was back in place. He sat up again, letting Emma help him. "I want to stand," he said.

It took several tries, but soon he was balanced on his feet, unsteadily. He could feel his pulse in his swollen finger, and his ribs were bands of agony. Looking around, he discovered what was left of his motorcycle wrapped around the trunk of a basswood tree about twenty yards away.

"I should be dead," he said.

"It is a miracle," Emma said, still with her hands on his arm.

"If it was a miracle I don't think it would hurt so much." He disengaged his arm and took a step. His legs seemed to work okay, but he felt as if the earth were undulating beneath his feet. "Who is this guy Tamm?"

"He is my husband."

Kosh nodded, taking it in like a pillow punch to the gut. "You say he'll be back?"

"Yes. But I will not let him hurt you again."

"Who *are* you?" he asked. "I know you're Emma, but where did you come from?"

"I am not supposed to say."

"You're one of them, aren't you? Those people in the park."

Emma nodded. "I am the Lamb Emma."

"So what are you doing here? At my brother's house?"

"It was assigned to us." She cocked her head. "Was that your brother who was here? The boy who looked like you? The one who said it was his house?"

"That was my nephew, I think. Why aren't you at the park with the rest of them?"

Emma looked away. "I do not like what they do. Even in Romelas I refused to attend the sacrifices."

Romelas? The girl, Lia, had told him she was from Romelas, supposedly in the distant future. "Do you know a girl named Lia? The Yar Lia?"

Emma shook her head. "The Yars are violent, wicked people."

Kosh smiled. "I don't know about wicked, but yeah, she's violent all right. How about Tucker Feye?"

"I . . . I know *of* Tuckerfeye."

"He's the boy who was here. Emily Feye is his mother. You look exactly like her."

"I am not her," she said.

"Then you must be her sister."

"I have a sister?"

Kosh took a few steps toward his wrecked bike, then stopped. There was no way that machine would ever roll again.

"You must leave," said Emma. "Tamm will come back."

On the grass, next to the wreckage of his bike, he saw the silver tube weapon he had taken from the priest.

"Let him come." Kosh limped over to the wreckage. As he bent down to pick up the weapon, blood rushed to his head and the world began to whirl. Black fuzz crowded the edges of his vision. He dropped to his knees, willing himself to come out of it, but the earth pulled him insistently downward, and everything went away.

The Lamb Emma looked at Kosh, sprawled facedown on the lawn, his arms flung to the sides. The blades of grass next to his mouth were moving. He was breathing. For a few seconds, she stood there undecided, then she rolled him onto his back, grasped his legs, and dragged him toward the house. He was a big man, almost twice her weight, but after several starts and stops, she got him to the porch, up the shallow steps, and inside. She tried to lift him onto the sofa but he was too heavy, so she left him on the floor and put a soft pillow under his head. She soaked a dish towel with cold water and laid it across his forehead. She considered the Medicant device, then decided not to use it. Whatever pain he was experiencing, he seemed able to handle it.

She went outside and picked up the *arma*. She had never before held one, but it looked simple to operate. There was only one button. She hoped she wouldn't have to press it.

Back inside, she sat beside Kosh. He was still asleep. His legs were twitching, and he was smiling. Emma wondered what he was dreaming about.

12 POTPIES

"Chicken potpies," said Emily, wiping her hands on her apron. "Come on in!"

The Ryans' home had a friendly sort of disorderliness. A large terra-cotta pot by the door held a motley collection: two umbrellas, a hand-carved walking stick, a garden hoe, and a broom. The living room furniture was mismatched and casually arranged. Not messy, but not rigid, either. He could smell the chicken cooking and a trace of Hamm's aromatic pipe tobacco. It felt like a place one could kick back and relax. There were books everywhere, most of them stuffed into bookcases built from old barn wood. Greta Ryan was a voracious reader, while Hamm was known as a man who let nothing go to waste.

"Your folks home?" Kosh asked.

"They went to an auction over in Zumbrota. They'll be back late."

Kosh followed Emily into the kitchen. He hadn't seen her since the night they went to the movie, two weeks ago. The night they had seen the man in black burst out of Hopewell House. Kosh felt bad about not calling. He'd meant to, just to see how she was doing, but it had felt too awkward. Every day since, he'd intended to call, but somehow never got around to it. Then, that morning, she had called and invited him to dinner. To pay him back, she said, for the goat-cheese-and-arugula burger.

Kosh watched her open the oven door and peek in at the five small pies baking on the center rack. "Another half hour," she said.

"Why five pies?" he asked.

"One for me, one for Hamm, one for Greta, and two for you."

"I get two?"

"You're big."

"Can I help?"

"You want some lemonade?"

"Sure."

Emily tossed him a lemon. "Start squeezing."

Happy to have something to keep his hands busy, Kosh set about making lemonade while Emily washed salad greens from the garden. It felt odd, in a good way, to be working alongside her. He wondered if it would be like this for her and Adrian once they got married. He tried to picture it: his brother making lemonade, squeezing a lemon with one hand, holding the

Bible in the other, Emily smiling as she sprayed cold clean water on the lettuce leaves.

In an effort to be nonchalant and clever, Kosh said, "So, you seen any ghosts lately?"

The smile fell from Emily's face. Kosh felt a familiar jolt of nausea, the way he always felt when he said something wrong or stupid. Quickly, he backpedaled.

"I mean, I was just thinking about what you said. I see stuff sometimes. Especially at night."

Emily turned to him, drying her hands on her apron. "The ghosts I saw had faces, and I was looking right at them. In broad daylight." She set her jaw, daring him to disbelieve her.

Kosh said, "Wow."

" 'Wow' like 'Wow, she must be insane'?"

"No! Wow like, just . . . wow."

Emily laughed and turned back to the sink to shake the water off the lettuce.

"One thing for sure," Kosh said, "that guy we saw was no ghost. Chuck Beamon saw him too, running across his soy field the next morning. Said the guy was being chased by a big pink pig. Like, *really* pink."

Emily's shoulders went stiff. *"Maggot,"* she whispered.

"Maggot?"

Emily laughed uncomfortably and shook her head. "I don't know where that came from. Probably some fairy tale from when I was little."

"I never heard of a fairy tale about maggots."

Emily shrugged as she piled the greens into a wooden bowl. "I guess I haven't, either. How's that lemonade coming?"

Kosh dipped his finger in the pitcher and tasted it. "A little tart."

"I like it that way."

While the pies baked, they sat on the front porch and drank their tart lemonade. Emily was good at talking about little things, a skill Kosh lacked. She told him about Hamm's latest project: making birdhouses out of coffee cans. She caught him up with the latest Hopewell gossip: Lorna Gingrass's divorce, the Friedmans talking about sending their daughter to a private school in Minneapolis, a family of opossums that had taken up residence in the old silo. Mostly things that were of little interest to Kosh, but he loved watching Emily talk, and the sound of her voice. She was sitting sideways on the swing, while Kosh leaned back in Hamm's homemade rocking chair. Although there was a wicker table and three feet of space between them, he had the sense that they were very close in a way that was more intimate than when she had been pressed against his back on his motorcycle, or when she had sat next to him in the movie theater. Maybe it was because he could see her eyes.

"Kosh?" She was leaning forward, looking at him intently.

"What?"

"You looked like you'd gone away for a second."

"I was just thinking, um, about what you were saying."

Emily cocked her head. "What *was* I saying?"

Kosh laughed self-consciously. "I have no idea."

Emily drew back in mock outrage, then burst out laughing. Kosh joined her, confused and—inexplicably—happy.

"Those pies should be ready about now," Emily said.

The potpie was delicious. Kosh didn't think he could eat two, but then he did.

"Can you show me how to make this?" Kosh asked as he savored the last bite of crumbly crust and tender chicken.

"As long as you promise not to put any arugula or goat cheese in it."

"I promise."

After dinner, they walked out to the raspberry hedge. Kosh asked her if she remembered anything about the day Hamm had found her.

"It's the strangest thing," she said. "I remember I was hiding in some bushes and crying, and this man walked over to me and squatted down and began talking to me. You know Hamm; he's half deaf now and talks like a foghorn, but on that day his voice was soft and quiet, and I felt safe right away."

"Do you remember how you got there?" Kosh asked.

"Not really. I don't remember anything about my life before Hopewell, except I remember *remembering*, you know? I remember remembering that I lived in a palace, and I was a princess." She laughed. "Isn't that silly? I guess every little girl wishes she was a princess. And I remember remembering that an angel came and took me through a magic door. But it's not like I really remember it; it's more like a dream. You know how you wake up and you think about a dream you just had, and later you don't really remember the dream itself but you remember thinking about it?"

Kosh nodded.

"I feel like my life before Hamm found me was chopped off, like it ended, and then started up again. I don't even know how old I am, not really. Hamm and Greta just picked a day and called it my birthday."

"Maybe you're actually forty-five," Kosh said.

Emily threw a berry at him.

They picked and ate berries until the mosquitoes drove them back to the house. Emily made a pot of strong black coffee and they talked into the night, about everything and nothing.

Hamm and Greta arrived home at eleven. Hamm had bought himself an old 1930s Ford tractor. Kosh helped him back it off the trailer and into the barn, where it joined Hamm's collection of seldom-used vintage farm equipment. Greta and Emily watched, clucking amusedly at the foolishness of men.

That night, as he lay in bed, Kosh thought about how his father's death had cut his life in half. His first ten years now seemed like a remembered dream. He wondered if it had been like that for Adrian when their mother had died. When Adrian and Emily married, would their lives end and start yet again? How many lives was it possible to live?

13 THE KLAATU FACTORY

ROMELAS, *ca.* 3000 CE

LIA OPENED HER EYES. THE SUN WAS PEEKING OVER A jagged horizon. Trees, as far as she could see. She sat up, stiff from sleeping on the hard stone surface, and looked for Tucker. He was standing a few yards away, at the edge of the frustum, looking down. Lia followed his gaze. A layer of mist lay pooled on the zocalo, snaking in and out of the broken buildings, filling the forest city.

Lia stood and stretched. Tucker saw her and said, "Good morning."

"Did you sleep?" she asked.

He shook his head. "I've been thinking."

Lia walked over to stand beside him. "About what?"

"We're in the future, right? Years after when you lived here, and even longer since Hopewell. But it's all one place."

"I think so."

"And when we were in the forest where Awn lives, that had to be even further in the future, because the pyramid was half buried."

"If it was the same pyramid."

"I'm pretty sure it was. And there were Boggsians there. So maybe there are Boggsians here."

Lia nodded reluctantly. Her experiences with the Boggsians had been mixed.

Tucker said, "I mean, I don't know where else we're going to go. I haven't seen any sign of people here. No smoke or anything. You know what else I haven't seen? Klaatu."

"They come and go," Lia said.

"Yeah, usually when something awful is about to happen."

"Then let's hope we don't see any."

Once the sun had burned away the morning fog, Tucker and Lia climbed down the steps of the pyramid to the overgrown zocalo. Tucker kept a rock in each hand. It wasn't much in the way of weapons, but it was all they had.

Lia wanted to check out one of the deteriorating buildings around the perimeter of the overgrown zocalo. "It's the Palace of the Pure Girls, where I grew up. There might still be something edible in the food storage area."

They passed though a crumbling entryway, stepping over the rusted skeleton of a gate. Inside, the floors were littered with decades of debris: dead leaves, dried mud, fallen stone, animal scat, and broken things that Tucker could not identify. The walls were mottled with mosses and mildew at the bottom; the remains of swallow nests clung near the sagging ceilings. Parts of the roof had caved in, as had several walls. Tucker had the feeling that if they kept looking, they would find a collection of human bones.

Lia climbed over a section of broken wall and followed a hallway toward the back of the building. There was less clutter there, but the invisible aura of death felt stronger. They found the food storage area, a large room filled with broken glass and clay jars, scraps of cloth bags, and the desiccated husks of ancient fruits. There was nothing remotely edible.

They continued through the disintegrating structure. Lia was being very quiet, her face tense and rigid. She stopped and looked into a small room. A sharp, acrid odor filled the air. The room had once had a single window; it was now blocked by rubble from an adjoining structure. The floor was dark with bat guano. Tucker looked up. The ceiling was alive with tiny, furry bodies and the soft rustle of leathery wings.

"My bedroom," Lia whispered.

"Let's get out of here," Tucker said.

They backed out, then returned the way they had come.

"How long do you think it's been?" Tucker said.

"Lifetimes," said Lia.

They emerged onto the zocalo. Tucker took a minute to tear a bar loose from the rusted iron gate. It felt good to carry something he could hit with, although he wasn't sure it would be much good against a three-hundred-pound jaguar.

They followed the perimeter of the zocalo to another building.

"This was the Convent of the Yars. There is—or was—a spring-fed fountain here," Lia said.

The convent was in even worse shape than the palace. The entire roof had caved in. Climbing over the rubble, they made their way to the center of the building and reached an open courtyard that was relatively undamaged. In the center of the courtyard stood a raised basin crowded with lily pads.

Lia let out a cry of delight and ran across the courtyard, not to the fountain, but to a gnarled old tree. She reached into the foliage and tugged, then tossed something round and green to Tucker. A green orange? She picked one for herself and joined him at the fountain.

The orange was not like any orange Tucker had seen before. The skin was bumpy and hard, and most of all, it wasn't orange. They peeled the fruits and gnawed on the pulpy, sour, slightly bitter flesh. It was delicious. Tucker hadn't realized how hungry and thirsty he had become. He looked suspiciously at the water pooled in the basin.

"Do you think it's okay to drink?"

Lia scooped up some water in her palm and sniffed it. "It is all there is." She sucked some of the water from her cupped palm. "It tastes like weeds."

Tucker palmed some water and drank. Definitely weedy.

Lia said, "The last time I was here, there was a war between the Yars and the priests."

"Who won?"

"The priests were driven off, but nobody won."

"Do you think that's what destroyed the city?"

Lia drank another handful of water. "It looks more like the people simply left."

"Then they must have gone *some*place, right?"

"I don't know. Maybe the Boggsians can tell us. But I want to see one more thing here." She walked over to one of the walls surrounding the courtyard and pushed aside a heavy curtain of vines, revealing an opening about a foot wide. "Do you think you can fit?" she asked.

Tucker was not eager to enter the dark slot. It reminded him of the tomb in Jerusalem.

"What's in there?" he asked. But Lia had already disappeared into the opening. Tucker took a deep breath and, with some difficulty, squeezed through into a tunnel only a few inches wider than the opening. It was pitch-black.

"Lia?"

"Right here."

He felt her hand brush his arm and grab hold.

"I don't think this is a good idea," he said. "What about that jaguar?"

"If there were beasts in here, we would smell them."

In the dark, they descended a stairway, felt their way along a damp passageway, then climbed a shallow ramp. After a few dozen paces, a faint light appeared ahead. They emerged into a large room with most of its roof collapsed onto the floor.

Between the chunks of roof tile and rotted wooden beams lay mounds of spongy, gray, flaking matter that looked like moldy papier-mâché. Several small dark rodents scurried into holes in the waste. Lia dropped Tucker's hand; her shoulders fell.

"What is this?" Tucker asked.

"It was a library."

They made their way through the forested streets slowly, every darkened doorway threatening to conceal jaguars or other dangerous creatures. Tucker had left behind his iron bar. He now carried a small rusted knife he had found, and a wooden pole with two sharpened ends. They had also found a wooden bow and some arrows in the convent. When Tucker flexed the bow, the brittle wood had splintered.

Lia was carrying an old rucksack she had found in a cabinet that had somehow resisted centuries of weather, insects, and rodents. She had loaded the bag with six green oranges and a stoppered clay bottle full of water. She stopped and pointed. A few yards in front of them was a tree growing up through the crumbled pavers. Several oblong fruits lay on the stones beneath it. "Mangoes," she said.

A number of green and yellow fruits were still hanging from the branches. They each picked one. Tucker cut away the rind with his knife, and they gnawed the sweet orange flesh.

"This is good," Tucker said as Lia added several mangoes to her bag, "but I don't know how long we can live on fruit."

They came across a large, low concrete building partially

covered with vines. The building had a metal roof, which was rusted through, and several wide, vine-swagged doorways along its side. Lia regarded the structure with a furrowed brow.

"This is not a Lah Sept building," she said.

Tucker used his pole to sweep aside some of the hanging vines and peered into the building's interior. A pair of swallows swooped out low over his head, startling him. He jumped back, then approached the opening cautiously.

Lia joined him in the doorway. Inside was a large open space littered with plant matter and unidentifiable junk. A few of the objects were recognizable as broken chairs and tables. As their eyes adjusted to the half light, they saw a row of boxy alcoves set into the far wall. Lia picked her way across the trash-strewn floor for a closer look. Each alcove was about the size of a shower stall. Most of them had glass doors, now streaked with white bird-droppings. Inside the alcoves were wires and other electrical apparatus.

"What was this place?" Tucker asked.

"I think," said Lia, "it was a place for making Klaatu."

14 THE DEAD PIG

THE URBAN FOREST GAVE WAY TO ROLLING LAND COVered with knee-high grasses and dotted with clumps of trees. They climbed a low rise to the top of a hill and looked back. Other than the stepped pyramid jutting up from the horizon, the city was invisible.

"I never want to go back there," Lia said. She swung her bag from one shoulder to the other.

Tucker shaded his eyes and looked to the east. At the base of the hill they were standing on, the land leveled out and met a dark line of tall trees.

"That's a creek down there," he said. "In the future, where we're standing now will be a hill covered with pine trees. The lower areas will be tamarack bogs. The climate is going to change back."

"That will be a long time from now," Lia said.

"The first time I met Awn she wouldn't tell me what year it was. She had a thing about numbers. She did this thing where she pounded her stick on the floor and said she was counting out the seasons. She did it for hours. I think she was telling me we were something like nine thousand years in the future."

"That is a big number." Lia still didn't like numbers, but Jonis, the librarian in Romelas, had taught her to use them. She had to admit they were useful at times. She could not quite grasp *thousands*, though.

"Long enough for this tropical climate to shift back to a northern forest," Tucker said.

"I wonder why the Boggsians haven't changed," Lia said. "The Boggsian I met in Mayo dressed and talked the same as the Boggsian who sent me here in Awn's time. But if that was thousands of years from now, you'd think that the Boggsians would talk different and dress different."

"There were people kind of like the Boggsians when I lived in Hopewell," Tucker said. "They were called Amish. I guess they have traditions."

"We will have to ask a Boggsian. If there are any to ask."

The creek was narrow and rocky; they crossed it easily, then entered a dense jungle crowded with large-leaved plants and alarming animal noises.

"Besides jaguars, is there anything living here we have to worry about?" Tucker asked.

"I never went outside Romelas," Lia said. "But I know there were snakes."

"Great. Snakes." Tucker climbed over a fallen tree. Every

stick, vine, and shadow now looked snaky to him. They picked their way through the tangle of vegetation, stopping every few steps to look for danger. The chatter of birds was constant, punctuated every few seconds by screeches, yowls, and clicking sounds.

"This is like a Tarzan movie," Tucker said.

"What is Tarzan?"

"Never mind."

The shape of the land seemed familiar at times, but mostly all they saw was a wall of green on every side. They tried to follow the high ground, searching for a vantage point, but even the tops of the ridges were vegetation-choked, leaving them to blunder blindly forward.

"I can't even see the sun. I hope we're still heading east." Tucker used his stick to push through a stand of head-high ferns. Behind the ferns was a ten-foot-tall rock wall. They climbed the wall and emerged onto a grassy knoll. At the center of the knoll stood the broken stone foundations of a building. A lizard the size of a cat perched on the crumbling wall, regarding them balefully.

"Iguana," Lia said. "People in Romelas used to eat them."

"Really?" Tucker raised his stick.

"I do not eat meat," she reminded him.

The lizard scrambled off the stones and disappeared into the grass. They walked over to the foundation. It looked as if it might once have been an old farmhouse.

"I hope this isn't what's left of the Boggsians," Tucker said.

"We haven't crossed the river yet."

"Yeah, if the river is there."

They found the river some hours later.

"I don't think we can wade across," Tucker said. "I don't think I'd want to swim it either. If there are jaguars here, there might be alligators. Or piranhas."

"I never heard talk of such creatures. They may have gone extinct."

"Still . . . let's follow it for a ways. Maybe there's a bridge or something."

They followed animal paths through the forest, keeping the river in sight. Tucker could see tracks that looked like they had been made by split hooves. Lia stopped and sniffed the air.

"I smell something dead," she said. The odor was unmistakable, and it was getting stronger. They rounded a bend and came upon its source: a pile of offal, topped by the hairy head of a wild boar, crowned by a swarm of flies.

"That doesn't look natural," Tucker said in a low voice. "Somebody must've put that head there. Maybe it's a warning." They backed away, looking around nervously.

"Boggsians?" Lia said.

"I don't know. It doesn't look like a Boggsian sort of thing."

They left the path, giving the dead pig a wide berth. After pushing their way through a nearly impenetrable copse of thorny bushes, they angled back toward the path, but either they'd gotten turned around, or the path had veered off to the right. The sky—what they could see of it—had clouded.

Tucker wasn't sure which way was east anymore. He didn't say anything to Lia.

A few minutes later, Lia stopped and said, "I think we're lost."

"Let's keep moving. We're bound to come across something."

"I can still smell that pig."

"We must be going in circles then. There's a big tree that looks climbable. Maybe I can get a look at what's around us. Wait here."

Tucker didn't know what sort of tree it was; it had smooth bark, large leaves, and some low branches he could reach. He climbed until he was above most of the other plants and could scan the surrounding forest. What he saw was more trees, in every direction. He climbed higher, until he feared the main trunk was too slender to hold him. He could see the river now, less than fifty yards away.

Lia screamed.

For a moment, Tucker didn't know what he had heard. The sound hit his ears and traveled down his spine; his body went rigid, then he heard her shout his name. Heart pounding, Tucker scrambled down the tree. He dropped the last ten feet to the ground. Lia was not in sight.

He shouted her name and listened, but heard nothing. Even the birds were silent. Looking down, he saw where the leaves had been trampled. Some of the fern fronds were bent. He grabbed his stick and followed the broken vegetation, thinking, *Jaguar!*

Slashing at the underbrush with his stick, he followed what

he hoped was her trail, stopping every few steps to call out her name, then listen. Moments later, he stepped out of the brush onto a trail. He was back with the dead pig. He ran around the pig and started up the narrow, twisting path. His foot caught on something. He heard a hissing sound, like wind in the leaves. Something struck him hard from behind. His first thought was that a jaguar had attacked, but he was still upright. He tried to move. Something was keeping him immobile. Frantically, he swung his head from side to side, trying to understand what had happened to him. His feet moved, but were touching nothing. He seemed to be suspended a few feet above the ground. The pain in his back and midsection was excruciating, almost as if a stake had been driven straight through him. He looked down and discovered the pointy end of a sharpened wooden prong, as big around as a broom handle, jutting from his abdomen, just below his rib cage.

Isn't that interesting, he thought, and then he fainted.

15 YACA

TUCKER WOKE UP SITTING WITH HIS BACK PROPPED against a tree trunk. Squatting before him with his arms crossed over his knees was a young man with long, dark brown hair and irises the same deep black as his pupils, looking at him curiously.

"What happened to me?" Tucker asked, his voice a whisper.

The young man cocked his head and furrowed his brow.

"Who are you?" Tucker said.

The man shook his head and waved a fly away from his face. Tucker looked past him. He could see the pile of pig guts on the trail.

"Lia . . . where is Lia? Where is my friend?"

The man licked his lips, then spoke in a strong accent. "You talk ugly like boggsey."

"Boggsey . . . Boggsian?"

The man nodded and stood up. He was naked except for a pair of black cutoff shorts. A machete with a leather-wrapped handle hung from his belt. "Why do you not die?" he said.

"Why did you attack me?" Tucker asked.

The man shrugged. "The trap think you are *el tigre*. I cut *estaca,* but I leave it."

"*Estaca?*" Tucker said.

The man made a jabbing motion with his forefinger, then gestured at Tucker's belly. Tucker looked down. The stake was still protruding from his abdomen, dark with half-dried blood. It didn't hurt. His entire midsection was numb. He thought he understood what the man was telling him—he had blundered into a trap designed to kill jaguars. A few yards away, a log was hanging from a tree. Several wooden spikes, each of them more than a foot long, were affixed to the end of the log, which now dangled six feet above the trail. He could see where one of the spikes had been cut off. When he had tripped the trap, the log had swung down from above and driven the stake through his body from behind.

"You do not bleed," the man said. "Are you a *bruja?*"

"No . . . I . . . what's a *bruja?*"

"Evil magic thing." The man looked up at the sky. "The sun is almost gone. You die soon, then I leave."

"What if I don't die?"

"Then you are *bruja* and I will kill you."

"What about my friend?" Tucker asked.

"Another *bruja*," said the man. He turned his head and spat. "She go with my brothers. Then I find you."

Tucker raised his hand and touched the bloody stake. The man was right—he should be dead, but he wasn't. The healing technology the Medicants had implanted in him must have stopped him from bleeding to death.

"Take me to her," he said.

The man laughed. "I do not talk to dead things." He turned his back and muttered something in a language Tucker did not understand. The man bent over a cloth sack by the side of the trail and tugged open the drawcord top.

Tucker wrapped his fingers around the bloody stake. It was sticky. He took a breath. *Just like a sliver,* he thought, and pulled. The stake came out of his body with a soft, sucking sound. There was no pain, but a wave of dizziness and nausea swept through him; he heard himself gasp. The forest spun crazily, then righted itself.

The young man whirled at the sound. His eyes went wide. Tucker staggered to his feet, still gripping the stake. The man grabbed the machete from his belt.

"Wait!" Tucker said.

The man didn't wait; he ran at Tucker, holding the machete with both hands, chopping down at Tucker's head.

Tucker threw himself to the side. He could feel the effort tearing something loose inside him. He hit the ground with his shoulder and rolled. He regained his feet just in time to dodge another slash of the machete. The man brought the blade back for another swing. Tucker moved in, knocked up the blade with the stake and delivered a sideways kick to the man's belly. The man staggered back against a tree trunk. Tucker hammered the dull end of the stake against the man's temple. The man's eyes rolled up as he collapsed.

Tucker took the machete from the man's limp hand and backed away, panting hard. Whatever had kept his abdomen from hurting before was not working so good now. He looked down and saw fresh blood welling from the wound. He could feel more blood seeping down his back. His legs were shaking, but he couldn't afford to rest. His attacker might recover at any moment.

Using the machete, he cut the rope that had triggered the trap, and tied up the unconscious man. By the time he finished tying the man's feet together, he was seeing spots in front of his eyes. He walked unsteadily to the tree where he had first woken up, and sat where he could watch the bound man. The bleeding from his wound had stopped; the sensation in his gut subsided to a dull throb. He could feel things moving inside him. He wanted desperately to lie down and let his body heal. Or not heal. *I could die here,* he realized, and was mildly surprised to find that his own death did not frighten him. What scared him was the thought that Lia might die, or be dead already.

I suppose I should pray, he thought, but he could not summon the desire to do so. What could God do? Why would God let these things happen? It made no sense to him. The machines inside his body would determine if he lived or died. Lia was dead, or she was alive. He would find her, or he would not. He did not think God could help him.

A new sensation radiated from his belly into his awareness. At first, he did not know what he was feeling, then he recognized it as hunger. He crawled over to the cloth bag. Inside was a glass bottle half full of water, and two leaf-wrapped packets. Tucker uncapped the bottle and drank. He unwrapped the packets. One held strips of dried meat, the other contained what looked like a yellow compressed sponge. Tucker sniffed, then tasted it. Like dense, stale angel food cake, but not so sweet. He washed it down with another gulp of water, then went to work chewing on the dried meat, trying not to think what sort of animal it might be. He ate all the meat, then finished the spongy, dry mystery cake. The food settled comfortably inside him. He examined the wound under his rib cage, which had nearly closed and was not bleeding at all. He sat back against the tree trunk and waited.

It was getting dark when the man finally stirred. His fingers twitched, he moaned, then tried to move. His eyes popped open and rolled around in sudden panic.

"I don't want to hurt you," Tucker said. He stood up. The numbness and discomfort in his abdomen had subsided — he felt almost normal.

The man struggled frantically against his bonds.

"I want you to take me to Lia. The girl."

The man shook his head, his shoulder and arm muscles

stood out as he strained to break the cord around his wrists. Tucker braced himself in case the man broke loose, but the rope held. The man glared at him and muttered something that sounded like a curse.

Tucker pointed the machete at the man's feet. "I'm going to cut your feet loose. If you run, I will catch you. You know I can." He hoped it was true. He was feeling much better, but chasing this man through an unfamiliar jungle in the dark might be beyond him. "I am a *bruja*," he said. "I will catch you with magic."

The man stopped struggling. Tucker could see in his eyes that the man believed him.

"If my friend is okay, I'll let you go. But you have to promise not to run."

The man licked his lips and nodded. Tucker sawed through the rope with the machete and stepped back. The man held out his bound wrists. "Cut?"

"No," Tucker said. "First, you take me to the girl."

The man lowered his hands and climbed to his feet.

"What is your name?" Tucker asked.

The man frowned and shook his head.

Tucker pointed at himself. "I'm Tucker. What is your name?"

"Yaca," the man said.

"Yaca. Okay, let's go, Yaca."

Tucker expected the man to follow the trail, but instead Yaca walked straight into the brush, sliding through and around obstacles with graceful familiarity. Tucker followed, staying a few feet behind him. He hoped that his talk of being a *bruja* and knowing magic had terrified the young man into obedience. If Yaca chose to run off in the darkening forest, there was no way he'd catch him.

They came to a well-trodden path. The path followed the side of a hill, then zigzagged down to the bank of the river. Without hesitating, Yaca stepped into the water. He picked his way across the river, his feet finding stepping stones just below the surface—a submerged bridge. Tucker followed, mimicking Yaca's footfalls. They reached the far side safely. The path continued on the other side, heading east. The surrounding forest had become a jumble of shadows. Tucker could barely make out the shape of the man ahead of him.

Yaca stopped.

"How much farther?" Tucker asked.

Yaca looked over his shoulder and Tucker saw a flash of white teeth—a smile.

"We are here."

Two shadows detached themselves from the underbrush and stood to either side of Yaca. Tucker took a step back. He heard a faint sound and turned. Two more figures were behind him on the trail. He could see the glint of their machetes.

Yaca spat out a string of words. The only one Tucker understood was *bruja.*

16 MARTA

Tucker almost made a break for it, but the men weren't attacking him—not yet. Yaca was speaking rapidly, repeating the words *bruja* and *boggsey* several times. One of the others, a man carrying a pitchfork, joined in. Tucker could tell from their tone that they were arguing.

"I'm looking for the girl," Tucker said. "I'm not really a *bruja.*"

They fell silent and stared at him. The man with the pitchfork stepped closer, peered into his eyes, then quickly backed away. He gestured with his pitchfork and started up the path. Tucker followed. The others, including Yaca, came close behind.

Shortly, they came to a small clearing. Several crude huts with roofs made of leaves and branches were arranged around the perimeter. A low fire burned in a pit in front of the largest hut. An older woman sat on a log arranged before the fire, talking to a younger woman sitting beside her. The two of them looked over as Tucker and his captors emerged from the forest.

The older woman said something. The young woman ran to one of the huts and disappeared inside. Yaca ran to the older woman and started talking. The woman looked from Yaca to Tucker, then back again. Finally she made a chopping gesture, and Yaca fell silent. The woman stood up. She was wearing a patterned green and gold sarong wrapped around her hips, and a loosely woven clay-colored shawl over her shoulders. She approached Tucker, her movements fluid and graceful. As she drew close, Tucker saw that the lines on her face were those that came with weather and hardship more than years. She may have been only thirty or forty years old, with intelligent black eyes, a strong jaw, and firm, narrow lips. Her dark, straight hair, spilling over her shawl, showed only a few strands of gray.

"Marta," she said, pointing at herself.

"My name is Tucker. I'm here to find my friend."

The woman drew back, frowning. "You are no boggsey."

"No, I'm just looking for my friend. The girl these guys grabbed." He pointed at Yaca and the others, who were standing a few yards away listening. "Is she here?"

Marta frowned, then spoke sharply to Yaca, who replied defensively and pointed at the man with the pitchfork.

"Malo!" the woman said sharply.

The man with the pitchfork came forward and launched into a long story. Again, Tucker heard the words *bruja* and *boggsey*. The woman listened. When he had finished speaking, she snatched the pitchfork from him and flung it into the fire. The man cried out and moved to retrieve it; Marta dealt him an openhanded blow to the face. The man jerked back, putting a hand to his cheek.

The woman returned her attention to Tucker.

"Your friend is not here."

"Do you know where she is? Have you seen her?"

"I will tell you a story. This I had from my son Malo." Marta gestured at the man she had struck. "Malo came upon a yellow-haired girl in the forest. He took her, though she fought back with the speed and strength of a *jabalina*. Malo is fast and strong and brave. He defeated her and carried her far through the forest to the place where the boggseys tear the earth with their plows. There, after much clever bargaining, he traded her to them for a pitchfork." She gave Malo a disgusted look. "This is the story my son tells me."

All Tucker could think to say was, "A pitchfork?"

"Yes. He is *idiota*." She regarded Tucker with narrowed eyes. "Yaca tells me a story as well. He says you were caught in his trap, and that the wooden tooth entered your back and burst out through your belly. He says he waited for you to die, but you refused. He says that you used magic to remove the tooth. He says you are a *bruja*. A witch. I do not believe in *brujas*, but I see blood on your garment. Show me your belly."

Tucker hesitated. The men with their machetes were still standing nearby. He feared that if the old woman thought he was a witch he would be killed.

"It was nothing," he said. "Just a scratch."

"Show me."

Tucker slowly opened the front of his coveralls and looked down. The wound below his rib cage had closed. She examined it in the firelight, then snorted.

"That is an old wound. Both my sons are *idiotas.*"

Yaca stared at Tucker as if he were a ghost.

"You speak English well," Tucker said.

"*Inglés* is our trading language. The boggseys speak it. You are not a boggsey. Come, sit with me." She walked over to the fire and sat down on the log. Tucker hesitated, then followed her and sat down a few feet away.

Marta motioned with her hand. "Who are you? Where do you come from? Tell me a story."

Tucker considered the many stories he might tell. He finally said, "My name is Tucker. I came from a faraway place called Hopewell. This morning I came from the city of Romelas."

"No one lives in Romas."

"Yeah, I kind of got that."

Her brow furrowed.

"I mean," Tucker said, "I didn't see anybody there."

"Tell me how you came to Romas."

"Through a disko. A Gate."

"A Gate!" Her eyes narrowed. "There are no Gates."

"You seem to have heard of them."

"They come in dreams." She stared into the fire for a moment. "I do not speak of them."

"Why is the city abandoned?" Tucker asked.

"The gods left. The people were eaten."

"Eaten by what? Jaguars?"

Marta laughed. "*El tigre's* appetite is not so great as that. I will tell you a story."

Tucker noticed that the men had moved closer, and were all squatting around the fire, listening intently. Marta cleared her throat and began.

"In a time long before my grandmother's grandmother's grandmother, Romas was a rich city ruled by the priests of the god Sept. People lived pressed together in stone buildings, while the priests performed miracles and dined on lamb liver and sweet persimmon. They lived this way for countless generations, and more. It is said the priests lived inside the great pyramid.

"Though they were powerful, the priests were small in their hearts, and they fought among themselves. There was a great battle, and the priests tore at each other like animals. When they saw that the people of Romas knew their pettiness, the priests were ashamed, and they climbed to a hole in the sky. Then a great beast appeared and devoured the hole, and the priests were no more."

She fell silent and stared into the flames. Tucker thought she was finished, but after a moment, she continued.

"For a time, the people of Romas were content without their priests, but then came the boggseys with their spirit-makers, offering solace to those whose joy in life had abandoned them. The boggseys claimed their machines would take people to a new life, a life without hunger or pain. They said their machines would make people into gods. They called it transcendence."

"Klaatu," Tucker said, understanding.

"*Klaatu* is the word for gods in our language. At first, few people were willing to give up their life in this world for promises of paradise. But some of the old, the sick, and the desperate gave themselves to the boggsey machines, and they returned as spirits and spoke of their new life. The people saw their friends and relatives living as gods, and they saw that they were happy—even those who had given themselves to the boggsey machines in despair. Soon, others began to enter the machines, hoping to join their departed ancestors, hoping to live without the discomforts of life. Lovers entered the machines together. Parents gave their children to the machines, then followed them. In time, there were so few remaining in Romas that the boggseys shut down their machines and returned to their farms, and the city died.

"My ancestors chose the bellies of the forest over the bellies of the machines. Now the forests have devoured us. We are few. We wait to die."

Her head slumped forward; she stared at the ground between her knees. One of the men added some sticks to the fire and it flared brightly. Tucker realized that there were now more than a dozen men and women squatting around the flames listening. He noticed there were no children.

Tucker asked, "These boggseys that made everybody into Klaatu, are they the same people who have my friend?"

"They are their mothers' mothers' mothers' children, yes."

"Why would they want her? Do they want to turn her into a Klaatu?"

Marta shrugged. "Who knows what the boggseys want. I do not even understand what my own children want. A pitchfork? Bah. We are not farmers." She glared again at Malo, who looked away angrily.

"Where do I find these boggseys?" Tucker asked.

Marta gestured vaguely. "Harmony is near. I will have Malo take you there in the morning."

"Take me now."

"It is too dangerous. The trap you blundered into is there for a reason. *El tigre* is a hungry beast. Tonight, you sleep in Malo's bed." She stood up. "No more stories." She walked tiredly to one of the huts and disappeared inside. By ones and twos, the other men and women also retired to their huts, leaving only Malo and Tucker by the fire.

"I don't want to take your bed," Tucker said. "I can sleep here by the fire."

Malo snorted and gave him a baleful look. "Marta speaks." He pointed to one of the huts. "My bed is yours. I will tend the flame."

17 CHICKEN

WEEKS PASSED WITHOUT KOSH SEEING EMILY. HE SPENT his time working at Red's, working on his bike, and keeping the house up.

Ronnie Becker had his court hearing and got off with probation. If he managed to make it to eighteen without getting into more trouble, his record would be cleared.

"You won't turn eighteen until January," Kosh pointed out. "When was the last time you went six months without getting in trouble?"

Ronnie laughed. "I'll be extra careful," he said. "I told the judge Jesus would be watching me."

"Yeah, but watching you do what?"

"The way I figure it, God wanted me to get off with probation, so I guess I owe him one. Or maybe God owed me one for letting me get caught. Next time I go to church I'll have to ask him."

Ronnie's peculiar epistemology was of little interest to Kosh. Adrian's over-the-top piety had put him off religion at an early age. He wasn't even sure he believed in God.

"Anyways, as soon as I can get a little scratch together, I'm leaving town," Ronnie said. "Arnold is making my life hell."

Arnold was Ronnie's father.

"Where are you going?"

"Anywhere. You want to come?"

"No thanks," Kosh said.

Occasionally, Kosh performed odd jobs for his neighbors—anything that required a strong back and the willingness to work cheap. Chuck Beamon, a bachelor farmer who had inherited a small spread from his mother, called Kosh one day and asked him to help with a fence repair. Kosh stopped by the next morning.

"Strangest thing," Chuck said as they toted tools and a roll of fencing across his soybean field. "You remember I told you about that guy being chased by a pink pig? The guy wearing the black coat? Well, this here is where I seen him, and the other day, I'm out and . . . well, you'll see."

They reached the edge of the field, which was bounded by a six-foot-tall welded wire fence. As they followed the fence line, Kosh remarked that it seemed an odd sort of fence for a soybean field. Chuck explained that he'd put it up because Henry Hall's pigs kept raiding his beans. "They make one heck of a mess," he said. "Course, Henry, he won't do nothin' about it. But lookie down here."

A perfectly round four-foot section of the fence was missing. Not broken, not collapsed, not hanging loose, but simply gone. A perfect circle of missing fence.

"Now, don't you think that's peculiar?" Chuck said.

"I do," said Kosh. He examined the ends of the cut wires. His first thought was that it was a practical joke—some kids had gotten hold of a pair of wire cutters and cut the circle out just to mess with Chuck's head. But the wires didn't look like they'd been cut. Wire cutters would have left the ends slightly uneven. These wires just . . . ended. And the circle was too precise to be the work of kids. Even Kosh, who was pretty handy, could not have performed such a flawless job of vandalism.

"I figure we can just slap on a new piece," Chuck said. "But I sure as shootin' would like to know what the heck did this."

It took only a few minutes to repair the fence. Kosh wondered why Chuck had bothered to call him, then realized that Chuck had simply wanted to show somebody the hole. He couldn't blame him—it wasn't the sort of thing you could describe and have anybody believe you. After they finished the repair and returned the extra fencing and tools to the barn, Chuck asked Kosh what he owed him.

Kosh waved him away. "Nothing," he said. "It didn't take but ten minutes."

"More closer to twenty some," Chuck said. "But I ain't going to force nothing on you. 'Less you want a chicken."

"Chicken?"

"Yeah. You like chicken?"

"A *live* chicken?"

"Nope. She's gutted, plucked, and ready for roasting. Had to thin the flock this morning."

"I have this chicken," Kosh said.

Emily laughed. He had never heard her laugh over the phone before.

"That's funny," she said.

"It is?"

"Yes. Chickens are funny. Especially when somebody calls you out of the blue and the first thing they say is they have one."

"This chicken isn't funny. It's dead."

"What on Earth are you doing with a dead chicken?"

"I was thinking I might eat it. I was thinking I might make it into chicken potpie tonight. Only I never made chicken potpie before."

"Are you asking me for a recipe, or inviting me to dinner?"

"Dinner, I guess. Only I need your chicken potpie recipe."

"Do you have flour and butter?"

"I think so."

"How about I come over around five?"

"That'd be great."

Kosh hung up the phone. He noticed his hands were shaking. What was that about?

18 TAMM

Kosh came to in starts and stutters. First, the voices—a distant, meaningless muttering, like waves breaking on a beach. Then the light, teasing at his eyelids. He opened his eyes. He was looking up at a ceiling. He had seen that ceiling before. He tried to sit up, but fell back when the pain hit, a racking ache from his neck to his feet. He gasped and squeezed his eyes shut and waited for it to subside. After a few seconds, he was able to sit up. He recognized the room, and remembered. This was the house where he had grown up.

The voices were coming from outside. Slowly, Kosh climbed to his feet and stood crouched for a few seconds as he waited for the dizziness to pass. When he felt able to move, he went to the window. A burly man wearing a yellow shirt was standing in the yard, talking. A black SUV with a dented front bumper and broken grille was parked in the driveway behind him. Kosh recognized the grille—he'd seen it last in his rearview mirror. The man had to be Tamm. Kosh shifted to the side and saw Emma sitting on the steps. She was holding the weapon Kosh had taken from the priest. Tamm took a step toward her. She pointed the weapon at him. He laughed, but didn't come any closer.

Ignoring the throbs and twinges from his battered body, Kosh made his way to the door and out onto the porch. His footsteps startled Emma. When she turned her head to look, Tamm darted forward and grabbed the weapon. Kosh threw himself at him before he could bring the tube to bear. Tamm staggered back and fell with Kosh on top of him. The weapon flew from his hands. Kosh pounded at him with both fists. He knew he was in no shape to win a prolonged fight—he had to knock the man senseless as quickly as possible. Already he could feel his strength draining away. Tamm was fighting back, but Kosh hardly felt the blows. He'd been in enough fights to know that if you feel it when they hit you, it's all over.

Tamm's fist connected with the ribs on his right side, and Kosh went rigid with pain. Tamm shoved him aside and jumped to his feet. Through a haze of agony, Kosh saw the toe of a boot coming at his head, but before it connected, the earth exploded, a blast of heat hit his face, and Tamm was thrown to the ground.

Kosh rolled away from the blast and managed to get up on his hands and knees. Tamm was collapsed next to a burned spot on the lawn. Emma, stunned by what she had done, was holding the silver tube. Ignoring the piercing stabs from his ribs, Kosh staggered over to her and took the weapon from her hands and aimed it at Tamm.

"Is he dead?" Emma asked. Tamm's yellow T-shirt was scorched, but otherwise he appeared intact. Kosh poked at his shoulder with the tube. Tamm's eyes fluttered open; he looked at Kosh and groaned.

"Nope," Kosh said, unable to keep a tinge of regret out of his voice.

Emma looked as if she was about to fall over. Kosh put his arm around her and together they walked unsteadily back to the porch steps. Emma sat down and hugged herself.

"I have never fired an *arma* before," she said.

Kosh looked at the tube in his hand. "Is that what this is called?"

"It is a dreadful device — the Boggsians built them for the priests. I do not understand why they would do that. I do not understand why people kill."

"You nearly killed somebody yourself just now."

"Am I, then, like Tamm?"

"Believe me, you're nothing like him." Kosh sat down beside her. Tamm started to sit up. Kosh pointed the *arma* at him. "Best you not move," he said. Tamm sank back onto his elbows and glared at them.

"The others will come looking for him," Emma whispered. "I will be punished."

"You can't stay here then."

She turned her head to face him. It was all he could do not to call her Emily.

"I have nowhere to go."

Kosh thought for a moment. "How do you feel about barns?" he asked.

19 TEMPLE GIRL

Trempealeau County, Wisconsin

Emma had hardly spoken to Kosh since they had left Hopewell in her husband's SUV, and she rarely met his eyes. She didn't seem to be afraid of him, but Kosh sensed that he made her uncomfortable.

He gave her the bedroom on the third floor of his barn. Tucker's old room. She thanked him and closed the door and did not come out for hours.

He tried to win her over with chicken potpie, coaxing her out of her room and to the table. She picked at her pie, then asked him if the chicken pieces were "dead bird parts."

"You don't eat meat?" Kosh said.

She shook her head, not looking at him. She sat at the table while Kosh threw together a bowl of rice with sautéed vegetables. He tried several conversational gambits, but got nothing back from her other than a few polite responses. He began feeling foolish, so he stopped talking. They ate in silence. Emma retired to her room.

The next morning at breakfast he offered her fresh-baked biscuits and homemade raspberry preserves. She ate listlessly, thanked him, then went back to her room. Kosh spent the rest of the morning reading his vegetarian cookbooks.

Dinner that second night was roasted vegetables and corn on the cob. While they were eating, Kosh asked her if there was anything he could do to make her more comfortable.

She did not say anything for several long seconds, then raised her chin and said, "You can stop staring at me all the time."

Kosh stared at her, then realized what he was doing and looked away.

"Have I been staring?" he said, knowing it was true. He couldn't help it. Looking at Emma was like traveling into the past, back to when he was seventeen, back to his days spent with Emily Ryan.

"I feel your eyes constantly," she said.

"I'm sorry. I can't help it. You look like someone who was . . . important to me."

"I am not her."

"I know that. I really do. You're Emma, not Emily."

Emma nodded.

"The corn is good," she said. "Our corn in Romelas was starchy and tough." She looked at him. "You seem familiar to me as well. I felt it the first moment I saw you. Have you ever been in Romelas?"

"Not that I recall."

"When I look at you, I get the most peculiar feelings."

"Was that why you defended me from your husband?"

"Perhaps." With that, she excused herself and retired to her room.

What am I doing? Kosh asked himself. *The woman is married, and perhaps deranged. She is not Emily. Have I kidnapped a madwoman? Or am I the one who's crazy?*

He read the papers, looking for news from Hopewell. His brother had been arrested and charged with murder, along with Gheen. Apparently the two of them had stabbed a boy on that stage in the park, but it wasn't clear whom they had killed. The news reports said that no body had been found. One article claimed that an unnamed local boy had been killed; another said that it had all been a magician's trick. He saw no mention of himself, of Tucker, of the girl Lia. The *Rochester Post-Bulletin* reported that Gheen had escaped from his jail cell, but this was not confirmed by any of the other papers.

With the arrest of "Father September," the Lambs of September had effectively ceased to exist. Many former members now claimed that they had never taken the whole thing seriously. "It was just something to do," said one former convert. "Now I got crops coming in and no time to talk to reporters."

When Kosh wasn't reading papers and cooking, he wheeled his '67 Triumph out into the yard and worked on it. He hadn't ridden the Triumph in years, but his Harley was a tangled wreck back in Hopewell, and it was driving him crazy not to have a bike to ride.

As he worked, he kept an eye on the top of the barn, but the disko did not reappear.

He noticed Emma standing at the window, watching him. She backed away and let the curtain fall closed. He decided to make fresh pasta with mushroom sauce for dinner.

As Kosh and Emma became used to each other, it got easier. Kosh managed not to stare at her so often, and Emma relaxed. The food therapy seemed to be working. Kosh discovered a world of meatless recipes. He tried to outdo himself with every meal. One night over a dinner of farfalle with braised acorn squash, he asked her about her childhood. In wistful tones undershot with bitterness, she told him, between bites, of the great city Romelas, of the pyramid, and of the Gates. At first he thought she was talking about regular gates made of metal or stone, but he soon realized that what she called Gates were the things Tucker had called diskos. Time portals. Like the thing that had appeared on top of his barn, or the one on top of the house in Hopewell. According to Emma, there were a number of these Gates in Romelas, and they were used by the priests in a human-sacrifice ritual.

"The Pure Girls are raised knowing that one day they will receive the sacrament of the blade, and be cast into the Gates," she said. "I was a Pure Girl."

"Is that how you ended up here? You got thrown into one of those things?"

"No. I was spared, and made a temple girl. I served the needs of the priests."

"Like an altar boy?"

"I do not know what that is."

"It's . . ." Kosh suddenly understood what she was implying. "Never mind."

"When I became too old for the priests, I was given to the deacon Tamm. He was not a bad man at first, but he changed. The Yars grew in power, and it made the priests and deacons fearful, and they did terrible things." She shuddered. "At first I blamed the Yars, but now I don't know. The Yars were raised as Pure Girls, like me. Who knows what awful things they experienced in the Gates? Still, it was they who caused the rebellion, and the destruction of the Gates. They have much to answer for."

"If the Yars were opposed to the priests, doesn't that make them the good guys?"

"There were no good guys," Emma said. "Yars killed priests; priests killed Yars. We fled Romelas to escape the Yar rebellion. The Yars tried to stop us. There was a terrible battle. Many were killed. Of the Lah Sept, only Master Gheen, a hand of deacons, and I were able to escape."

"Lah Sept? I thought you were called Lambs."

"That is what we are called now — the Lambs of September, because of Father September — but in the future we will be called the Lah Sept."

"The guy you call Father September is my brother," Kosh said.

Emma put down her fork and gave him a searching look. "Father September is the founder of the Lah Sept."

"He's a nutcase."

Emma shook her head. "I grew up being taught that Father September was a great prophet. I don't know what to think anymore. When I first met him, I thought him a madman as well."

"Maybe you should trust your first impression."

Emma nodded thoughtfully. "After we fled through the Gate, we found ourselves in a great forest. I had never seen such trees, with needles instead of leaves. Master Gheen said we had traveled to the distant future. He said he had been there before. He led us through the forest. There were Gates everywhere — hands and hands of Gates."

"What do you mean, 'hands'?" Kosh asked.

Emma held her palm toward him and spread her fingers.

Five, Kosh thought. He had noticed that Emma did not use numbers.

"We arrived at an abandoned cabin, where we spent the night. The next day we came upon the remains of a pyramid in the woods. It was much smaller than the pyramid in Romelas, the stone was crumbling, and there were trees growing from cracks in the steps. Later, Master Gheen told us that it was the Cydonian Pyramid, the same pyramid that had once stood proudly in the center of Romelas, ravaged by time, sinking slowly into the forest floor.

"On top of the pyramid stood a rickety scaffold woven of branches, sticks, and vines. An old man was clinging to its side, tying on more branches. Several man-heights above him was a Gate, floating in midair.

"Master Gheen called on the old man to come down. As he descended, the tower of sticks creaked and swayed. I thought it would collapse. When he reached the bottom, Master Gheen asked him what he was doing.

" 'I am going *home,*' the man said.

" 'And where is this home?' Master Gheen asked him.

"The old man's eyes welled with tears. 'Hopewell,' he said. We were all astonished by this revelation, as ancient Hopewell was said to be the birthplace of the Lah Sept.

"Master Gheen asked him who he was, and the old man said, 'I am Adrian, a sinner.'

"Master Gheen was stunned. We were all stunned. Adrian the Sinner is the author of the Tribulations, the final book of *The Book of September.* Furthermore, Adrian the Sinner was believed to be one of the many aliases used by Father September, the founder of the Lah Sept.

"Master Gheen said, 'Why do you believe this Gate will deliver you to Hopewell?'

" 'The Archangel Gabriel guides me,' the man said. He could have said nothing more astounding, as the Archangel Gabriel is an important figure in *The Book of September,* and the one who lighted the way for Father September's journey through darkness, as is described in the sacred text.

"Master Gheen asked, 'Are you he who wrote *The Book of September?*'

"The man said, 'I do not know this *Book of September.*'

"'Perhaps you have yet to write it.'

"The old man said, 'I would not know what to write.'

"Master Gheen said, 'I will tell you what to say. Trust me, Father.'

"The man said, 'I am not your father. My name is Adrian!'

"'Your name,' said Master Gheen, 'is Father September.'

"The old man appeared to be very confused, and I remember thinking that he could not possibly be who Master Gheen claimed. But Master Gheen took him by the hand and knelt down before him and said, 'You are our greatest prophet.'

"And the old man said, 'I am?'"

Emma sat back in her chair. "That is how I first met the man you say is your brother."

Kosh, shaking his head, said, "Adrian is no prophet."

"Master Gheen would disagree with you."

"But . . . how did he get so *old*?"

"I suppose he lived a long time. I know of no other way." Emma tipped her head, then continued her story. "For hands of days, we stayed in the cabin in the forest. Master Gheen gave Father September the bed. The rest of us slept on the floor. There was food in the cabin, grains and beans, and berries in the forest. During the day, Tamm, Koan, and the others worked on the scaffold the old man had started, building a tower to reach the Gate above the ruins of the pyramid. And every day and every night, Master Gheen talked with Father September. Master Gheen can be very persuasive. He speaks with God's voice."

"He sounded kind of whiny to me."

"Father September did not think so. He listened with both ears open. Master Gheen told him of the Medicants, of the Plague of Numbers. When the old man realized that his lost wife had fallen to Plague, he was filled with righteous anger. In time, he came to accept that he was Father September.

"Master Gheen had a plan. He wished to use the Gates to return to the time and place of the birth of the Lah Sept. But there were forces at work that tried to stop us. A maggot appeared outside the cabin and attacked Master Gheen. He destroyed it with his *arma*. This happened several times."

"Maggot—you mean like that thing in the park?"

"Yes. Creatures sent by those who would destroy us. We could sense them coming by their sound. Master Gheen became very skilled at destroying them with his *arma* before they reached their full size.

"Finally, the scaffold was complete. We climbed the scaffold one at a time and entered the Gate. Tamm and I were the last to go. As I was about to enter, I looked down and saw a strange woman standing at the base of the pyramid. She waved to me. It was very odd . . . She looked like me."

Kosh's heart lurched. How many Emilys could there be?

"But she was older. Tamm didn't see her; he was looking up at me. He yelled for me to go, and I stepped into the Gate and came out here. I mean, on the roof of the hotel in downtown Hopewell.

"We took over the small church downtown, and Father September began preaching the gospel of the Lambs. At first, people came to the church out of curiosity, but soon they were amazed. Father September told of marvels and tribulations to come — the arrival of the pigeons, the coming of the Digital Plague, and the tornado that tore through the town of Ghentburg. These things we knew from *The Book of September,* and when the marvels he prophesied came to pass, word spread quickly. The congregation grew, and soon we had to hold our services in the park, where Master Gheen declared the Cydonian Pyramid would one day rise.

"One night after services, a maggot appeared above the altar. This time, Master Gheen was prepared. Tamm and Koan captured the maggot and affixed it to a metal frame. The maggot could not move or close its maw. It was rendered helpless, as you later saw in the park.

"We waited then for the arrival of Tuckerfeye, Father September's son, as was foretold by the scriptures. It is the most important story in the Book, and Master Gheen was determined to see it come to pass. It is called the Shaming, when Father September becomes a martyr by sacrificing his only son, and he is imprisoned. It is the first and greatest tribulation of the Lambs. Only a chosen few would pass the test."

"What test is that?"

"In the scriptures, Father September commits the greatest

of sins by killing his own son in full view of his flock, and those whose faith is weak turn away from the church. The Lambs enter a period of darkness—those who stay the course are few, but their strength is great."

"How does that make Father September a martyr?" Kosh asked.

"He sacrifices his pride, his good name, and the respect and love of his people. As it is written, 'Any man can give his life, but to give up the love of one's own people is the one true sacrifice.'"

Kosh shook his head. "I can't believe that Adrian, crazy as he is, would kill Tucker. Anyway, it didn't happen. Tucker and Lia went into that maggot thing."

"A boy was sacrificed."

"Yeah, I read that. But it wasn't Tucker."

"You cannot know that. Master Gheen's plan was to have Father September perform the sacrifice, then send the boy into the maggot. According to the scriptures, Tuckerfeye returns from the dead to continue his father's work."

"Then the scriptures are wrong."

"Perhaps." Emma looked down at her plate of cold pasta. "Perhaps not."

20 WAHLBERG

KOSH GOT THE TRIUMPH RUNNING THE NEXT MORNING. He celebrated by going for a quick ride, just a few miles, to see how it rolled. When he got back ten minutes later, there was a Hopewell County Sheriff squad car in the driveway.

The cop was still sitting in the car. Kosh got off his bike and hung his helmet on the handlebar. The cop shouldered open the car door and climbed out.

"Morning, Jeff," Kosh said, keeping his voice casual.

Sheriff's Deputy Jeff Wahlberg, a hefty, red-faced man about Kosh's age, hitched up his implement-laden belt and nodded. "Hey, Kosh." He looked around. "Nice spread."

"It's got a ways to go, but I'm working on it. What's up?"

The deputy puffed out his cheeks, then let out the air with a soft *phtt.* "Understand you had a little accident a few days back."

Kosh had gone to high school with Jeff Wahlberg, but they'd never really been friends. He chose his words carefully. "Well, my bike got sort of bunged up. Totaled, actually."

Wahlberg looked at the Triumph. "New bike?"

"Refurbished."

"How many you got now?"

"Just a few. Mostly in pieces."

"I heard you had your nephew living with you."

"I did, but he's gone. You haven't seen him, have you?"

"Nope. You the only one here now?"

Kosh considered how he might answer that. If he said yes, would the deputy leave? Probably not. He decided to counter with a question of his own.

"Can I ask you what you're doing here? Kind of out of your jurisdiction."

Wahlberg shrugged and held up his palms. "Seems there's a missing woman. Thought you might know her whereabouts."

"You think I kidnapped somebody?"

"Nah, don't figure you for a kidnapper. But if you run off with a fellow's wife, *that* I wouldn't put past you."

"And what if *she* ran off with *me*?"

Wahlberg shrugged. "Is that what happened?"

Kosh said, "Is there something I should know? Outstanding charges? Am I in trouble?"

"You tell me. We found the husband tied to a tree in front of your old house. He says you assaulted him." He looked pointedly at the scabs on Kosh's knuckles. "Can't say I'd blame you. The guy's a piece of work. One a them Lambs."

"He rammed me with his truck and wrecked my bike. Nearly killed me."

"I figured something like that. He says you stole his SUV, too."

"I don't know anything about that," Kosh said, hoping Wahlberg wouldn't look behind the barn. "You here to arrest me?"

Wahlberg laughed. "You see a SWAT team? Nah, the guy declined to press charges on the assault. I figure he's got something to hide. I'm just here to find the woman, make sure she's safe."

"She's safe," Kosh said.

"Mind if I talk to her?"

Kosh couldn't see any way around it. He looked up at the third-floor window. Emma was standing there, watching. He waved for her to come down. A minute later, Emma emerged from the barn, walking as if she were headed for her own execution. She stopped several steps away from them.

Wahlberg smiled. "Are you Emma?"

Emma nodded.

"Your husband is worried about you."

"I have no husband," Emma said.

"That a fact? Pretty quick divorce."

"Our marriage was not legal. Not here."

"Oh." Wahlberg shifted from foot to foot. "Well, either way, I guess you got a right to leave him. I just stopped by to make sure you weren't being held prisoner against your will. This guy treating you okay?" He looked at Kosh.

"He is very kind," Emma said. "I am here of my own free will."

* * *

As soon as the deputy's car headed off down the driveway, Emma started to shake. Kosh put his arms around her and held her until the police car was out of sight.

"I was afraid he would take me back," she said.

"You haven't done anything wrong," Kosh said.

She stepped from his embrace. "So you say. I am not so sure. To my people, leaving one's husband is a sin against God."

"You're not with your people now."

"That is a sin as well. I am destined for *infierno.*"

"What is that?"

"You call it hell."

Kosh removed the sensor from the motion-detector light above the barn door. He attached it to the mailbox at the entrance to his long driveway, then strung several extension cords from the mailbox to the barn. He found an old clock radio on his junk shelf and plugged it in to see if it worked.

Emma appeared in the doorway and stood watching him with a puzzled expression.

"What are you doing?" she asked.

"Hacking together an alarm system. We get any visitors, I want a heads-up."

He tuned the radio to a moldy-oldies station out of Whitehall.

"The Lambs believe digital devices are evil," she said, watching the numbers flickering on the display.

"Can't say I blame them." He finally found the station. They were playing an old Aerosmith tune. "You like music?"

"Is that what that is?"

"Not a classic-rock fan, huh?" He unplugged the radio from the wall and plugged it into the extension cord that led to the sensor on the mailbox.

"I'm going out to trip that sensor. Will you let me know if the radio comes on?"

"How will I know it's on?"

"Sound will come out of it. If it comes on, wave to me."

Kosh hopped on his Triumph, drove to the end of the driveway, and stopped at the mailbox. He looked back at the barn. Emma was waving to him from the doorway. He drove back.

"The digital device is making noise. A man is shouting 'la vida loca' over and over."

"Must be nineties week," Kosh said.

The music stopped.

"Good. I got it set so it only comes on for thirty seconds. Now if anybody comes in the driveway, I'll be ready for them. I got a feeling when Jeff Wahlberg tells your ex you're okay, he might just let slip where you went to."

"You think Tamm will come here?"

"Yeah, I do. To get his truck back, if nothing else."

21 TAMM

KOSH WAS NAPPING ON THE BEAT-UP SOFA IN HIS SHOP the next day when an old Duran Duran song, "Hungry Like a Wolf," invaded his dreams. He had never liked that song. Why was the wolf hungry? It made no sense.

He opened his eyes and sat up. The radio! He jumped up and ran to the open doorway. An SUV was coming up the driveway fast, raising a cloud of dust. Standing at the head of the driveway, Emma was holding the *arma* in her hands.

"Emma!" Kosh shouted. She ignored him.

The SUV skidded to a stop. Emma raised the weapon and fired. Shards of hot metal exploded in every direction. The front of the truck leaped into the air liked a rearing horse. The truck thumped back down. Kosh could see the glowing, molten remains of the engine—the grille and bumper were gone. Both front tires were in flames.

Kosh ran to Emma and tried to take the *arma* from her hands, but she would not let go. Her face was as bloodless as stone, jaw rigid, lips a tight line. Kosh released his hold on the weapon and took a step back.

The passenger door of the SUV opened and a man jumped out. Tamm. A second man tumbled out of the truck headfirst. Kosh recognized him as one of the men at the park. Tamm grabbed the man under the arms and dragged him away from the burning truck.

Emma pointed the weapon at them.

"Emma, don't!" Kosh pushed the tube down so that it pointed at the ground. "It's not worth it."

Her jaw loosened. "They will keep coming," she said, a slight quaver entering her voice.

"I'll talk to them," he said. He walked toward the two men. Tamm was standing unsteadily, stunned and bewildered, watching the truck burn. The other man was on the ground, holding his leg, his face a mask of agony. His right knee had a brace on it.

Tamm saw Kosh coming toward him and put his hand to the stun baton at his waist.

"You're in no shape to fight me, son," said Kosh. "With or without your stun stick." He hoped it was true—his rib cage was still fragile, and the stun baton would give Tamm an advantage. "You maybe figured this out all on your lonesome, but you're not welcome here." Kosh stopped with about twenty feet between them. He knew from experience that confidence and bluster won more fights than fists.

"I came for my wife," Tamm said, looking past Kosh at Emma.

"Consider yourself divorced."

"Lambs do not divorce."

"You had best make an exception. Unless you want me to kick your butt from here to *infierno*. You hear me?"

Tamm glared at him.

"And if I don't" — Kosh jerked his head toward Emma — "she will."

Tamm looked at Emma, who was pointing the *arma* at him. Tamm then looked at Kosh, and at the truck. The upholstery had ignited; the interior of the vehicle was a mass of flames.

"I recommend you drag your buddy a little farther away," Kosh said. "That gas tank might go any second."

Tamm did as Kosh suggested. Moments later, the back end of the truck exploded with a soft *whoosh*. A pillar of black smoke rose to the sky.

"Now you should maybe think about leaving," Kosh said.

"How? Koan cannot walk."

"Your other truck is behind the barn. I've been saving it for you."

Kosh was not happy about the pile of slag the burning SUV would leave in his driveway, but he felt good about the way things had gone. Tamm and his friends would think twice before returning. Or so he hoped.

"He won't be back," he told Emma, trying to sound confident.

Emma nodded, but he could see she didn't believe him.

The following morning, the first hard frost arrived. Kosh went to work on his neglected garden, harvesting several buttercup squash and some of the kale. He pulled up the spent tomato plants and threw them on the compost pile, then turned the soil to make it ready for next spring. He was digging up onions when he felt a sharp, violent tug on his left arm.

Almost simultaneously, he heard a sharp *crack*. For a moment, he wasn't sure what had happened. He looked at his arm. A blotch of bright red had appeared on his shirt sleeve. Confused, he raised his head and saw movement behind the old woodshed, fifty yards away. His right leg collapsed, followed instantly by another *crack*. By the time he hit the ground, he knew he'd been shot.

A man wearing a camouflage jacket stepped out from behind the woodshed, holding a rifle. The man came slowly toward him, dragging one leg. *Koan*. A second man came into view. The priest known as Gheen. Knowing it was hopeless, Kosh tried to drag himself back to the barn. The men smiled grimly at his feeble effort and kept coming.

Funny thing—it didn't even hurt. *I must be in shock,* Kosh thought. He kept moving, leaving a streak of blood on the frosted grass. He didn't stop until the two men were standing over him. They were talking, but he couldn't make sense of the words. Seconds later, he heard another voice. He looked toward the barn. Tamm was coming out, holding a baton in one hand and Emma's wrist with the other. Tamm gave Kosh a contemptuous look and walked past him, pulling Emma along.

Am I dreaming? Kosh wondered. It felt like a dream, but he knew it wasn't. Still, it was more as if he were watching things happen from a distance. He wondered how much blood he had lost, and why the sky had become so distant and blue, and how long it would take him to die.

He did not have to wonder long. Gheen said something to Koan, who pointed the rifle at Kosh's chest and pulled the trigger.

22 HOPELESS

BISCUITS, BLUEBERRY PIE, CORN CHOWDER, SWEET tomato sauce, zucchini cake, shell bean fritters, creamed potatoes, raspberry scones, fresh cucumber pickles — Emily showed him how to make them all. Kosh, in turn, showed Emily how to butterfly a chicken, make sourdough pancakes, and stir up a delicate herb omelet. Every Sunday afternoon they would cook together for Hamm and Greta. It became a ritual, the centerpiece of Kosh's week.

Kosh had been cooking since he was a kid, teaching himself from cookbooks inherited from the mother he had never met. He had cooked for Adrian, for himself, and at Red's Roost. But this was different. Cooking with Emily Ryan was a labor of love.

During the week, Kosh would experiment at home, trying new recipes and techniques to share with Emily. One of his more ambitious efforts was chocolate soufflé. One week he made six attempts, progressing from muddy sludge to light and heavenly deliciousness. He tried to duplicate his success the next Sunday, but a slamming oven door reduced his soufflé to a puddle of chocolate. He served it anyway, covering the collapsed soufflé with large dollops of fresh whipped cream. Greta said it was the best pudding she had ever eaten.

One hot August afternoon, Kosh and Emily were working on a special dinner for Hamm, who was celebrating his eightieth birthday. Emily was kneading bread dough while Kosh seasoned a pork roast. They joked about making such a meal on the hottest day of the summer, but pork roast and fresh-baked bread were Hamm's favorites. All the kitchen windows were open, flies dotted the screens, and an inadequate fan oscillated from its perch atop the refrigerator.

Kosh paused in his work to watch Emily folding, pressing, and refolding the dough, occasionally slapping it to see her handprint on the smooth surface. She said you could tell when the kneading was done by how long the fingerprints stayed visible. She had been working for several minutes, making small, almost inaudible sounds of effort. He could see the muscles in her forearms, and a sheen of perspiration on her brow. Her long hair was tied back in a loose ponytail. Her lips were slightly parted. Kosh felt something rising up inside him, a bubbly sensation in his chest, a quickening of his breath.

Emily, sensing his attention, looked over her shoulder.

"What?" she said, smiling quizzically.

"Nothing," Kosh said, and went back to rubbing salt and spices into the roast.

It was in that moment, he later realized, that he had fallen completely and hopelessly in love with his brother's fiancée.

PART THREE
THE KISS

The refusal of Netzah Whorsch-Boggs to build the diskos did not dissuade Iyl Rayn from pursuing her goal. She contacted other Boggsian technicians, and even approached a small enclave of technocrats in the far north, to no avail. Some months later, as Iyl Rayn considered other options, she was contacted by Whorsch-Boggs.

"I have some technology for you," he said.

It is not known what happened to change Whorsch-Boggs's mind. Records of diskos appear throughout known history. This, it is argued, may have been sufficient to convince Whorsch-Boggs to proceed with the project. Others maintain that the historical presence of the diskos did not exist prior to their construction. Chayhim, representing the Klaatu faction known as the

Gnomon, suggested that the collision of incompatible timestreams may have been responsible. Others in the Cluster, most notably the artist Iyl Rayn, disagreed.

In any case, so far as is known, the diskos were present prior to their conception, and so stands the ineffable paradox of our existence.

— **E**³

23 HARMONY

TUCKER LAY ON THE CRUDE MATTRESS OF MOSSES AND straw, but sleep proved to be impossible with Malo and his machete outside. He lay still and alert on the lumpy pallet, thinking about the old woman's story. He had seen the ruins of the Klaatu-making machines. But why would the Boggsians want to turn everybody into a Klaatu? Why would the Boggsians living in this time trade a pitchfork for a girl? Were there other tribes like Marta and her people? Had the Boggsians in this time devolved as well? Were there any Medicants left?

As he lay there thinking, he could feel things happening inside his body. He imagined tiny machines gallivanting through his blood vessels, stitching microscopic tears. He wondered if he was still human. He *felt* human, but he wondered how much he could trust his own thoughts. Maybe in addition to healing him, the machines had changed the way his mind worked. Was that what had happened to his father when the Medicants had taken his faith? Had they done it by putting tiny robots into his brain?

Whatever they had done, it hadn't lasted. His father had found a new faith—a sick, twisted religion that told him to murder his own son. Had the machines driven him mad? Would they drive *him* mad as well?

Better crazy than dead, Tucker thought. If it wasn't for the Medicant modifications, he would be a human popsicle on the North Pole.

At first light, Tucker emerged cautiously from the hut. Malo, tending the fire, shot him a glum look, then ignored him. No one else was awake. Tucker sat on a log, across the fire from the young man.

"I'm sorry you had to sleep outside," he said.

Malo stirred the coals vigorously, sending a shower of sparks in Tucker's direction. "I did not sleep."

Tucker leaned back and brushed the cinders from his lap. "I just want to find my friend, then I'm out of here."

Malo did not seem to hear him. Tucker got up and walked to the edge of the encampment, staring out into the forest shadows, listening to the morning songs of the birds. When he turned back, Malo was digging in the fire with a stick. He fished out the head of the pitchfork. Its handle was completely burned off. Malo tossed it on the ground to cool. Tucker suppressed the surge of anger rising within him. It would do no good to get mad at these people. He needed Malo to guide him to the Boggsians.

Malo threw the stick in the fire, then went into his hut. A few minutes later, he came out with a bag over his shoulder and a machete in his hand. He gestured for Tucker to follow, then walked off down a narrow path leading into the forest. Tucker started after him, then stopped, went back to the fire, and picked up the head of the pitchfork. It was still hot, but not too hot to hold. He hurried after Malo, who was waiting for him just inside the forest. Malo saw the blackened fork in Tucker's hand and scowled. He seemed about to speak, then pressed his lips tightly together, turned his back, and continued down the trail.

The trail was a twisted maze. They moved in a generally northeast direction, judging by the sun. Tucker stayed several yards behind Malo, who occasionally used his machete with unnecessary vigor to cut through foliage that had grown over the trail. He asked Malo how far they had to go, but received no reply.

Soon the trail widened and opened onto a hillside cultivated with something that looked like corn. Malo pointed with his machete.

"Boggseys."

Tucker could see the top of a silo peeking up over the brow of the hill. Without a word, Malo turned and was swallowed by the trees.

Tucker followed the base of the hill until he came to a rutted track leading over the top. Several buildings came into view. It looked very much like the Harmony he had visited before, but it was bigger, and there were more people. He counted a dozen men and women performing various tasks—cutting, picking, toting, hoeing, and pounding. Two men were setting a fence post at the corner of a large corral. Two draft horses were feeding from a trough inside. As Tucker approached, the horses noticed him and raised their heads. The men turned to see what the horses were looking at.

"Gutmorgen?" one of them said. The men, a few years older than Tucker, looked like brothers. They had the same broad, open faces, the same small crinkly blue eyes, and they were dressed the same: Black trousers with suspenders, and white linen shirts with the sleeves rolled up. They regarded Tucker with open curiosity, their work forgotten.

"Hello," Tucker said.

One of them noticed the fork in Tucker's hand and said something in a low voice to his companion.

"I'm looking for my friend," Tucker said. "A girl. I was told she was here. That she'd been traded to you for a pitchfork."

The men looked at each other, then at the fire-blackened fork in his hand. The man on the left laughed. "Netzah," he said.

One of the men led Tucker through the settlement. It was larger than Tucker had first thought, almost like a small town. There were dozens of homes and other buildings. They turned onto a stone-paved street lined with shops. None of the shops had signs, but people were going in and out, many of them carrying packages. They all looked at him curiously as they passed. He smelled baking bread. His mouth began to water — he hadn't eaten since yesterday, when he'd eaten Yaca's trail food.

On one side of the street was a large building that looked like a cross between a church and a warehouse, and next to that, a blacksmith and an open-front building containing burlap bags filled with grain and bales of livestock feed. A man loading sacks onto a wagon greeted them without pausing in his task. Tucker's guide waved back cheerfully. They continued through the town.

"How many people live here?" Tucker asked.

"Two hundred twenty-six," his guide said. "But Herman's wife is bursting with life, and soon we will be two hundred twenty-seven. Of course, you are welcome to stay with us, and that would make us two hundred twenty-eight."

"Are you counting the girl I came here to find?"

"You will have to ask Netzah about the girl. It is nothing to do with me."

"Who is Netzah?"

"Netzah Whorsch-Boggs is our technologist. He and his sons trade with outsiders." He made a wry face. "It is an ugly business. Fortunately, these days their services are seldom requested."

The paved street ended at a low, metal-sided building the size of six garages set end to end.

"We are here," the man said. A faint hum came from within the structure.

"What is that sound?" Tucker asked.

"Netzah uses electrical machines for his work. A necessary evil, but we make sure he keeps it within his domain."

"The rest of you don't have electricity?"

"It is not needed. You may enter through the door at the end. I'm sure Netzah will be pleased to tell you what you wish to know. He is not half so mad as he seems." With that, the man headed back down the street.

24 NETZAH WHORSCH-BOGGS

TUCKER KNOCKED ON THE DOOR AND WAITED. WHEN NO one answered, he knocked louder. A muffled voice from inside shouted something unintelligible. The tone made it clear that Netzah Whorsch-Boggs—or whoever was inside—did not want company.

Tucker took a breath, turned the latch, and opened the door. He stepped into a brightly lit alcove containing several chairs, like a waiting room. At the far end of the room was another door. From beyond it, he heard muttering and an occasional *bang*, like someone pounding a desk with a fist.

"Hello?" he called out.

The muttering stopped. A moment later, the door opened just wide enough to admit a man's head: a narrow, pointed, scantily bearded chin; a sharp, arched nose like the beak of a small hawk; a shaggy set of eyebrows; an unruly mop of gray hair; and dark, energetic eyes, one of which was surrounded by a large purple bruise.

"Go away," he said, and slammed the door.

Tucker crossed to the door and pulled it open. The next room looked like a computer lab. Long desks with number-filled screens mounted on them ran down each wall. There were no wires, keyboards, or peripherals visible. The man who had yelled at him was sitting before one of the screens, stabbing at it with his finger. His finger kept disappearing into the screen, and Tucker realized that the screens weren't really screens, but projections.

The man gave Tucker a sideways glare. "I told you to go away."

"Are you Netzah?" Tucker said.

"I am Netzah Whorsch-Boggs, and I do not care who you are. Please leave." The man turned back to the projection and poked at it again, muttering beneath his breath.

Tucker felt himself squeezing the pitchfork head so hard it hurt. He took two steps forward, raised the fork, and stabbed it into the desk. The tines punched through the desktop and nearly impaled the Boggsian's knees.

Whorsch-Boggs sprang back from the desk, with an outraged cry. He was shorter than Tucker had thought.

"What are you doing!" the man raged. "You are a monster!"

"I'm returning your pitchfork," Tucker said. "Where is the girl you traded it for?"

"Are you mad? I do not want your . . . your . . . What happened to the handle?"

"It was defective. Where is my friend?"

142

Whorsch-Boggs collected himself and gave Tucker a measuring look. "Friend? One such as you, I am surprised you have a friend."

"The girl you traded this pitchfork for."

Whorsch-Boggs blinked and scratched his sparse beard with thin, delicate fingers. "The *maidel* brought by the savage? Feh! He brings her to me trussed like a pig ready for roasting. What does he think, I eat children? I take her from him so that he will go away."

"Where is she?"

Whorsch-Boggs spread his hands and performed an exaggerated shrug. "Where she wants to be."

Tucker noticed that the man's face was going out of focus. For a moment he thought he had been drugged, then he realized that something foggy had come between them. He took a step back. A Klaatu. Whorsch-Boggs saw it too.

"Klaatu, bah! Always asking for the impossible and paying with *bupkis*. I pixilate them!" He waved his hands frantically through the cloudy figure, breaking it into thousands of glittering particles. The cloud dissipated. "I spin them in their graves! Hah!" He glared at Tucker. "What do you want?"

"I want to know where my friend is."

"This is valuable information. Nothing is free."

"I gave you your pitchfork. Do you want me to give it to you again?"

Whorsch-Boggs glanced at the ten-inch tines penetrating his desk.

"Feh, I tell you what I know. The girl was a termagant, a she-demon. I give the savage an old tool, I untie the girl, and she gives me this!" He pointed at his black eye. "I try to help her and she attacks me. She is gone. Good riddance!"

"Gone where?"

"I should know this? She ran off. I know no more. Go away."

"You don't know where she went? What direction?"

Whorsch-Boggs pointed at the door.

Tucker suppressed the urge to give the man a second black eye. Where would Lia go? Back to the place where she had been abducted, he decided. Back to where they had been separated. If he could find his way back to the village, he might be able to retrace his steps to the river, to the tree he had climbed when he had last seen her.

Tucker started for the door, but Whorsch-Boggs called him back.

"What is that on your feet?" He was looking at Tucker's blue Medicant boots.

"That is valuable information," Tucker said. "Help me find my friend."

Whorsch-Boggs threw up his hands. "Feh! You are a mono-maniac. I will give you my son Shem to help you find your *maidel*. Now tell me of your peculiar footwear."

"I got them from the Medicants."

"That is absurd. There are no Medicants." He bent over to examine Tucker's boots. He touched the plasticky substance, then jerked his hand back and stood up. "This is ancient technology. Tell me how you acquired it."

"I told you. From the Medicants, in Mayo."

"Mayo is long gone."

"Yeah, well I was there. And before that I was in Hopewell."

"Hopewell! Another name from the histories. And you came there how?"

"Through a disko."

"What is this *disko*?"

"Diskos are portals that go back and forth through time."

Whorsch-Boggs looked puzzled.

Tucker said, "You know, like what used to be on top of the pyramid. The Lah Sept called them Gates."

The Boggsian shook his head. "This is sheer fantasy. You are worse than the Klaatu."

Tucker was surprised. How could the man not know about the Gates? According to Lia, the Boggsians had traded with the Lah Sept. Even if that had been a couple hundred years ago, it was not likely that the Gates had been forgotten.

"The diskos are real. I've been through them a bunch of times. I was in Romelas, and even here, in Harmony, in your future after all the Boggsians are gone. Yesterday, a disko dropped me on top of the pyramid."

Whorsch-Boggs looked unconvinced, but uncertain. He walked unsteadily to a chair and lowered himself onto the seat. "Diskos," he said, shaking his head.

"How can you not know about them?"

"I cannot know of that which does not exist." Whorsch-Boggs's brow furrowed. The color began to return to his face. "The Klaatu told me it could be done, but I did not believe. Why should I believe? But now . . ." He drummed his delicate fingers on his knee and began to nod. "I am not such a one as cannot learn new things. You say there is one of these diskos in the old city?"

"There was, but it disappeared a few seconds after it dumped me there."

"Yes . . . it cannot exist when it has not yet been made . . . that makes sense."

"How does that make sense?"

"Because I have not yet built it, of course! Leave me now, I must meditate."

"You said your son would help me find my friend."

Whorsch-Boggs rolled his eyes. "Yes, yes I did. How is your hearing?"

"It's fine," Tucker said.

"That is unfortunate. Shem fancies himself a philosopher."

25 SHEM

SHEM WHORSCH-BOGGS WAS A YOUNGER AND CONSIDER-
ably taller version of his father, with similar features, a somewhat more substantial beard, and a proud, self-important
demeanor. He was not pleased about being Tucker's guide.

"You wish me to locate a *tree*? In a forest *filled* with trees?
Are you *mad*?"

"It's near the river."

Shem rolled his eyes. "My concerns are allayed. Instead
of sorting through an infinity of trees, we must find your tree
among millions!"

"If you can guide me to the village where the forest people
live, I think I can find my way from there."

"It is a simple matter to locate the savages," Shem said with
a flutter of his long fingers. "You simply enter the forest and
follow your nose. I do not know why I must go with you. I do
not care for their reek."

They were standing on the street outside the metal-sided building. The other residents of Harmony were going about their business with their usual intent self-absorption. The sun was at its peak. A Klaatu, hard to see in the daylight, swooped between them. Shem jerked back, waving his hand through it. The Klaatu broke up.

"It is rare for them to show themselves outside," Shem said.

"Where do they live?" Tucker asked.

"Live?" Shem sniffed contemptuously. "I do not call it living. They are everywhere and nowhere."

"You mean we're surrounded by Klaatu but we can't see them?"

"Your question is meaningless," Shem said. A second Klaatu appeared in the air just behind his shoulder. Tucker didn't bother to point it out.

"Are we going?" he said.

Shem inflated his cheeks, then expelled the air with a *pop.* "If you insist." He set his flat-brimmed hat low on his forehead and started toward the trees.

The Klaatu followed Tucker and Shem to the edge of the forest, then stopped and drifted back toward Harmony. Tucker was relieved not to have it trailing after them, but also a bit insulted. He had gotten used to the idea that the Klaatu found him *interesting,* as Awn had once suggested.

Shem quickly found a trail and set off with long, loose-limbed strides.

"You know there might be traps," Tucker said, hurrying to catch up.

"Feh! The savages and their crude devices do not concern me," Shem said, but he slowed down slightly.

"What about jaguars?" Tucker asked.

"They are night creatures. In any case, I am prepared."

"Prepared how?"

"That is not your concern."

For a time, they walked without speaking. Shem kept up a steady pace. Tucker stayed about ten feet behind him. Shem might not be worried about traps and jaguars, but that didn't mean they weren't there.

At the intersection of two trails, Shem halted abruptly.

"Are we lost?" Tucker asked.

"I know exactly where we are," Shem replied. "*Lost* is a subjective concept. Does the ant know north from south? No. He follows his antennae. Eventually he finds himself where he is, as do we all."

"So you're saying we're lost."

"Every path is connected to every other path." Shem gestured to the right. "One way is as good as another."

As they walked, Tucker thought about the story Marta had told him, about the people of Romelas giving up their lives to become Klaatu.

"Why did you make everybody into Klaatu?" he asked.

"I have made no Klaatu," Shem said.

"I mean, your ancestors. Why did they turn the people of Romelas into Klaatu?"

Shem said nothing. After a few paces, Tucker said, "I guess maybe you don't know."

"I know," said Shem. "I was debating whether it was worth the time and effort to speak, as I am quite certain you would not understand."

Tucker bristled. "I'm not stupid."

Shem snorted. "It is a matter of perspective. I will tell you some history. Transcendence technology was invented by my seventeen-times great-grandfather Artur, who offered his services to those who desired to enter Olahaba before the natural end of their time on Earth."

"What's Olahaba?"

"It is what we call the nonphysical realm where the Klaatu reside. It is said to be a pleasant enough place, or so the Klaatu tell us."

"How do they tell you? Can you talk to them?"

"We have technologies that enable us to communicate with them. As I was saying, transcendence was made available, first to the people known as the Medicants, and then to all peoples. It proved to be quite popular, as it offered a way to avoid the travails of physical existence, and promised a continuation of consciousness.

"The religious fanatics known as the Lah Sept, however, refused transcendence. And, of course, we did not use it on ourselves. When the Lah Sept priests fell from power, the creed of the Lah Sept fell with it, and the people of Romelas developed new epistemologies. My great-grandfather Herman sought to service those who wished to become Klaatu. It was before my time."

"Why do . . . why *did* you offer transcendence when you don't use it on yourselves?"

"A few of us have transcended, but only those whose lives have become unbearable—as you are making mine at this moment."

"What are Boggsians, anyway? Is it like a religion?"

Shem laughed. "We have no religion."

"You believe in God, though, right?"

"How can one believe in that which one cannot comprehend?"

"Lots of things I don't comprehend are true."

"That is different. Most things you don't understand are *not* true, so how can you know which things to believe? It is better to believe in that which you know. All else is futility. Prayer is for those too desperate and frightened to think for themselves."

"If you don't have a religion, then what's a Boggsian?"

"We are a simple folk who live in harmony with our environment."

"But you build complicated machines that turn people into Klaatu."

"If you do not want to be bitten by a snake, you must know the snake. To avoid technology, one must understand it. My father, for example, intends to build a time portal, but that does not mean he wishes to travel though time."

"Then why build it?"

Shem stopped and turned to Tucker. "You are a flea asking questions of a bull. The answers would be meaningless to you."

"Tell me anyway."

"Feh, why do I waste my time?" He sighed. "I will tell you this. A Klaatu wishes to witness historical events, so it has asked my father to build a device that will transmit coherent nodes of information—that is to say, Klaatu—through time. Quantum science tells us that this is possible. All of what exists is information. You are yourself a collection of irreducible bits. Smaller than the things atoms are made of. You are composed of on and off, left and right, something and nothing. This is the basis of our existence. Transcendence technology is based upon the interruption of the matter/information entanglement—the Klaatu are Klaatu because the information of which they are composed is suspended in a pre-matter state. In other words, they exist in a sort of limbo.

"The Klaatu believe that their nonmaterial state means that they should be able to travel backward in time without creating paradoxes. They want my father to build them devices by which they can do so. However, matter is simply an expression of organized information, therefore if one can move information, one can move a particle. Essentially, time travel is simply a matter of altering the history of said particle."

"Does that mean that if I travel back in time, I change what will happen to me later on?"

"No, because there will have been nothing to change. This

is why time travel is unlikely. If the information existed in the past, then there is no need to move it there, and if it did not exist, then it follows that it was not moved. History demonstrates that time travel has never occurred at a non-quantum level, and if it has not been done, then it will not be done. The Klaatu offered a theoretical solution, but such theories are no more solid than the Klaatu themselves. My father refused their request. It seems he has changed his mind."

Shem turned his back to Tucker and continued up the path. "Apparently, you have inspired him."

26 SEVERS

Kosh woke up to the sound of a heartbeat, but faster and sharper. Like hands clapping, but deeper. Like castanets, but not so resonant. *Clop, clop, clop.*

A creaking of wood on metal. A shifting, jerky vibration. The smell of hay. The smell of horse.

Clop, clop, clop.

How many times can I be killed and not be dead? Kosh Feye wondered.

He opened his eyes. Above, a sky so pure and blue and alive it took his breath away. Or maybe something else had taken his breath away. He was not breathing at all. Maybe he *was* dead. He had felt no pain when Koan had fired the rifle at his chest. He remembered only sudden pressure, then falling into the abyss, the walls of his life passing by with increasing speed. He had been certain he was dying. *It is only fair,* he thought, *that one should die aware.*

He became conscious of another sensation, a heaviness upon his chest emitting a subsonic thrum, felt more than heard. He tried to move his arm, to grope at whatever was pressing down on him, but his will was not sufficient to activate his muscles.

A wisp of cirrus came into view, moving slowly from his head to his feet. He watched the cloud until it passed from view. He heard the fluttering exhalation of a horse, the distant cry of a meadowlark, and the hiss of wind passing through dry cornstalks. He pictured himself in a wagon, traveling down a country road.

Maybe instead of being ferried by boat across the river Styx or carried to heaven in a golden chariot, he was being transported from this life on a hay cart. Serve him right. He had failed to protect Emma. Failed to save himself.

I cannot move, and I have no heartbeat, he thought. *Why am I not afraid?*

More clouds came and went. After a time, the cart stopped. He heard a horse snort, then some soft clanking. A shadow fell upon his face, then the sky was blocked by the head of a man wearing a broad-brimmed black straw hat. The man looked into his eyes, then withdrew. Hands grasped his ankles and dragged him off the cart and onto some other surface. Again, they were moving. He could hear the creak of wheels turning. The sky became a rough plank ceiling. Kosh caught glimpses of the man's black-hatted head moving in and out of his vision.

A crackle and buzz filled the room; the light became greenish, then warmed to yellow orange. The buzzing settled to a staticky hum. Kosh could not turn his head to see the source of the sound and light. He didn't need to; he knew what it was even before he was lifted and cast through the disko.

The next time Kosh became aware, a silver-haired woman was bending over him, looking into his eyes.

"Do you know who you are?" asked the woman.

"Kosh," said Kosh. He was speaking, therefore he must be breathing. "Kosh Feye."

"That is correct." The woman made a notion on a tablet. "I am Severs Two-Nine-Four. You may call me Severs. I am pleased to meet you, Kosh Feye."

Kosh cleared his throat. "Where am I?"

"Mayo Two." She raised her eyes from the tablet. "By your reckoning, it is the year twenty-three ten."

Kosh took a moment to absorb that. His thoughts moved sluggishly, as if the juices in his brain had thickened.

"I have to get back," he said, and tried to sit up. Severs put her hand gently on his chest; the weight of her hand was enough to put him back down.

"You are weak," she said.

"How did I get here?"

"You arrived through a portal."

"Portal . . . is that the same as a disko?"

"Portal, disko, Gate—it is all one. Your body was severely injured. The damage has been repaired, though you will require time to regain your former strength."

"How much time?" He was thinking of Emma.

Severs consulted her tablet. "We estimate twenty-three days to reach ninety percent of your estimated former strength and endurance."

"I can't wait that long."

"You are agitated. Do you want to be sedated?" She displayed a small handheld device and made as if to apply it to his neck. Kosh waved it away. It took a tremendous effort just to raise his hand.

"Sedation may augment the healing process," Severs said. "This is a relatively primitive point in our technological development. We do not yet have the nanotech required to accelerate the process. In my time, you would be healed in a matter of days."

"What do you mean, *in your time?*"

"I will not be born for another seventy-three years. Like you, I have been displaced."

"I have to get back to where I came from."

"You must enter a portal to do so," Severs said. "There is no reason to hurry. Wherever the portal takes you, there you will be. What was your point of origin?"

"You wouldn't know it. A place called Hopewell, back in the twenty-first century."

"Mayo was once called Hopewell."

Kosh let that sink in, then said, "I never liked the name Hopewell, anyways."

"I think we have an acquaintance in common," Severs said. "Do you know the Yar Lia?"

Kosh nodded. "I just saw her about a week ago, in Hopewell, kicking butt on some priests."

"I am certain we are talking about the same person," Severs said. "She spoke of you on several occasions. Was she well?"

"Last time I saw her she was jumping into a disko. She didn't show up here, did she?"

"I have not seen her since the Terminus. She was searching for Tucker Feye. Do you know him as well?"

"Tucker is my nephew."

"I treated him once, after he stumbled into one of our recycling centers."

"Kind of a coincidence, you and me being here."

"It is no coincidence. I am assigned to Mayo Two because this is where the portal is kept. I am a specialist, you might say. A fellow traveler. This is why I was assigned to you."

Kosh felt something cool touch the side of his neck. A wave of tranquility moved down his spine. "I don' wanna be sedated," he said, his tongue growing thick.

"Heal," said Severs.

27 SOUFFLÉ

"I DON'T UNDERSTAND," EMILY RYAN SAID. "LAST WEEK you said you wanted to see it. It's about aliens, I think."

"Well now I don't," Kosh said. "I gotta go." He hung up the phone and sat staring at it, waiting for his breathing to go back to normal. Last Sunday, Emily had asked him if he wanted to go see *Contact* with her. It was playing at the multiplex in Rochester. He'd said yes, because he could not say no to her. Not to her face. But now he didn't think he could stand it, sitting next to her for two hours. Smelling her hair. Feeling the heat of her body. It was best to simply not see her at all, because it hurt too much to know he could never have her.

The phone rang. He let it ring five times before picking up.

"Hello." He made his voice go dead.

"Kosh, are you mad at me?" It was Emily again.

"No. I've just got. . . . Look, I'm really busy, okay?"

"That's fine, I understand. I just wanted to make sure it wasn't something I'd done."

"It's nothing to do with you," Kosh said.

"We can go see it another time."

"Okay."

"Are we still cooking next weekend?"

"I might be busy."

Emily didn't speak for a moment. "I think you're mad at me," she said at last.

"I'm not mad." Kosh was squeezing the handset so hard his fingers hurt. He forced his hand to relax.

"Well . . . I was thinking about doing a pot roast Sunday, so, call me if you want to."

"Okay. Good-bye." Kosh set the handset back on the phone cradle with exaggerated delicacy, as if presenting a perfect soufflé.

28 JAGUAR

". . . QUANTUM SCIENCE, OF COURSE, IS NOTHING MORE
than an extension of kabbalistic philosophy, as Jonathon Boggs
realized, and so applying the numerological constructs of the
medieval Kabbalah one must be led to conclude that quantum displacement of matter, reverse or otherwise, is both
true and untrue, and therefore without value, which is why
Schrodinger's felicidal inclinations existed purely as a thought
experiment. The man did not even own a cat. My father, however, chooses to overlook the self-evident, and sends me on this
fool's errand to—"

"Do you even know what you're talking about?" Tucker
asked.

Shem stopped walking and looked back at Tucker. "Why
would I talk if I did not know what I was saying?"

"That's what I was wondering."

Shem compressed his lips. Tucker could see that the
Boggsian was formulating a scathing and verbose reply. He had

become increasingly weary of Shem's supercilious attitude and nonstop prattle.

Shem said, "You are as ignorant as the forest savages. I—"

"You know, we've been here before," Tucker said.

They were standing at the intersection of two trails.

"It does look somewhat familiar," Shem admitted.

"I think you just led us in a big circle."

"The savages have been playing tricks on us." Earlier, Shem had been going on about the "forest savages" and their ignorant, unclean ways. Tucker had no great love for Marta and her people, but they weren't nearly so *irritating* as this Boggsian.

"I thought you knew how to get to their village."

"As I indicated previously, every path is connected to every other path," Shem said with a haughty wave of his hand. "Er . . . which way did we go last time we were here?"

"That way." Tucker pointed.

"That was incorrect," Shem said. "Why did you not say something before?" He set off in the opposite direction. Tucker followed, thinking that he would have been better off alone.

"Now, where was I?" Shem said.

"You were explaining the gobbledygook of the gibberish," Tucker said.

Shem stopped and turned on him. "You are a philistine! I share my most sublime thoughts purely as an act of generosity!"

"Whatever," Tucker said.

Shem sniffed and continued walking, muttering to himself. Shortly thereafter, they reached the collection of huts where

Tucker had spent the previous evening. Shem halted at the edge of the open area and cleared his throat.

"Greetings, savages, I bring you a distinguished visitor with whom you have much in common!"

In full daylight, the small encampment looked even shabbier than Tucker remembered. The huts were little more than lean-tos, and several of the leaf-frond roofs were falling in. The fire pit at the center of the circle of huts was a mound of ashes and charred pig bones. There were no people.

"Hah!" said Shem. "They heard us coming and have fled. I am not surprised."

"I don't think it was us." Tucker pointed. "I think it was that."

On the far side of the dead fire, a few inches above the trampled earth, hovered a disko.

Shem stared at the disko. "My eyes perceive a disk-shaped object."

"Your eyes perceive a disko," Tucker said.

"Disko?"

"Disko, Gate, time-travel portal."

Shem walked around the fire pit for a closer look.

"I wouldn't get too close," Tucker said.

Shem reached out with his hand. The disko buzzed and turned orange. Shem snatched his hand away and backed up a few paces. He looked frightened.

Tucker said, "Or, if you want, you can step into it. It might take you someplace interesting."

"No thank you," Shem said.

"I wonder if the people that lived here went into it. The woman, their leader, told me they were waiting to be transported. Maybe they decided that this was their transportation."

"More likely, they ran off in terror." Shem recovered his confident demeanor. "Ignorance breeds fear. This"—he gestured at the disko—"is my father's doing."

"How so? It's only been a few hours since he decided to build a disko. How could he do it so fast?"

"Is it not clear? Once he made the decision to proceed with his plans, the technology became inevitable. In the same sense, you were conceived in the moment your father first met your mother. Intent is the platform upon which reality teeters. We are dealing with displacement of information in time, therefore events appear to occur out of sequence. No doubt my father is at this moment back in Harmony attempting to build his device. Even if many months pass before he achieves success, the devices already manifest themselves."

"A while ago you were saying he would fail, that the diskos were an impossibility."

"I adjust my thinking to account for observed realities," Shem said with a flutter of his fingers. "And now, I will return to Harmony to assist my father."

"What about me?"

"I have brought you here at great inconvenience to myself. I wish you luck."

Shem began to walk away. Out of the corner of his eye,

Tucker saw something move within the dark interior of one of the huts.

"Shem!"

The Boggsian glanced back at him, annoyed. Tucker pointed toward the hut. Two greenish-yellow eyes were gazing out at them. Shem saw the eyes and went rigid.

"Get on the other side of the disko," Tucker said.

Shem, transfixed, could not move. The jaguar oozed out of the doorway like slowly flowing liquid, taking soft, silent steps with its enormous paws. Tucker had seen housecats stalking birds exactly that same way.

"Back up slow," Tucker said. Shem took a step back, fumbling in his pocket with his right hand. The jaguar froze in midstep, its tail twitching.

"Two more steps," Tucker said. "Come on, Shem!"

Shem pulled a metal object from his pocket. Tucker could see the cat was about to leap. He ran to Shem, grabbed him by the shoulders, and pulled him back behind the disko. Startled by Tucker's speed, the cat hesitated. Tucker watched it through the wavery lens of the disk. Shem was panting loudly.

Keeping one eye on the jaguar, Tucker grabbed a charred stick from the fire pit. The jaguar's mouth opened slightly, showing the tip of its pink tongue. Shem raised his arm. The metal object in his hand looked like a small version of a Lah Sept *arma*.

The jaguar hunched its back and sprang. Its leap took it straight toward the disko. Shem screamed, and a gout of blue fire erupted from his hand. The jaguar and the flame hit the disko from opposite sides. The disko hissed and flared brilliant orange, swallowing both fire and cat in the same instant.

In the stillness that followed, Tucker could hear his own heartbeat. The disko returned to its diaphanous, semitransparent state. Shem dropped to his knees and began muttering in the Boggsian language. It sounded like a prayer.

So much for no religion, Tucker thought. He scanned their surroundings. Every shadow looked as if it might hold another jaguar. A crackling buzz interrupted Shem's chanting. The disko had turned to green. Tucker grabbed Shem and dragged him away just as a smoking apparition jumped out of the disko and landed in the middle of the fire pit, sending ashes scattering in all directions. For a fraction of a second, Tucker thought the jaguar had returned, then he realized it was a man with a sooty face and wisps of smoke trailing from his collar and hat brim. The man looked a great deal like Shem's father, Netzah Whorsch-Boggs, only with much of his beard singed off.

The man's eyes moved from Tucker to Shem and fastened upon the weapon, still in Shem's hand.

"Dummkopf!" he shouted. "Idiot!"

It was definitely Netzah Whorsch-Boggs. He stepped out of the fire pit, grabbed the weapon from his son, shook it in his face, and threw it to the ground, all the while delivering a stream of Boggsian invective. Tucker didn't understand any of the words, but the tone was clear. The man was apoplectic.

He was also, Tucker noticed, considerably older than the Netzah Whorsch-Boggs he had met that morning.

29 AWN

It took Lia the better part of the day to find a place to cross the river. Eventually she came upon a bridge. She crossed, then headed downstream. The banks were tangled with roots and brush; in some places she had to veer well away from the river to get around impassable snarls. She kept moving, and by early afternoon she detected the reek of decaying pig offal.

The pig's head was gone, along with most of the entrails. Some animal or animals had been at it. Lia looked around nervously, hoping that whatever had eaten the pig was not still around. It took her a few minutes more to find the tree where she had been grabbed. She called Tucker's name, softly at first, then louder.

She listened, but heard no response from Tucker. He might be searching for her. He might have been captured by the forest people. He might be injured. He might be dead. The only sounds were the mindless chatter of birds, the scurry of small ground creatures, and a distant rapping noise. Lia at first thought it was a woodpecker, but the *tok, tok, tok* was too irregular, and not so fast as a woodpecker. It sounded more like someone chopping wood.

Her curiosity soon overcame her fear. She gathered some sticks and made a large arrow on the ground, pointing in the direction of the rapping sound. If Tucker showed up while she was gone, it would tell him where she was headed.

Using her ears to guide her, Lia wound her way through the woods. The sound became louder, then stopped abruptly, and was followed by the crackle of breaking branches, and a decisive thump. Lia moved forward, slowly and silently, and soon arrived at a small sunlit clearing. The underbrush was trampled. Several stumps jutted from the earth. She could smell the bright odor of fresh-cut wood.

At the center of the clearing, almost invisible in the bright sunlight, was a Gate. At the far edge of the clearing, Lia saw a neatly stacked quantity of trimmed, debarked logs, each of them as big around as Lia's waist and several arm-spans in length.

From the forest beyond, she heard a new sound, a ripping, scraping noise that went on for a few minutes, then stopped. The Gate went from translucent to gray-green. Lia concealed herself behind a bush. The end of a log emerged from the Gate, then the person who was carrying the log: a woman wearing plain, earth-colored trousers and an identically hued long-sleeved shirt. She carried the log, four times as long as she was tall, on her shoulder, balancing it with one hand as if it were weightless. She rolled the log off her shoulder onto the pile of logs, where it landed with a heavy thump.

The woman had only a shadow of colorless hair on her head. Her facial features were smooth and regular, as if they had never expressed an emotion. Clearly she was not a Boggsian, nor one of the forest people. A Medicant, perhaps? Lia did not think so. Even Medicants carried more expression on their faces than this.

The woman walked back into the disko, stepping into it with the ease and confidence of one entering a familiar open doorway. Seconds later, the distant chopping resumed.

Lia crossed the clearing. Behind the stack of logs, a rectangular area had been cleared down to the dirt, and leveled. Along each side of the rectangle, logs had been placed, overlapping at the ends. The woman was building a log cabin.

Lia returned to her hiding place. The chopping resumed, then another crash, and the sound of scraping. Again, the woman came through the Gate with a trimmed log. This time, she was carrying a double-bladed ax in her left hand. Lia wanted to ask the woman who she was and what she was doing, but caution kept her still. The woman was immensely strong, and therefore potentially dangerous.

The woman unloaded the log, then went to work with the ax, carving a deep notch into each log end. Lia did not like the look of that ax. It might slice through muscle and bone as easily as it cut through wood. Best to leave this frightening woman to her work, and return to the place where she hoped Tucker would come looking for her. She edged back from her vantage point until she could no longer see the woman, then began to walk quickly through the forest. She found the path she had been on earlier, but had gone no more than a few hands of paces when the woman appeared before her, leaning on her ax, standing calmly on the trail as if she had been waiting for some time.

"*Trackenspor? Septan? Deutsch?*" the woman said.

Too surprised to speak, Lia simply stared back at the woman. Close up, her features looked more unformed than ever, as if she had been pressed from a mold, like a mannequin. Her voice was familiar, however. Lia was certain she had heard those words before.

"*Inglés? Español?*" the woman said.

"I am from Romelas," Lia said.

"Ah." The woman smiled. Her cheeks stretched oddly, as if she had never smiled before. "You are Lah Sept?"

"Not anymore . . . Are you *Awn?*"

"An awn is a bristle growing from a grass flower. I am an Augmented Whorsch-Novak golem. You may call me Awn."

"Are you human?"

"That is a very good question. Are you?"

"Yes!"

"Then I am human, as well, though I have been modified."

"I think I met you before."

"That is unlikely. I am new."

"You were a lot older."

"Ah, you have been traveling."

"I met you in the future. Thousands of years."

Awn blinked and waved a hand in front of her face. "Please keep your numbers to yourself."

Lia was puzzled. She had never met anyone outside the Lah Sept who did not use numbers.

"You must live a long time," she said.

"My enhancements include a telomere regenerator. Still, I will age, and I will die. The Terminus will go on."

"This is the Terminus, then?"

Holding her ax by the blade with one hand, Awn swept the handle slowly through the air, indicating all that surrounded them. "Already the diskos arrive."

"When I was here before—I mean, later—there were lots of them. Everywhere."

"Yes. My creator is busy."

"Your creator? Somebody *created* you?"

"Are you not made?"

"I suppose I was. By my mother."

"And so it is with me. Why are you here?"

"I'm not sure. I came here with my friend, and we got separated. I'm trying to find him."

"Who is this friend?"

"His name is Tucker Feye."

"Ah yes, a figure from your Lah Sept mythology."

"He's a real person."

"I did not say otherwise. When you find him, what will you do?"

"We hope to find a disko that will take us to Hopewell. There are things we need to do there."

"Hopewell was long ago. Perhaps you have already done them."

"Only if we go back. Can you help us?"

"Possibly. Where did you last see your friend?"

"He was climbing a tree, and I was on the ground. Then the forest people grabbed me and tied me up and sold me to a Boggsian. I got away and went back to the tree, but Tucker wasn't there. It's not far from here."

"There are many trees."

"It was close to a place where somebody killed a pig."

"Ah! I know that place. The forest people trapped a pig not long ago." A few yards behind Awn, a Gate materialized on the path. Awn walked up to it and pushed her ax handle into the swirling gray surface. Lia expected it to be sucked in, but the disk remained inactive. Awn removed the ax and looked at the handle.

"This disko is local. Come, I will help you find your friend, and we will talk." She stepped into the Gate.

Lia hung back. Could she trust this half-human woman? Entering a Gate was not something to undertake lightly, but Awn was promising to help, and she had helped Lia twice before.

Awn stuck her head out of the disk. This was an effect Lia had never seen before. It looked like a disembodied head sticking out of a big swirly gray plate.

"Are you coming?" the head asked.

Lia took a breath and entered the Gate.

30 FATHER AND SON

TUCKER WATCHED, FASCINATED, AS NETZAH WHORSCH-Boggs tore into his son. It was a magnificent performance—the sooty old man shouting insults and jabbing Shem in the chest with his long forefinger, as Shem flapped his hands helplessly and tried to apologize. After having endured hours of Shem's pontificating, Tucker rather enjoyed seeing him on the defensive.

Netzah Whorsch-Boggs now appeared to be a man in his seventies, whereas before he had looked some twenty years younger. After another minute or two, the old man ran out of invective. He wrapped his arms around his son and hugged him fiercely. Tentatively, Shem hugged his father back. Netzah took Shem by his shoulders and looked into his eyes. "Go back. Make yourself useful. Clean up the mess you have made. I will join you shortly." He shoved his son into the disko. Breathing heavily, he glared at the disko until it settled back to gray translucence.

"*Dummkopf!*" he spat on the ground, then began brushing bits of charred fabric from his shirt.

Tucker said, "Um . . . hello?"

Netzah Whorsch-Boggs whirled. Tucker braced himself, thinking the old man might try to throw him into the disko, too.

"Feh. It is *you*. I should have known."

"What happened to you?" Tucker asked.

Whorsch-Boggs threw up his hands. "Someone's idiot son fired an energy weapon into this disko is what happened." He picked up Shem's hand weapon and put it in his pocket.

"He was shooting at a jaguar," Tucker said, feeling a little sorry for Shem.

"Do I look like a jaguar? If not for the filters I would be *asche*. One moment I am working peacefully, then *boosh!* I will have to make some adjustments." He looked back at the disko. "At least I now know what happened to the *verdammt* fool. I thought the forest savages had eaten him for their breakfast. Seventeen years my wife has been mourning him. *Dummkopf!*"

"Where did you send him?"

"Shem is back in my crèche, cleaning up the damage he has caused."

"Crèche . . . Is that like your laboratory?"

"It is where notions are bred. Now, if you will excuse me, I must join my son to spend my golden years suffering his nitwit philosophies." Whorsch-Boggs turned and disappeared into the disko.

Tucker had a momentary urge to follow Whorsch-Boggs into the disko. He had more questions. Why had the Klaatu asked him to build the diskos? How did Whorsch-Boggs know where each disko went? How could he get back to Hopewell?

His questions would have to wait. First, he had to find Lia. Once they were together again, perhaps they would find some answers.

He looked into the hut where he had spent the night. The bedroll was gone. He searched the other huts. Everything of possible use had been taken. Marta and her people would not be coming back soon, if ever.

Tucker set out along the trail leading west, toward the last place he had seen Lia. He had gone only a few steps when he heard a familiar hissing, popping sound. A bright orange blob, about the size of his fist, coalesced on the trail ten steps behind him. The blob swelled rapidly, then lengthened and turned from orange to pink.

The maggot swiftly reached its full size, then raised its front end as if sniffing the air. It pointed itself directly at Tucker and moved toward him. Tucker turned and ran.

The last time he had been chased by a Timesweep, Tucker had been able to outrun it easily, but that maggot had been damaged. This maggot moved with remarkable speed. Tucker left the trail and sped though the trees, leaping over fallen logs, zigzagging around brush piles, leaping over a small stream, doing everything he could to put obstacles between himself and the maggot. It wasn't working. The maggot never fell more than a few dozen yards behind, and it didn't seem to be getting tired. He figured he could keep up the pace for another few minutes, but sooner or later he would run out of energy and the Timesweep would be on him. His only other option was to climb a tree, but he would have to climb fast, and even then, he wasn't sure what the thing was capable of. The ease with which it sped through the tangled forest suggested that climbing a tree might be well within its capabilities.

Tucker scrambled up a steep hillside. His hand fell upon a grapefruit-size stone. He turned and hurled the rock as hard as he could. It hit the maggot dead center — and bounced off like a pebble. Tucker kept running, his breath rasping, his heart hammering. It was only a matter of time.

The moment Lia stepped out of the disko she could smell death. A few feet away, Awn stood on a trail, looking down at the scattered remains of the dead pig.

"As a Pure Girl," Awn said, "the Sisters would terrify us with tales of such carnage."

"You were a Pure Girl?"

"Yes. No. I possess fragments of memory from another's life. Now, where is this tree?"

"This way." Lia moved off the path to the spot where she had been abducted. The arrow she had made of sticks was undisturbed.

"He's not here," she said.

"There are many possibilities," Awn said. "He may have encountered the forest people, or the Boggsians."

"Or a jaguar," Lia whispered.

"Or a jaguar." Awn sniffed the air. "Though I detect no odor of cat nearby. But there is something . . ." She walked back to the trail, around the pig entrails, and up the path. After a few paces she stopped and bent over.

"What is it?" Lia asked.

Awn touched her hand to the earth, then held her fingers to her nose. "Blood has been spilled here." She stood and examined their surroundings. "There has been violence. See this?" She pointed her ax at a wooden appendage dangling from the limb of a tree. "It is the remains of a device built by the forest people. A trap for large animals. The pig entrails may have been left as bait."

"Are you saying Tucker got caught in a trap?"

"This trap was not made to catch. It was designed to kill." Awn stood and looked off into the trees. "The forest people are coming."

"I think they're here," Lia said.

A woman wearing a mottled green and gold sarong and mud-colored shawl had materialized from the leaves and shadows.

"Hello," said Awn.

The woman regarded Awn warily as a hand of men emerged from the underbrush behind her, all carrying machetes. Lia's eyes narrowed as she recognized the man who had attacked her and delivered her to the Boggsian.

"I do not know you," said the woman.

"I am Awn."

"You are very odd-looking. Are you a *bruja*?"

Awn smiled; creases formed on her unlined face. "Does it matter?"

"I suppose not," said the woman. "We are leaving this place, and you are welcome to it. Evil things have invaded our forest." She looked at the disko on the trail behind Awn. "We do not wish to be devoured."

"So long as you do not approach the diskos, they will not harm you."

"So you say. We are leaving." The woman made as if to turn.

Lia said, "Wait. Have you seen a boy with blue feet?"

The woman did not reply, but the expression on her face made it clear that she had.

"Do you know where he is?" Lia asked.

"He is with the boggseys," she said, then melted into the forest along with the rest of them. A moment later it was as if they had never been there.

Lia looked at Awn. "He's alive," she said.

"So it seems." Awn sighed. "I suppose we now must deal with the Boggsians." Her face suddenly changed, bland features going hard and tense. She tipped her head, listening. A moment later, Lia heard it too. Something large, crashing through the woods, coming straight toward them.

31 COURAGE

On the sixteenth day of Kosh's stay in the Medicant hospital, Severs 294 visited him during his physical therapy session. The therapists had clamped him into one of their devices and were exhorting him to various physical contortions as the machine did its best to resist him. Kosh entertained himself by attempting to break the machine. Twice so far, he had succeeded, to the tongue-clucking irritation of the therapists, whom he had dubbed Thing One and Thing Two. Kosh thought Thing One was a woman, but he could not be certain. Thing Two, judging from the shadow of beard tracing his jaw, was male.

On this day, the Things were asking him to straighten his leg while the straps and metal springs fought his efforts.

"Do not push so hard that it causes pain," said Thing One, who had been saying the same thing for two weeks.

Kosh tried to straighten his leg. His thigh muscles corded, sweat popped out of every pore, pain rocketed up and down his leg from ankle to hip. The machine groaned.

"You are pushing too hard," said Thing Two. "You will damage yourself or the machine."

Kosh grunted in reply and pushed harder.

"Your pulse and blood pressure are reaching dangerous levels," said Thing One.

Kosh gritted his teeth and pushed harder yet. "Resistance is futile," he growled. The machine emitted a gratifying squeal, followed by the smell of overheated plastic. Kosh straightened his leg completely, to no resistance whatsoever.

"Did I bust it again?" Kosh asked, breathing heavily.

The Things were examining the readouts anxiously, twittering back and forth in their weird technical jargon.

Looking over their shoulders, Severs read the displays.

"I see our patient is getting stronger," she said.

"Stronger?" Thing Two gave Kosh his bland version of the stink eye. "He is a berserker bent on destruction."

"If he is too strong for your equipment, then perhaps we should consider our work here complete."

"He is scheduled for seven more days of therapy," said Thing One.

"I will unschedule him."

"That is not proper procedure," said Thing Two.

"Do you want him to break *all* your machines?" Severs said.

Thing One and Thing Two looked at each other.

Thing One said, "We will not object if he does not return."

Thing Two added, "But we will not sign a formal discharge."

"I will take responsibility," Severs said.

"I can walk, you know," Kosh said as Severs guided his wheelchair along the hospital hallway.

"There are rules."

"So you keep reminding me. It's pretty cool, this chair having only one wheel. It would be even better if it had no wheels, like a hover chair. This is the future, right? Don't you have flying cars?"

"Flying cars would lead to accidents. The use of maglev transport within our hospitals has been explored, but it proved impractical. Even in my time, a century from now, we will rely on wheel-based patient transport."

"I thought the future would be cooler," Kosh said.

Over the past two weeks, Severs and Kosh had spent several hours talking. Severs had told Kosh about the coming Lah Sept destruction of Mayo, and of her time with the Yars in Romelas after the overthrow of the priests. Kosh had told her about his life, and about Tucker, and Emma, and about how he had been shot. Kosh liked Severs. They had something in common — both of them were castaways in time. Severs was living seventy-odd years before her birth, while Kosh was stuck three centuries in the future.

"Your recovery is going well," Severs said as she wheeled Kosh into his room. "The damage to your heart and lungs is nearly healed, and your strength is at one hundred seven percent of optimum. Are you still experiencing pain?"

"I feel great," Kosh said. He hopped off the chair, ignoring the sharp twinge from his hip and the grating sensation from his chest.

Severs regarded him doubtfully. "The more time you give your body to repair itself, the less likely you are to reinjure yourself. Your journey through the portals may be arduous."

Kosh opened and closed his fists. "I'm ready."

"You cannot know that, because you cannot know where the portal will take you."

"Yeah, well I'm ready to give it a whirl. Not that I haven't enjoyed your company."

Severs smiled. "It has been a pleasure to know you as well."

"What about you? Do you ever think about leaving here?"

Severs shook her head. "It is a peculiar thing to be here, helping to build and maintain this society all the while knowing that it is likely to come to a bloody end. Still, day to day, the work is gratifying. Who knows? Perhaps something I do will change the dark future I remember."

"Thinking about that kind of stuff makes my head hurt," Kosh said. "I figure I just do what I have to do, and what has to happen happens."

"That is as valid an approach as any," Severs said.

The next morning, Kosh saw his own clothes for the first time since he had arrived at the hospital. They had been cleaned, but not repaired. He pushed his finger through the bullet holes in his shirtsleeve, the right front pocket of his jeans, his jacket, and his shirt, shaking his head in wonder. How had he lived through that?

He dressed himself slowly, with a sense of ritual. Pulling on his jeans made him feel stronger. He peeled off the odd blue stockings they had given him, put on his old socks, and pulled on his motorcycle boots. The boots increased his height by two inches, making the floor seem far away. His jacket gave him a sense of invulnerability. He felt good.

When Severs showed up, Kosh was gazing at himself in the mirror.

"You look quite frightening," Severs said.

"Thank you," said Kosh.

Severs led Kosh to a large room deep in the hospital sub-basements. In the center of the space was a massive metallic armature surrounding a disko. Several men and women were milling about, making adjustments to the equipment and working on small handheld tablets.

"This is the first portal we captured," Severs told him. "And the only one, so far. Our engineers are still trying to understand how it works. All they know for certain is that several people have emerged from the disk. Some, like you, were badly injured. Some were dead. Those who survived all claimed to be from other times, some as far back as your Hopewell, some, like me, from the future. We do not know where it will take you, but the fact that you came out of it is encouraging. They have sent a number of probes into the portal, but none have returned. If you enter it, you will be the first person to enter from our side. Our scientists have arranged for you to carry some devices in your body. We have implanted several small recording capsules. They should cause you no discomfort."

Kosh frowned. "Thanks for asking first!"

"Consider it payment for the services you have received."

"What are these capsule things supposed to accomplish? I mean, I'm not coming back."

"You cannot know that for certain. And even if you don't return, as soon as you enter the portal we will search the historical archives for information about your eventual demise. We may be able to locate your body and extract the information from the capsules. That is, assuming you die in the past."

"Are you saying that for the rest of my life, these things inside me will record what happens to me?"

"To a limited extent, yes."

"Not so sure I like that."

"If we remove the devices, you will not be permitted to enter the disk."

"Great. I guess I have to make sure I get cremated when I die."

"That is your prerogative."

"Why do you have to wait for me to enter the disko before you look for records of my death?"

"We have looked. We can find no such records." Severs consulted her tablet. "You do not have to go."

She can read my heart rate, Kosh thought. *She knows how scared I am.*

"Yes, I do." He managed to keep his voice level.

Severs looked him up and down. "You are very courageous."

Kosh did not feel courageous. Looking at the disko, it was all he could do not to collapse into a quaking, blubbering puddle of terror. He was half certain he was going to die. He would die, and no one would ever know, and based on his recent near-death experiences—falling off the barn, wrecking his bike, getting shot—it would hurt. A lot. But the alternative—leaving Emma in the hands of Gheen and his deacons without even trying to rescue her—was unthinkable. He would not want to live if he had to live with that.

"It's not courage," he said, "if you have no choice."

32   HOPEWELL

Another roof. This time, to Kosh's vast relief, he was not on the World Trade Center, or tumbling down a steep barn roof to a forty-foot drop. This roof was flat, and the building was not on fire. He looked out over the low parapet. He was on top of the old hotel in Hopewell. The sky was low and gray, with a late-morning feel to it, and that biting autumn cold that comes just before the November snows. It had been early October when the Lambs had taken Emma.

Last time he had been up there, he'd been sixteen years old. He and Ronnie Becker had broken into the abandoned hotel and hauled a twelve-pack up to the roof. That had been a fun night — until Ronnie tossed a can of Grain Belt off the roof and hit Elwin Frahlen's Ford LTD smack on the windshield. Elwin had called the sheriff, and Kosh had spent his first night in jail. They'd caught Ronnie, too, but he'd been in jail before — it was nothing new for him. Kosh could still remember the expression on Adrian's face the next morning: a frozen mask of contemptuous condemnation.

Kosh pulled open the trapdoor and climbed down into the fourth-floor hallway. There were lights inside, and the smell of carpet cleaner. Somebody must have opened the hotel again, probably because of all the bird-watchers and religious nuts that had flocked into town. The tinny sound of a television came from behind one of the doors, but Kosh sensed that the hotel was sparsely occupied. He took the stairs down to the first floor. As he entered the lobby, the young woman behind the desk looked up from painting her nails. Her eyes went wide. She put her hand on the desk phone.

"Um, if you're not a guest, you're not supposed to be in here." The girl was gripping the telephone handset hard. Kosh figured if he so much as narrowed his eyes at her, she'd be punching in 911.

"I'm just leaving." He moved toward the front door, then hesitated and turned back to her. "Tell me one thing. What's the date today?"

She frowned warily. "November first?"

Kosh nodded, taking it in. A little over two weeks since he had been shot.

"Those Lambs of September, are any of them still around?"

Her eyes widened and she drew back. "Are you one of them?"

"I'm just trying to find them."

"You have to go."

"Okay, okay," he said. "I'm leaving."

Kosh looked back as he left the hotel. The girl was talking on the phone. He left the hotel and crossed the street to the Pigeon Drop Inn. He noticed a poster taped to the inside of the window, just below the Budweiser sign:

Kosh stared at the poster, trying to make sense of it. Henry *Hall*? For *Mayor*? Henry hadn't been sober in twenty years. It had to be a joke. Kosh pushed though the door and stepped inside. His first impression was that nothing had changed. Same dingy walls, same fake neon signs, same cracked vinyl booths. Then he noticed that none of the five people sitting at the bar were Henry Hall. That was different.

Red spotted him. "Curtis! Back from the dead!"

"You thought I was dead?" Kosh said.

"Figure of speech," Red said. He was the same beer barrel of a man with bushy gray hair, black eyebrows, and a bulbous, vein-shot nose. Kosh had last seen him the day he'd picked up Tucker, just after Adrian and Emily had disappeared. Was it only months ago? It felt like years. Kosh took a stool and propped his elbows on the bar. He had a lot of questions, but the first one that came out of his mouth was, "Henry Hall for mayor?"

Red chuckled. "Can you believe it?"

"No," said Kosh.

"Believe it," Red said. "The old sot quit drinking a few months back and now he's making like Abe Lincoln." He shook his head. "Took a piece out of my bottom line, I can tell you— he was my best customer. But what the heck—I'm gonna vote for him. For one thing, ain't nobody else wants the job."

"What happened to Ed Hammer? He die?" Ed Hammer had been mayor of Hopewell for thirty years.

"Ed got his self mixed up in that cult business. It was him that let the crazies use the park for their revival. After what happened, people got kinda upset. Anyways, he's pushing eighty. What're you doing back in town?"

"I have some business with the crazies."

"You?" Red's smile turned flat and his forehead crinkled. "You ain't with that bunch, are you?"

"No. A friend of mine got mixed up with them. I'm trying to find her."

"A girl, huh?"

"Yeah. You know where they are?"

"Well, folks around here are done with that whole thing. You won't see a yellow T-shirt in the county no more. The ones

189

running the show, they all took off, except for the old man, that Father September fellow. He's in jail now. The cops don't quite know what to do with him. More'n five hundred people saw them kill some kid, but the kid disappeared. But they got a blood sample and it matches up with a local boy, Tom Krause. In fact, they're having a funeral for the kid right this minute. As for that Gheen fellow, him and his cronies took off. Nobody knows where."

Kosh nodded slowly. He would have to talk to Adrian—he could see no other way to get the information he needed. If he could find the Lambs, he would find Emma. That is, if he didn't get himself killed all over again.

"Hey Red, you by any chance got a car I could borrow?"

"I might could do that," Red said after a moment. "Long as you plan to bring it back."

As Kosh walked out of the bar with the keys to Red's delivery van, a sheriff's cruiser pulled abruptly over to the curb. Jeff Wahlberg climbed out.

"Kosh Feye!"

"What's up, Jeff?"

Wahlberg hitched up his belt, not quite putting his hand on his gun.

"I could ask you the same."

"Nothing's up. I came back for a visit. Why?"

"We got a call you were harassing the girl in the hotel."

Kosh laughed. "I did no such thing."

"That's not what she says."

Kosh sighed. "Look, Jeff, I went in the hotel and asked her a couple of polite questions. She was kind of freaked out, so I left. End of story."

Wahlberg relaxed slightly. "People are touchy these days, ever since that business with the Lambs," he said. He gave Kosh a squint-eyed, calculating gaze. "So why *are* you here?"

"Do you remember the woman who was staying with me?"

"The runaway wife, sure."

"Her husband and some of the other crazies came by my place and grabbed her."

"Grabbed?"

"Kidnapped."

Wahlberg stared at him. Kosh knew what he was thinking. To a small-town cop, a kidnapping was like hitting the lottery. He probably wished it had happened in his jurisdiction.

"You report this?" Wahlberg said.

"Oh, yeah." Kosh improvised quickly. "But the Wisconsin cops . . . well, as far as they're concerned, she took off with her husband. They asked around some, but they're not doing much, so I'm looking around on my own. You haven't seen that guy Tamm around, have you?"

"Not since he complained about you kidnapping his wife. She sure does seem to get kidnapped a lot."

"You talked to her. She was with me of her own free will."

Wahlberg shrugged that off. "I don't know anything for sure. But for what it's worth, I hope you find her."

"What about the rest of the Lambs? Gheen and so forth."

"Gone."

"What about the one called Father September?"

Wahlberg laughed nervously. "Funny story, that. You know he was charged with murder, right?"

"The Krause kid."

"Yeah, well, I just came from the memorial service, and you'll never believe it. The kid showed up! At his own funeral! I mean, we must've mopped six quarts of his blood off that altar, and got a DNA match and everything, and now he shows up alive and healthy a month later. Unbelievable."

"Yeah, unbelievable," Kosh said, thinking about the bullet he had taken to the chest. He wondered if Tom Krause had experienced a similar resurrection.

"But here's the weirdest part," the cop continued. "That Father September? I just heard over the radio he's escaped. They say the dude just evaporated. Nobody can figure out how he got out of his cell. I swear, Hopewell these days is like the Twilight Zone."

Kosh felt defeated. Without Adrian, every last link to the Lambs was broken.

Wahlberg, sensing Kosh's despair, said, "You know who you might talk to? Ronnie Becker."

Kosh said, "What?" The last time he'd seen Ronnie had been during the fight at the park. Tucker had blown Ronnie's leg off at the knee, then Gheen and Koan had thrown both Ronnie and his leg into the disko. "He's back?"

"Living with his folks," Wahlberg said. "We interviewed him, but he claimed to know nothing about where the rest of the Lambs went. But you guys were tight, right? Maybe he'll talk to you."

33 RONNIE

RED GRAUBER'S VAN WAS LOADED WITH CASES OF BEER. Kosh supposed he should have unloaded it for Red back at the bar, but he could do that later. First things first, and Ronnie Becker was at the top of his list, for more reasons than one. As he drove toward the Becker place, Kosh tried to level and organize his anger, and it kept coming back to Ronnie. If not for Ronnie, things might have gone differently at the park. Lia wouldn't have been forced to enter the disko. Tucker wouldn't have had to follow her. They could have dealt with the Lambs then and there, and he would not have been shot in the chest a few weeks later, and they would not have taken Emma.

Kosh was dimly aware that his logic was not flawless. He could as easily blame himself for allowing Ronnie to hit him with the stun baton, for not going after Tucker when he'd entered the disko above his parents' house, for putting up the weathervane on his barn—leading to his own first trip through the diskos—for causing the rift with Adrian that had made him leave Hopewell all those years ago. The cycle of blame never ended. He could blame Adrian; he could blame his father for dying too young; he could blame Emily Ryan for ever having been born. But at the moment, he was consumed with blaming Ronnie Becker, because that was who was available.

As he approached the Becker farm, he mentally rehearsed what had to happen. First, he had to convince Ronnie to tell him about the Lambs. That was the important thing. Once he found out where Emma had been taken, *then* they could talk about other things. Like how it felt to have a shock baton stuck in your gut.

Kosh hadn't been to the Becker place in fifteen years, and he almost missed the turnoff. He hit the brakes at the last second and skidded into the driveway. He heard glass breaking and the wet hiss of foaming beer—one of the cases in back had tipped over. He didn't care.

The place looked different. The cedar trees flanking the driveway had tripled in size, there was a new silo, and the house had been painted a creamy yellow. As he entered the farmyard, he spotted Ronnie twenty feet up a ladder rolling red paint on the side of the barn. He parked next to Ronnie's pickup and walked over to the base of the ladder, resisting the temptation to kick it out from under him. *Stay cool,* he told himself.

Ronnie looked down. "Kosh Feye." He grinned. "I hoped I'd see you again." He balanced his roller on the paint can and climbed down, jumping to the ground from the third step up.

Both his legs seemed to be working fine. "How are you doing, bro?" Ronnie held up his hand for a high five.

Kosh hit him as hard as he could in the face.

So much for staying cool, Kosh thought.

Ronnie was sitting with his back against the barn, holding a paint rag to his bleeding nose. He'd been unconscious for only a few seconds.

I must be losing my touch, Kosh thought.

So far, neither of them had said a word. Ronnie watched warily as Kosh clenched and unclenched his fist, trying to get some feeling back into it, studying the split skin on his knuckles. Why had he ever thought it would make him feel good to hit somebody? It never did. Well, maybe a little. He hoped he hadn't busted his hand.

"I bid id arder," Ronnie said, his voice distorted by the rag pressed to his nose.

Kosh just looked at him. Ronnie took the cloth away from his face.

"I said, I been hit harder." He wiped at the runnel of blood still coming from one nostril, looked at the red paint- and blood-soaked rag, and added, "But it's been a while."

"Just wait," said Kosh.

Ronnie said, "Listen, I know you got cause to be upset."

Upset? Kosh didn't trust himself to reply. Did Ronnie not remember the last time they'd seen each other?

"You want to hit me again? Go ahead. Have at it." His lower face was streaked with red. "I wouldn't blame you."

Kosh could feel the rage draining out of him. How could he hit a guy who would just sit there and take it?

"How's that leg?" he asked through gritted teeth.

"Check it out." Ronnie leaned forward and pulled up the left leg of his jeans. From the knee down it was metal and plastic. "Works better than the old one."

"Let me guess. You were in a high-tech hospital in the future."

"You know about that? Yeah! Changed my life. They fixed me up and sent me back. Did something to me so I don't want to get high no more, too. Cost me a kidney, though."

"So now you're like a teetotaling bionic jerkwad?"

Ronnie laughed. "Same old Kosh. Listen, I made some bad decisions. You know how it is."

Kosh thought of all the times Ronnie had talked him into doing something stupid.

"Yeah, I do. Sort of your specialty."

"Anyways, I'm sorry. I'm done with all that. I'm a new man."

"Right."

"Seriously. I'm done with the Lambs. I don't know how I ever got involved with them. I think about it now, it's like a nightmare."

Kosh wanted to not believe him, but Ronnie really did seem different.

"Do you know where they are?"

Ronnie cocked his head. "The Lambs? Why?"

Maybe not so different—still looking for the angle.

"I got business with them," Kosh said.

Ronnie thought for a moment, then said, "If I was you, I wouldn't mess with those guys." His eyes went to Kosh's fists, and he reconsidered. "Tamm showed up here a week ago, trying to convince me to join up again. I told him to take a hike. They're off in Wisconsin someplace, living in some big old barn. If I wanted to live in a barn, I'd live in this one."

"Wisconsin's a big state," Kosh said.

Ronnie dabbed at his nose. "Tamm said it was off Highway 88, on something-or-other Hill Road."

Kosh felt the hairs stand up on the back of his neck.

"*Blank* Hill Road?"

"That sounds right," Ronnie said.

Several years ago, Kosh had sewn a hundred-dollar bill into the lining of his jacket for emergencies. He tore the stitches loose and used the bill to pay for a tank of gas and a burrito in Winona. He stopped at a sporting goods store and bought a pair of cheap binoculars, then headed across the river to Wisconsin with Arnold Becker's double-barreled twelve-gauge shotgun balanced on the console beside him. He ate the burrito as he drove, chewing and swallowing mechanically.

Kind of sad, he thought, *if my last meal is a microwaved gas station burrito.*

He drove up Highway 88 toward Blank Hill Road. He had driven that route hundreds of times, but now everything looked eerily unfamiliar, as if reality had slipped a cog. All the colors were too bright, the edges of things too sharp and focused. Was everything more vivid because he was seeing it for the last time? Would Emily be proud of him?

Not Emily, *Emma!* He was getting them mixed up in his head. "Emma is not Emily," he said aloud. He thought back to the last time he had seen Emily — the real Emily — and felt his gut begin to churn. It wasn't the burrito. He'd been, what — seventeen? And Emily had been only a couple of years older. Too young to have their hearts ripped out and stomped on. But that was what had happened.

34 A MATTER OF THE HEART

"KOSH?" IT WAS EMILY, HER VOICE SHAKING.

"Yeah?" Kosh gripped the phone, sensing that something was horribly wrong.

"It's Greta. She's—I think she's having a heart attack. Oh my god, her face is all red!"

"Did you call an ambulance?"

"Yes!"

"Is she breathing?"

"I think so, yes. Dad's with her."

"Do you know CPR?"

"I don't know. I think so. Oh, please, Kosh, can you come?"

Kosh was already pulling his boots on. Seconds later, he was on his bike. He kicked the starter a dozen times. Nothing. In a fury, he jumped off and kicked the bike, denting the gas tank and knocking the bike onto its side. With a roar of frustration at the unjust universe, he went back inside for the keys to Adrian's Mustang.

The ambulance was there when he arrived. Greta was on a gurney in the kitchen. The paramedics were putting an IV line in her arm. She looked scared. Hamm was hovering over them, ignoring the paramedics' pleas to give them room to work. Emily stood with her back to the stove, white-faced, gripping the oven door handle with both hands. Kosh put his arm around her shoulders.

"We were just sitting down to eat," she said, her voice small. "She just crumpled up."

"She'll be okay," Kosh said, hoping it was true.

"I know," Emily said, though she clearly didn't believe it.

Hamm rode to the hospital with Greta in the ambulance; Kosh and Emily followed in Adrian's car.

"She said she wasn't feeling good," Emily said. "This morning she was complaining about twinges in her chest. I just thought it was being old. She and Hamm are always saying how creaky they are. I should've listened."

"It'll be okay," Kosh said, because he didn't know what else to say.

Emily fell silent, sitting hunched forward, her red-rimmed eyes fastened on the back of the ambulance. Kosh kept the car dead center in his lane, arms stiff on the wheel, concentrating on driving perfectly. He had never driven Adrian's Mustang before. It wasn't as nice as he had thought — just a clunky econobox with some fancy details. The ambulance was traveling at a sedate sixty miles per hour, with no siren. That was a good sign. If Greta had been dying, they'd be going faster. He opened his mouth to share this thought with Emily, then thought better of it. He glanced at Emily and cleared his throat.

"About another ten minutes," he said.

Emily nodded. Her face was drawn and brittle. Even so, she was as beautiful as ever.

They were at the hospital all night. Hamm would not leave Greta's side. After the first hour, when the doctor assured them that Greta would live and that it was a minor cardiac event—something called angina—Kosh and Emily went to the hospital cafeteria for coffee and a bite to eat. They talked about little things. Neither of them brought up that Kosh had been avoiding her. Later, they brought Hamm a turkey sandwich, then went to the hospital lobby and sat on a sofa and pretended to read magazines. Sometime around midnight, Kosh noticed that Emily's *People* magazine had fallen to her lap. Her eyes were closed. He put his arm around her and cradled her head on his shoulder, and for several hours they did not move.

When Kosh woke up, his arm was dead. He gently pulled himself free and replaced his arm with one of the sofa pillows. Massaging his arm, he went down the hall to Greta's room. Hamm was slumped in the visitor's chair, head back, snoring. Greta was snoring too, though not as loudly.

Kosh went back to the lobby. Emily's eyes fluttered open.

She saw him approaching and she smiled. An instant later, she realized where she was, and why, and sat up.

"Greta's fine," Kosh said quickly.

Emily relaxed slightly.

"They're both in there snoring to each other."

Emily laughed. The sound of it echoed through his bones.

By the end of her second day in the hospital, Greta Ryan declared herself "fit as a fang-dang fiddle" and convinced the doctors to send her home, much to the relief of her harried and abused nurses. Kosh was surprised and amused to see Greta, the sweetest, gentlest woman one could ever hope to meet, become a hospital-bed harridan. As they walked her out to the car, Greta looked over her shoulder with contempt and said, "Those girls don't know which side their bed is buttered on!"

Kosh, worried that Greta was having a stroke, looked at Emily.

Emily said, "You're always saying that. You don't butter bed."

"Somebody should tell *them* that," Greta snapped.

It was getting dark by the time they got back to the house. Greta ignored the doctor's prescription for bed rest and immediately set about cleaning the kitchen. Emily had cleaned it that morning, but apparently not to Greta's exacting standards. Kosh and Emily tried to help, but she shooed them off. Hamm, exhausted by his two-day vigil, put up a feeble protest, but she sent him away as well.

Kosh and Emily went outside and stood awkwardly on the front porch. Moths and other night insects flitted around the dim yellow porch light. A light, cool breeze came out of the west, bringing with it end-of-summer smells and the promise of fall.

"I guess I should get going," Kosh said. "I got a busted bike and a pickup to fix."

"Kosh . . ." Emily was staring at something behind him. Kosh whirled. For an instant, he thought he saw a small cloud, about the size of a person, hovering off the end of the porch. But when he looked at it directly it seemed to be no more than a wisp of condensation, or a cloud of gnats. Kosh blinked, and it was gone.

"Did you see it?" Emily said in a small voice.

"I'm not . . . sure," Kosh said. The skin on his forearms prickled, and he became aware of his heartbeat. "I saw something."

Emily breathed out shakily. "I've been seeing more of them," she said.

Ghosts. She was talking about her ghosts.

She laughed. "Oh, I'm just being silly," she said.

"You're not silly."

"Well, I feel silly. I'm just upset about Greta, and . . ." Emily cupped her palms around his right hand. "Thanks for being here, Kosh. I don't how I could have gotten through it without you."

"I didn't do anything," Kosh said, embarrassed.

"You know what I mean." She raised herself on her toes and

kissed the side of his mouth. Clumsily, he moved to kiss her back, then realized what he was doing and jerked back. They stared at each other. Emily's green eyes looked black in the yellow light.

"Silly Kosh," she said in a husky voice. She put her hands on either side of his face and pulled him to her and kissed him full on the mouth.

35 DEATH ANGEL HOLLOW

BEHIND THE WHEEL OF RED'S VAN, KOSH LET HIS REC-ollection of that kiss linger in his conscious memory, then shook his head hard, casting it into the dungeons of his mind, where he kept things too sweet and painful to revisit. He pulled into an abandoned logging trail just south of his property and followed the bumpy, rutted, overgrown road along the ridge of a coulee, moving slowly, branches dragging noisily along either side of the van. Twice he had to get out and drag fallen limbs off the road.

About half a mile in, he was stopped by a fallen elm tree too big to move. He loaded two shells into the shotgun. Bird shot, but at close range it would stop anything. A few more shells went into his jacket pockets. He shouldered the gun and hiked up the trail toward the knob.

The knob was a relatively bare elevated hilltop that had once been an oak grove, but ten years back, the owner, a farmer named Emil Blatz, had logged it. Kosh had been sorry to see the oaks go, but the knob now provided a beautiful panorama of the valley including, on the far side, a view of his property. Most of the leaves had fallen, and he had a clear view of the back of his barn. He sat on a stump and focused the binoculars on the bank of second-floor windows, but saw only reflections. Shifting his view to the left, he saw a dark gray SUV parked next to the barn. He saw no sign of Emma.

Patience, he told himself. He raised the binoculars slightly to view the weathervane on the roof. If the disko was there, he couldn't see it. Did the Lambs know about the disko? He had never mentioned it to Emma, but if it had shown up, they might have seen it.

Kosh returned his attention to the windows. A cloud had drifted over the sun, and he could now see indistinct shapes through the glass. He watched for movement and was rewarded by a figure crossing from the kitchen area toward the fireplace. Emma? He couldn't be sure.

The smart thing to do might be to drive into town, call the cops, and tell them his home had been invaded. But he didn't trust the cops. He could see it turning into a bloodbath, with Emma getting killed. Or maybe Gheen had spent the past weeks brainwashing Emma, and she was back to being one of them, and even if the cops kicked them out, she would stay with the Lambs. No, it was best to first find out for sure if she was there, get her to safety, and deal with the Lambs later.

He hung the binoculars around his neck, picked up the

shotgun, and made his way down the steep hillside into the valley.

The local name for the valley behind Kosh's property was Death Angel Hollow. Emil Blatz claimed it was named for the Death Angel mushroom, which grew in abundance locally. Kosh had always liked the name—it suited his somewhat morose world view—but on this day, he feared that it was entirely too appropriate.

It had been a few years since Kosh had explored the hollow. It was rough going, all fallen trees and slippery moss-covered boulders. Heavy rains often turned the bottom into a treacherous, muddy torrent. It was reasonably dry now, the forest floor covered by a carpet of fallen leaves, but he had to climb over several old log jams left by the spring floods. The far side of the valley rose steeply. Kosh made his way up the slope, grabbing on to vines and saplings when he could. Halfway up, he came to a rusty barbwire fence. Using the gun barrel to press down the top strand, he climbed over the wire onto his own property.

Standing upon his own land gave him strength. It flowed up from his feet to his legs, and filled his chest with a sense of ownership, pride, and power, overlaid with a seething anger at those who had invaded his home. *Stay cool,* he reminded himself. This wasn't like confronting Ronnie Becker. These guys were armed, and he had to consider Emily's—*Emma's*—safety. As he neared the crest, he slowed. The barn came into view.

The woods were bordered by a raggedy copse of honeysuckle

and prickly ash. Kosh concealed himself and considered his options.

The barn was only about thirty feet from his hiding spot. He would have to cross an open expanse of unmown grass to reach it. Looking up at the windows from below, he could see only the glare of reflected sky. Impossible to see inside. If someone was looking out he wouldn't know.

He could wait until dark, or approach the barn by circling through the woods to the east side, where there were no windows. He decided to risk it. He broke cover, ran across the lawn to the barn, and flattened himself against the wall. A low hum, like a laboring refrigerator, was coming from inside. Staying close to the wall, he crept toward the west end. He peeked cautiously around the corner. The SUV was still there, and something else that nearly stopped his heart.

His Triumph, tipped on its side in a mud puddle next to the driveway. Outraged by seeing his bike treated that way, he started toward it, then saw a man walking from the barn toward the SUV.

Kosh raised the shotgun. A Lamb? The guy was dressed like a local: jeans, a heavy flannel shirt, and a seed cap. He wasn't much older than Tucker, and as far as Kosh could see he wasn't armed. Kosh lowered the gun.

The young man turned and looked directly at Kosh. They stood staring at each other for a few seconds, then the man broke and ran. Kosh started after him, then thought better of it. He didn't know how many others were inside. Cursing, he turned and ran back into the woods.

36 EX MACHINA

Tucker burst from the forest onto a trail. His Medicant-enhanced legs propelled him at a tremendous pace, but not fast enough to lose the maggot. He rounded a bend and saw someone standing on the trail. A woman, her head shaven, carrying an ax. Before Tucker could veer away, the woman leaped into the air, straight toward him. Tucker ducked, lost his footing, and rolled. The woman flew over him and landed between Tucker and the maggot. She jabbed the handle of her ax into the maggot's gaping mouth. The maggot came to a sloshing, jiggling halt.

"This is the Terminus," said the woman. "You have no business here."

The maggot shuddered. Its mouth slowly contracted around the ax handle, then puckered and began to roll inward. Tucker, gasping for breath, watched, fascinated, as little by little the maggot swallowed itself, gathering into a pink ball on the end of the handle. When it had reduced itself to the size of a basketball—it looked to Tucker like a giant pink cake pop—the woman withdrew the ax and the maggot winked out of existence. The woman sniffed the ax handle, wrinkled her nose, then looked at Tucker.

"I assume you did not wish to visit a Boggsian crèche?" she said.

"No . . . thank you." He heard footsteps pounding up the trail, and turned to see Lia running toward them. She stopped a few feet away, breathing heavily.

"Tucker Feye," Lia said between breaths. "I have been looking for you."

Tucker put his hands on Lia's narrow shoulders and pulled her to him. She stiffened, then relaxed. The embrace lasted only a few seconds, but it was enough to make their reunion real, and it held the promise of more.

Lia said, "Please do not go away again."

"I won't," Tucker promised. "Only it wasn't me that got kidnapped and swapped for a pitchfork."

Lia smiled. "I had little choice."

"The Yar Lia tells me you wish to return to your time," the woman said.

"Awn says she can help us," Lia added.

"Awn?" Tucker peered closely at the woman. She looked nothing like Awn. For one thing, she was young. No, not so much *young*—more like she was *new*. Her face was smooth and mannequin-like, as if she had just been pressed from a mold. Could this really be Awn?

"You don't look like the Awn I know," he said.

"I am not." Awn's mouth curved into an unpracticed smile. "Though perhaps I will become so. Your answer, therefore, is yes, and no."

"Okay, you're definitely Awn," Tucker said.

"Told you," Lia said.

Tucker noticed the disko hovering over the trail. "Does that disko go to Hopewell?"

"That is a local," said Awn. "The disko you need is in the old city, atop the pyramid."

"The same one we came out of? It's gone."

"It has returned."

"Won't it just take us back to Harmony?"

"It will take you to where you need to be," Awn said. "But you must go soon. Outside forces are meddling with the diskos. The creature you just observed, for example."

"The maggot," Tucker said. "You once told me they were made by Boggsians for something called the Gnomon."

Awn thought for a moment, then said, "The Gnomon are a conservative faction of the Klaatu. It is no surprise that they will object to the diskos. Already their future actions echo back through the timestreams."

"What does that *mean*?" Tucker asked.

"Intent and the ability to perform a task is sufficient," Awn said. "Consider your footfalls upon the earth. You intend to step forward. You have the capability to do so. Therefore, it is as if done. In this fashion, we both control the future and cause it to occur."

"But suppose I intend to step forward and something stops me."

"Then you did not have the capability in the first place."

Tucker and Lia looked at each other.

"She can be very irritating," Lia said in a low voice.

"Yes," said Awn. She propped the ax on her shoulder. "Come. I will take you as far as my dwelling. From there you must proceed on your own." She set off down the trail, walking swiftly.

Tucker and Lia followed. On the way, they told each other about what had happened while they were apart.

"That Boggsian, I think he's the guy who built the diskos," Tucker said as they climbed a slope toward the crest of a hill. "It's like, as soon as I told him about the diskos, he decided he had to build one, and all of a sudden they're popping up everywhere. Like what Awn said, as soon as he *intended* to do it, it was done."

Awn turned to them and said, "It is more than intent. The means must also be at hand. The Boggsian had already developed the technology, but he had yet to apply it. Now, however . . ." she pointed her ax at a disko perched upon the top of the hill. Tucker could have sworn it had not been there a moment ago. "The diskos come." She stepped off the trail and approached the disko. "This disko has a malevolent aspect." She prodded its surface with the ax handle, then backed away. The disko spat out a handful of reddish dust.

"A genocide," Awn said, rejoining Tucker and Lia. "And the death of any unfortunate creatures who should pass through it. The Klaatu have a taste for the macabre." She continued along the path, speaking over her shoulder. "The Klaatu believe themselves to be superior creatures, and in many ways they are. However, they lost something of themselves when they transcended. One might say they worship the lives they left behind."

"Like a religion?" Tucker asked.

"Not in the sense that you mean."

"One of the Boggsians told me *they* have no religion, either," Tucker said.

"The Boggsians cannot be trusted to say what is true," Awn said. "They do not even trust themselves."

"I once believed in the religion of the Lah Sept," Lia said. She turned to Tucker. "I used to think you might be the prophet named Tuckerfeye. But now I am not so sure. According to *The Book of September,* Tuckerfeye saved the Lah Sept from the Digital Plague."

"What is *The Book of September*?"

"*The Book of September* is the Holy Bible of the Lah Sept. It is like your Bible, but different. According to the teachings, it was written by Father September. Your father. According to the Book, Father September sacrificed his only son, and then the son rose from the dead and saved the Lah Sept from the Plague."

Tucker said, "Wow."

"Yes. Wow."

"So that's why my dad wanted to kill me?"

"Yes, to make *The Book of September* true. But you were not sacrificed. You escaped."

"Does that mean we changed history?"

Awn stopped again and faced them. "History is what is written. We do not know whether the diskos are capable of changing that which may have happened, nor can we ever know, for were an event to be undone, it would never have occurred."

Tucker said, "So if we change something that happened, it never happened?"

"One may experience only a single timeline, though it is possible that multiple timelines exist."

"You mean there are other versions of me in other timelines?"

"This is a theory that may never be provable. Judging from their actions, the Gnomon believe that such timelines exist independently of one another, and that any entanglement could be catastrophic."

"But we *can* change what happens?"

"Yes. No."

The trail led into a meadow studded with tree stumps. On the far side of the meadow was a pile of logs, and what looked like the start of a log cabin.

"My home," said Awn.

In the future, Tucker thought, *this is where Awn will die.*

Awn said, "As I stated, my ability to manipulate the diskos is limited; I cannot create them at will, nor guarantee their destination. The disko atop the Cydonian Pyramid will take you to your own time, though I cannot promise that you will arrive in Hopewell."

"You mean it might take us to the top of Mount Everest?" Tucker said.

"A disko on Everest has yet to be conceived by the builder, so no, you need not fear that."

"But we might end up someplace not in Hopewell?"

"Hopewell is a place of special interest to the designer. You are likely to find yourself near your home."

"Who is this designer? Is that another word for God?"

"Only if your concept of God is very limited. The designer of the diskos, and my creator, calls herself Iyl Rayn. She is a Klaatu."

"I have met her," said Lia. "She is no god."

PART FOUR
THE BLACK BARN

During the third phase of their debate, Iyl Rayn and the Gnomon Chayhim discussed the fate of Tom Krause.

"Memories," Iyl Rayn maintained, "are not reality."

Chayhim disagreed. "Are you suggesting that the qualities that make us who we are can exist independent of our memories?"

"I am suggesting that memories simply model reality for our edification and amusement. They are not in and of themselves the sum total of who we are. I, for example, was transcended without my full complement of recollections. Does this make me any less real?"

Chayhim emitted a dismissive pulse, indicating a complete rejection of Iyl Rayn's argument. "Even if your assertion were true, you cannot deny that memories influence action, and action implies reality. The boy Tom Krause, for example, acts in accordance with memories which are not reality-based in his timestream. He is caught in a time stub. The boy is disturbed. Your actions have inconvenienced him."

"He will adapt," said Iyl Rayn.

"You cannot know this to be true."

"Neither can you know it to be untrue."

"A moot point. The Timesweeps will right matters."

"Your Timesweeps are more likely to exacerbate the problem."

"Ah, so you admit there is a problem?"

"Yes. A problem that did not exist before you unleashed your Timesweeps."

— E³

37 PRETENDING

Krazy Krause, they called him.

At first, when Tom had returned to school, everybody wanted to hang with him. They all wanted to know what had happened. Tom just kept saying he didn't remember. But then Will had opened his big mouth. Tom wished he'd never told Will about the things he remembered—about Tucker, and the rope swing, and being in the futuristic hospital, and getting zapped by those two guys with the black coats and hats. But Will had wheedled it out of him, and now his bigmouthed little brother had the whole school thinking he was as crazy as old Mrs. Benson.

Krazy Krause. He had found it scratched into the paint on his locker. Nobody said it to his face, but he knew they were talking about him. The fact that maybe he *was* crazy made it worse. He was living in two different worlds. There was the world that arrived through his senses—the world people told him was real—and the world that existed in his memories. The world where there was a rope swing at Hardy Lake, and a boy named Tucker Feye. At times, he was ready to accept that he had dreamed the whole rope swing adventure, but what about Tucker? He hadn't made up Tucker Feye, but nobody seemed to remember him.

The Feyes' house was still there, but it was vacant. He asked around, but no one could remember who had lived there.

Tom remembered being in a hospital in the future. He remembered seeing Tucker that snowy night in downtown Hopewell, and all the old cars, and seeing a younger version of the Reverend Feye. And the two men in black who had zapped him with something. He remembered falling into Hardy Lake. Suppose it had all really happened just the way he remembered? Did that mean everybody *else* was crazy?

He had started cutting himself with his pocketknife. Just little cuts on his arms, to feel the pain, to see the blood, to know he was alive. When his mom noticed the cuts, he told her they were thorn scratches.

Did crazy people *know* they were crazy? He thought about Mrs. Benson, with her house full of cats and wearing galoshes year-round and talking about her husband, who had died before Tom was born, as if he were still alive. Did she *know* she was crazy?

One day over dinner, he asked his dad if he ever remembered things that had never happened.

His dad gave him a concerned look and said, "Of course not."

His mother laughed. "Yes you do, Jack! Just last week you said you thought you'd paid the electric bill, when in fact you had done no such thing."

"That's different," his dad said.

"Memory plays tricks on all of us," his mother said.

What he *should* do was just act like everything was normal, and do normal things, and try not to think about Tucker or the rope swing, and not cut himself. People pretended all the time—pretended that things had never happened. The Lambs of September, for example. That had been in the papers, and just about everybody he knew had been in the park that day, and half his friends had been calling themselves Pure Boys or Pure Girls. Everybody remembered that. But none of them wanted to talk about it. He'd talked to Kathy Aamodt one day in the lunchroom, back when everybody was trying to get him to say what had happened to him while he was gone, and he said something about how stupid it was that they had gotten involved with the Lambs. Her face went all stiff and red.

"That's really rude," she said.

"Why?" Tom said, genuinely confused.

"As far as I'm concerned, none of that ever happened." With that, she turned away, and had not spoken to him since.

Not only could he not talk about the things that nobody else remembered, there were things he couldn't talk about that *were* real.

It's all about pretending, he thought. *Maybe if I just believe what everybody agrees is real, then everything will be okay.*

He tried. But most afternoons he found himself back at Hardy Lake, sitting under the cottonwood, making shallow cuts on his arms, remembering things that had never happened.

One evening, he returned from Hardy Lake and found his parents and Will already sitting at the dinner table, eating chicken casserole. There were only three place settings. His mother looked at him with a puzzled expression.

"Well, who do we have here?"

"Will, is this one of your friends?" his dad asked.

Tom thought they were messing with him. Was he late for dinner? Then he saw the bewildered expression on Will's face and he knew they weren't kidding.

"I don't know him," Will said.

Tom was too shocked to breathe, let alone speak.

"Young man," his father said, standing up, "may I ask what you are doing walking into our home without knocking?"

"Maybe he's lost, dear," his mother said, looking at Tom with an utter lack of recognition.

"Mom! It's me!" Tom said. "Tom!"

Mrs. Krause blinked, her face blurred, then snapped back into focus.

"Tom," she said. "Where have you been?" She stood up. "Let me get you a plate."

His dad grunted and sat back down, shaking his head in confusion. Will was staring at Tom as if he had sprouted antlers.

"What *happened* to you?" Will asked.

"Nothing," Tom said, even as he was thinking, *Everything happened to me!* Either he really was Krazy Krause, or the entire universe was going nuts. Numbly, he sat down at his usual place. His mother set a plate and utensils before him, and he served himself some chicken casserole. It tasted the same as always — a favorite comfort food — and the rest of the meal went on as if nothing odd had happened.

38 DAMAGES

THE TWO-LANE HIGHWAY RAN DEAD STRAIGHT INTO THE setting sun. Kosh brought the Mustang up to one hundred miles per hour. Pedal to the floor, he leaned back in his seat and stared at the rapidly advancing horizon. On either side, snow-dusted fields of harvested corn, white, gold, and black, blurred to flickering yellow-gray. One oh two. One oh four. He came up over a low rise; at the top, the weight came off the wheels, and for a moment he was flying. The Mustang touched down. One oh five.

Ahead, a yellow sign announced a coming curve. He eased back on the accelerator, disappointed. He'd gone faster than that on his bike. He'd hoped for more from the Mustang. He touched the brake, brought the car down to thirty, eased onto the shoulder, and pulled a tire-screeching U-turn.

The dash clock read 6:36. Emily was expecting him at seven. He brought the Mustang back up to eighty and headed back toward Hopewell.

He was so dead. So totally, irredeemably dead.

Emily's best friend, Karen Jonas, lived just south of Hopewell in a house set into a cornfield that had once been part of the Hauser farmstead. George Hauser had been selling off parcels of his land for years, some to other farmers, some to folks looking to build homes. Karen's father had a job with the county, something to do with taxes. He'd put a three-story home on a half acre notched into Hauser's east field—a blocky square house sitting on a square half acre of perfect lawn walled on three sides by dry cornstalks.

Kosh pulled into the short driveway and beeped his horn. Seconds later, the front door opened and Emily ran out to the car, her open parka flapping in the wind. She hopped in and kissed Kosh on the cheek. Kosh put the car in gear and backed out onto the highway.

"What's the plan, Stan?" she said.

"Chicken cacciatore," Kosh said.

Greta had remarked, a few weeks earlier, on how much time Emily had been spending with Kosh.

"It's unseemly," she said.

"Oh, Greta, leave the girl alone," Hamm said.

Greta pursed her lips and gave her head a shake. "People will talk," she said.

It was true. Kosh and Emily spent every available hour together, more than she and Adrian ever had, and people noticed. They were careful how they behaved in public, but it was hard. People noticed how closely they walked with each other—close enough to hold hands, though they never did. People noticed how they looked at each other. It was a small town. Greta was right. People talked.

Kosh and Emily took to meeting in secret. On this night, Emily had told Greta she was spending the night at Karen's. Karen, of course, knew what was going on. Tonight, as on many other nights, Emily would go to Kosh's, and they would cook, and she would act as if this was her life. As if it was real.

Like little kids playing house, she thought.

Kosh drove Adrian's Mustang all the time now. His pickup had a bad clutch, and it was too cold to ride his bike, and what difference did it make? When Adrian got back from Jerusalem, the car would be the least of it. Again and again Kosh imagined the occasion.

Welcome back, brother. Your fiancée and I are in love. Sorry about that.

The fact that he was using the Mustang against Adrian's express wishes was nothing, a tiny pimple on the vast, bloated sin of stealing his brother's fiancée.

Kosh had tried to talk Emily into running away with him.

"I'll be eighteen in a few months," he said. "I can get a job up in Minneapolis. We can get an apartment."

"Oh, Kosh," Emily said sadly, putting her hand on his forearm. "It wouldn't be fair to Adrian."

"But you can't marry him now!"

"I know." Emily sighed. "I'll break it off with him after he's home and gets settled. I can let him down easy."

"Adrian doesn't do *anything* easy."

"We'll work it out, Kosh. For now, can't we just be happy?"

He *was* happy. But he was also miserable. Adrian's return was hanging over them like a time bomb, and even though it was more than two months away, he thought about it constantly.

The chicken cacciatore was a disaster. Kosh burned the chicken, Emily's salad was oversalted, and the ice cream they'd bought for dessert turned out to be fat-free frozen yogurt that had spent too many months in the freezer at Economart. It didn't matter. They laughed their way though the awful meal, and talked about things that had nothing to do with Adrian and the coming apocalypse, and for a time, Kosh was as happy as he had ever been since before his father died.

It was after two in the morning when Kosh dropped Emily back at Karen's. He turned off the headlights as he approached the house so as to not wake up Karen's parents, kissed Emily good night, then sat in the car and watched as she let herself in the side door. Driving home, the weight of what he was doing filled his belly and dragged him down, as if the burned chicken in his gut had turned to mud. Why did something so pure and clean and wonderful as his feelings for Emily have to have such a monstrous consequence attached? Why hadn't he fallen in love with someone else? The answer was clear. There *was* no one else for him. Kosh was not big on fate or karma, but being with Emily. . . . If anything in this universe was inevitable, if anything were truly meant to be, it was his arms around Emily Ryan, his lips on her lips, his soul and her soul together forever.

It's not my fault, he told himself. *It just happened.*

He knew that was a cop-out, but he clung to it as the mileposts flashed by. *I could die now,* he told himself, *and my life will have been worth living—*

A gauzy white figure appeared in front of him, holding its arms out as if telling him to stop. There was no time; it was too close. Kosh didn't even have time to touch the brake pedal. The Mustang blew through the apparition. Kosh laughed shakily—it was just a bit of thick fog. He checked his rearview mirror, but saw nothing. When he looked at the road ahead he saw a deer trotting casually out onto the highway.

Deer!

Time slowed. Kosh's foot moved from the gas pedal to the brake.

A big buck.

Tires locked, the nose of the Mustang dipped. The deer looked up and froze.

Look at the rack on that thing!

The screech of rubber on asphalt seemed muffled, as if this were happening to somebody else. There was no way he could stop in time. Lifting his foot from the brake, he jerked the wheel to the left, crossing the oncoming lane, heading for the ditch. The rear tires lost traction; the Mustang went into a spin. The rear end of the car struck the buck with a nauseating wet thud. Kosh fought the wheel, turning into the skid, and seconds later, he was motionless, the only sound that of the still-running engine, and the gasping sound of his own breathing. Kosh closed his eyes and swallowed. He sat there for a few seconds, waiting for his heart to slow, then got out.

The deer was gone. Kosh examined the Mustang. Rear quarter panel bashed in and streaked with blood. The tire was still holding air. Kosh took the tire iron from the trunk and pried the sheet metal away from the wheel. It was still drivable, but it would need bodywork. He could fix it. Adrian would never know.

Not that it mattered. A dent in the Mustang was nothing compared with the damage he and Emily were about to inflict upon his brother's heart.

39 FIVE MAGGOTS

ROMELAS, *ca.* 3000 CE

THE GATE WAS BACK, AS AWN HAD PROMISED.

Tucker and Lia climbed the pyramid slowly, Tucker going first and helping Lia up the giant steps. She didn't really need his help, but it was an excuse to touch her.

The disko was now positioned over a different facet of the pyramid. Tucker stood a few feet from its shimmering surface, staring into it as if the swirls and coruscations could tell him something.

"Do you trust Awn?" Lia asked.

Tucker shrugged. "I'm not even sure she's the same Awn I met before." He turned to Lia. "She's kind of odd-looking, don't you think?"

"She is very smooth."

"Like she just popped out of a mold."

"She told me her name stands for Augmented Whorsch-Novak golem. Whorsch-Novak sounds like a Boggsian name, but what's a golem?"

"A creature made out of earth or clay, or something. I think it's an old Jewish legend. Awn — the other Awn — once told me that the Boggsians are Amish Jews."

"And they make *golems*?"

"I don't know." The disko changed color from gray to green. "Something's coming." Tucker backed away. The disko pulsed and buzzed, and a Klaatu emerged, an indistinct blobby-looking shape, like the one that had guided Tucker into the disko in Harmony. The Klaatu drifted up until it was suspended about twenty feet above the disko.

"What do you think it wants?" Lia said.

"Mostly, I think they just like to watch." Tucker raised his voice. "Hey! Can you hear me up there?"

The Klaatu did not respond.

"I think you can only talk to them through a machine," Lia said.

The Klaatu drifted down to the level of the disko. The disko pulsed orange; the Klaatu was gone.

"Are you ready?" Tucker asked.

"Hold my hand," Lia said. They entered the portal together.

Tucker and Lia landed on either side of the ridge on Kosh's barn. If they hadn't been holding on to each other, one or both of them might have tumbled off. Tucker grabbed the weathervane and pulled Lia up beside him.

"I've been here before," Lia said.

"This is Kosh's barn. I used to live here." It was cold. Not as cold as the North Pole, but after the tropical climate of Romelas, the wind felt frigid. Judging from the nearly leafless trees, it was late fall. A thin, steady stream of smoke rose from the chimney at the far end of the barn.

"Looks like he's home." Tucker let go of Lia's hand, worked his way around the weathervane, and followed the ridge to the chimney. One of Kosh's motorcycles—the Triumph—was lying on its side in a mud puddle to the side of the driveway. It wasn't like Kosh to leave his bike like that. Next to the bike was an SUV.

Tucker backed away from the edge. Lia said, "What is it?"

"I'm not sure," Tucker said. "But it's not good. We'd better get down. Come on." They edged around the weathervane, crawled under the disko, and followed the ridge to the far end of the barn.

"Uh-oh," Tucker said. The rungs nailed to the side of the barn only went down halfway. He remembered Kosh ripping off the bottom rungs. "How did you get down last time you were up here?" he asked Lia.

She peered over the edge. "There was a ladder."

"Well, it's gone." The bottommost rung was a good twenty feet above the ground. Tucker figured he could hang from the last rung and drop to the ground safely—he'd fallen a lot farther than that when the disko had dropped him onto the ice pack at the Pole—but he would have to find a way to get Lia down.

They heard voices coming from the back side of the barn.

"That is the language of Romelas," Lia whispered.

Tucker nodded. It was as he feared. The Lambs were here, which meant that Kosh was in serious trouble. If he was alive.

"There they are," Lia said. They ducked behind the roof ridge. Three men dressed in hunting garb were entering the woods. One of them was limping.

"Do you know them?" Tucker asked.

"I can't tell."

"I might have to leave you up here for a bit," Tucker said.

"No," Lia said flatly. "We will both go."

"I can drop down from the bottom rung. I'll have to find a ladder for you."

"I'll jump too," Lia said.

"It's too high."

"I'll climb down you."

For a moment Tucker was confused, then he got it.

"Okay, let's go." Tucker let himself over the edge and descended the rungs. Lia followed. When Tucker reached the bottommost rung, he grabbed it with his hands and hung from it. Lia put her feet on his shoulders, then held on to his arms and lowered herself, wrapping her legs around his body and slowly sliding down until she was hanging on to his ankles. This brought the bottoms of her feet to within ten feet of the ground. She hung there for a few seconds, then released her grip, hit the ground, and rolled. Tucker waited for her to get out of the way, then dropped. He landed lightly on his feet. He gestured for Lia to follow him around to the front. He peeked around the corner. The door leading into the barn was standing open.

"I'm going to take a look inside," Tucker whispered. "Wait here." He eased around the corner. Staying close to the wall, he approached the nearest window and peeked inside.

Kosh's workshop was illuminated by a familiar glow. Diskos. Tucker counted five of them lined up against the back wall. He ducked below the level of the window and moved to the open door. Seeing no one in the workshop, he entered. Kosh's tools, parts, benches, and cabinets had been shoved aside, blocking the big double doors at the end of the barn, to make room for the row of diskos. Each disko was confined by a metal armature and surrounded by a flabby pink band of maggot flesh, like the captive maggot at Hopewell County Park. He heard soft footsteps from upstairs, then the sound of someone descending the spiral staircase. Quickly, he concealed himself behind an upended bench.

The person coming down the steps was a woman. Tucker stopped breathing. It was his mother—or rather the younger version of his mother he had met in his house in Hopewell. Emma, she had called herself. She stopped at the bottom step, glanced toward the diskos, then crossed to the doorway. She looked out, to the left, to the right. After a moment, she turned and approached the row of diskos.

Tucker was struck by the expression on her face, which seemed to contain both fear and sadness, with sadness predominating. She stopped in front of the leftmost disko. She gazed into its churning gray surface for a few heartbeats, then moved to the next. Tucker sensed that she was trying to decide which one to enter. She looked into each of the portals. When she reached the last one—so close Tucker could have reached out to touch her—he saw her make a decision. It was a small thing; her jaw became firm, her shoulders squared, her eyelids tightened, her knee bent slightly, and she began the forward lean that would take her into the disko. Tucker leaped over the bench and grabbed her—one arm around her waist, one hand clapped over her mouth—and dragged her back.

In a low voice, he said, "I won't hurt you. If you want to go through the disko, I won't stop you. But I have some questions. Do you understand?"

Emma nodded, her eyes wide.

"Do you remember me?" Tucker asked, taking his hand from her mouth.

She nodded again.

"The men outside, who are they?"

"Master Gheen. Koan. Tamm. The acolyte Jonas."

"Do you know the man who lives here?"

"Kosh," she said, almost too quietly to hear.

"Is he here?"

She bit her lip. Her eyes filled with tears. She looked away.

For a moment Tucker felt nothing, then the bottom seemed to drop out of his gut as he read her expression.

"No," he said, backing away from her and holding up his hands as if he could stop her from saying more. His butt hit the bench he had been hiding behind. He grabbed it—something solid to hold on to.

"They killed him," Emma said.

40 GHEEN

Kosh crouched behind a fallen tree and listened to the men, calling to one another in a strange language, tramping clumsily through the woods, looking for him. He thought there were four of them, but he wasn't sure. One of them was the young guy he had seen before. The others he couldn't get a look at, but he suspected one of them was Koan, the man who had shot him, and maybe Tamm and Gheen as well. Kosh waited, shotgun safety off, half hoping Koan would find him. He hadn't been able to bring himself to shoot the kid, but he figured Koan wouldn't be a problem.

The men moved off. Kosh raised his head. He saw one of them from the back, moving toward the barn. Had they given up? He considered his options. From where he was hiding, he could see the top half of the barn. Something on the roof caught his eye. Two figures, moving along the roof ridge toward the ladder end of the barn. Tucker and Lia! What were *they* doing here? And if Kosh could see them on the roof, then the guys who were hunting for him might spot them too. Kosh stood up. The three men were walking away from him, back toward the barn.

Tucker and Lia were no longer visible — they were probably on the ladder. Kosh snatched up a piece of broken limestone and threw it. It hit a tree just downhill from the nearest man. He stopped moving and looked toward the sound, calling softly to the others.

Kosh ducked back behind the fallen tree and watched. He could see Koan clearly now, less than fifty yards away. The men spread out and moved toward the place where they'd heard the rock hit. Good. As long as they stayed in the woods, Tucker and Lia would have time to make it to the ground unseen, and — he hoped — get their butts out of there. Kosh waited until the men were out of sight, then moving silently downhill, away from the barn, he found another rock and threw it in their general direction. Kosh peered through the trees, trying to see how they would respond.

He heard the slug thud into the hickory tree next to him at the same moment he heard the flat crack of the rifle. Kosh ducked low and ran. A second shot ripped through the brush. Kosh leaped over a small ravine and kept running.

"Kosh is *dead*?" Tucker said. His voice sounded hollow and distant.

Emma nodded. "I saw Koan shoot him. I am sorry. He was your uncle, yes?"

Tucker nodded, drawing a shaky breath. Kosh was all the

family he had. The air around him seemed to thicken; the sound of his breathing rasped at his eardrums. He felt his heart beating raggedly, as if it couldn't decide whether to speed up or slow down.

A muffled bang came from the woods outside. Emma flinched at the sound. A second shot rang out.

"Those were rifle shots," Tucker said. He felt things inside him hardening, crystalizing. "I need a weapon."

"There is an *arma* upstairs," Emma said. "Guns as well."

"Is anybody up there?"

She shook her head.

"Show me. Quickly."

They ran up the stairs. The second floor was much as Tucker remembered, although the furniture had been disarranged, and four mattresses were lined up in front of the stone fireplace. A small fire was burning.

Emma checked on the living room table, then in the kitchen, then between the mattresses. She found a shock baton, but no *arma,* no guns. She handed the baton to Tucker. "The other weapons are gone."

"That must have been them in the woods shooting. But shooting at what?"

"I don't know. A few minutes ago Jonas came running inside and said something to Master Gheen, and they all went outside, very excited. It was the first time I had been left alone since they came here. I thought to escape through the Gates."

"Do you know where the Gates will take you?"

"It does not matter. I only know I cannot stay here, not after all the things they have done. Kosh was not the first man they killed, nor will he be the last."

"We'll see about that," Tucker said. "Whatever else happens, they can't have Kosh's barn." He went to the stove, blew out the pilot light, and turned the gas jets to all six burners on high. The skunky smell of propane filled the air. "Let's go."

Back in Kosh's former workshop, the diskos were buzzing and flickering with unusual vigor, as if they sensed the upstairs filling with explosive gas.

"If you want to take a chance on the diskos, you'd better do it now," Tucker said.

Emma looked from Tucker to the diskos, then back. "You are going to fight them?"

"I'm going to do *something*," Tucker said. "I have a friend outside. She's going to be wondering what happened to me. You can come with me if you want, or take your chances with the diskos. But I wouldn't recommend hanging out in here."

Emma hesitated, then said, "I will come with you."

They started for the door, but were stopped by the sound of voices just outside. Tucker grabbed Emma's arm to pull her back behind the bench where he had been hiding before. She said, "No. They will expect me to be here. I will not betray you."

Tucker looked into the face that was the face of his mother, and he believed her. He jumped over the bench and hid himself behind it.

* * *

From the corner of the barn, Lia watched the open doorway through which Tucker had entered. What was he *doing* in there? She stepped out to follow him inside, then ducked back when she heard a gunshot from the woods. A second later, another shot came from the same direction. Again, she started for the open doorway.

"Yar."

Lia spun around. A few yards away, a clean-shaven man wearing a camouflage jacket, matching trousers, and a blaze-orange hunting cap stood holding an *arma* pointed at her midsection. The man's lips drew back from large white teeth. With a jolt, she recognized him.

"Master Gheen," she said, the words catching in her throat.

"I did not think to see you again," he said. He looked younger without the beard.

Lia looked at the *arma*, measuring the distance between them. Not close enough — it would be suicide to rush him.

"I like your hat," she said.

Gheen smiled. Was he really her father? She saw nothing of herself in his leering face. "I like to blend in with the locals," he said. "Where is your weapon?"

"I have no weapon," Lia said.

"So you say. Turn around. Put your hands on the barn."

Seeing no alternative, Lia did as she was told. She sensed him moving closer. Close enough for her to donkey kick him? Not quite.

"Are you alone?" he asked her.

"Yes," she said.

Gheen chuckled. "I think not."

The base of her skull exploded. Her face hit the barn. She fell to her hands and knees, and bright lights flashed behind her eyes. *He killed me!* she thought. But no, she was still alive. *He must have hit me with the butt of the* arma. She heard a grunt of effort and Gheen's boot crashed into her gut, knocking her onto her side. Lia forced herself to ignore the pain and lie still, feigning unconsciousness. Gheen stood over her, breathing heavily.

"I owe you that and more, Yar," he said. "Best pray to whatever bitch god you worship. You'll meet her soon."

Through slitted eyes, Lia watched him back away two steps, keeping the *arma* trained on her.

"I know you can hear me," he said.

Lia did not move, hoping he would come closer. She imagined planting her boot in his groin. Just one step closer.

"Your Yarish tricks won't work this time. On your feet." Gheen put his thumb on the *arma*'s trigger button. "Or we can end it now."

Sullenly, painfully, Lia climbed to her feet. Her neck was on fire and her belly felt as if something inside had broken.

"You are in pain," Gheen observed. "Good. Tell me, who is the man in black?"

Man in black? She shook her head. Tucker was not wearing black. That meant that Gheen didn't know about him. But who was the man in black?

Gheen said, "Do you wish to die sooner than is necessary?"

"I don't know who you're talking about." It hurt to talk. Breathing shallowly, she waited for whatever was to come. She would find an opportunity to act, or she would die.

Gheen turned his head slightly, glancing toward the woods behind the barn. He waved. Three men emerged from the trees, two carrying rifles, the other holding a baton. One was limping. He wore a brace on one leg. Lia remembered him from the park. As he drew closer, recognition widened his eyes.

Lia said, "How is your knee?"

The man raised his rifle. Gheen held up a hand. "Brother, restrain yourself."

"This one crippled me," the man said.

"She has information. Your time of reckoning will come." Gheen turned to the other man. "Did you see anything, Tamm?"

Tamm shook his head. "We thought we heard him. Koan got a couple shots off, but woods are impossible—all fallen trees and brambles. It might've been a deer. He could be anywhere." He looked nervously toward the trees.

"He is armed," said the younger man, an acolyte named Jonas. Lia remembered him from her days as a Pure Girl. He had often carried messages from the temple to the palace.

"We had best get inside," Koan said.

Gheen nodded. "Perhaps we can persuade this Yar to tell us some things."

41 HISTORIES

Lia entered the barn, Koan shoving her along with the barrel of his rifle. Inside, she stopped, astonished to see a row of five Gates. Five captive maggots! Standing beside the Gates was a young, red-haired woman. Lia remembered her from Romelas—the temple girl with amazing blue-green eyes. They had spoken once, in the east garden.

Koan gave Lia a vicious jab with the barrel of his rifle; she pitched forward onto her hands and knees. He hit her again, between the shoulder blades, and she fell flat.

"Restrain her, Jonas," Gheen ordered, entering the barn behind Jonas and Tamm. Jonas found a length of nylon cord and wrapped it around her arms, pulling them behind her back. She could not restrain a cry—every part of her body hurt.

Pain exists only in the mind, Yar Song had once told her. She tried to believe it.

"Legs too," said Gheen. Jonas ran the cord down to her ankles and bound them together. "Sit her up," Gheen said. Jonas and Koan dragged her roughly over to one of the barn posts and propped her against it.

"You keep watch," Gheen said to Jonas, handing him the *arma*. The young man went to stand at the doorway, holding the *arma* nervously.

"Who is this?" the temple girl asked.

Tamm noticed her for the first time. "Emma? What are you doing down here, woman?"

"I wondered where everyone had gone." She looked at Lia, her eyes wide and frightened. "What will you do with her?"

Tamm grunted. "It is not your concern."

Gheen had returned his attention to Lia, his heavy-lidded eyes boring into her.

"And now," he said, "let us talk."

Lia glared defiantly back at him. The aching in her gut and the sharper pains from her neck and back made it easier to not be afraid. *Fear is pain, and pain is fear.* Yar Song again. *Two edges of the same blade. Use them against each other.* Interesting how so many of the things that had made no sense to her when Yar Song had first said them now seemed like the most important words she had ever heard.

"Why should I talk? You are going to kill me."

"You are not so important as you think," Gheen said. "Our work here is almost done. If you help us, we may allow you to use one of the Gates. If you do not, things will go badly for you. Now, who is the man Jonas saw?"

Had he seen Tucker? If so, they apparently hadn't caught him. And where was Kosh? What had they done with him?

"I don't know," she said.

"Why do I not believe you?" Gheen smiled.

"Because you are a fool."

Gheen colored slightly, but held his smile.

"And a murderer," Lia said.

"Murderer?" Gheen frowned. "I have defended myself, certainly. I have acted as the hand of the Lord at times. But I have *murdered* no one."

"You killed the Lait Pike," Lia said. "You tried to kill *me.*"

"The Lait was an accident. The man was hysterical. As for you . . ." he cocked his head. "You are already dead. Your fate was determined the day you were born."

"Determined by *you.*"

"Determined by *scripture.* But I spared your life in Hopewell, as I recall. I may do so again, if you cooperate. Why did you come here?"

"I had no say in the matter. A Gate spat me out."

Gheen raised his eyebrows and looked at the row of captive maggots. "One of these?"

Lia hesitated. *When in doubt, lie to your enemies.* "Yes," she said.

"Interesting," he said, stroking his chin as if his beard were still there. "Which one?"

246

"The one on the end, or the one next to it. I did not look back."

"And from where did you come?"

Lia shrugged, wincing at the pain from her neck. "I will tell you the truth, but you will not like it. I came from a future in which the Lah Sept no longer exist."

"Ah!" Gheen seemed pleased. "Here we are at the nub of the matter. What is the future but the inevitable product of the present? Today we make choices; tomorrow we reap the benefits. This is the basis of our faith, is it not, Brother Koan?"

Koan shifted his weight onto his good leg and nodded, glaring at Lia.

"Let me ask you, Yar. Do you know why we chose to risk the Gates and come here to this primitive time?"

"Because you were driven out of Romelas. Because you are hated and feared."

Gheen opened his mouth in mock astonishment. "Such passion! You remind me of your mother."

Lia strained against her bonds, but only succeeded in nearly passing out from the pain in her side.

"That dark future you speak of," Gheen said, "will never arrive. That is why we are here — to ensure a glorious future for the Lah Sept. To ensure that the Lambs will rise, that Plague will be vanquished, and that in this new future, the Yars will never exist. I have made certain of this. Father September has done his part. During his incarceration, he inscribed the words that will become scripture. I have contributed my own words, as well. *The Book of September* is now as it should have been."

"The book of *lies.*"

Gheen sighed. "You are indeed an apostate. I will pray for you."

"Pray all you want," Lia said. "The Lah Sept will fall. I have seen it."

"You have seen but one future. *Our* future is still to come. *Woman!*" he snapped.

The red-haired woman, who had been standing silently to the side, jerked as if she'd been prodded. "Yes, Master Gheen?"

"Bring me the Book."

The woman nodded, walked over to the spiral staircase, and climbed upstairs.

"There is a saying with which you may not be familiar," Gheen said to Lia. "'History is written by the victors.'"

"The Lait Pike quoted it differently," Lia said. "He said, 'History is the lies of the conquerors.'"

Gheen shrugged. "It is all the same. Once events pass from the memory of the living, history becomes truth. You, for example, will exist only in the words that are written about you."

The woman came back down the stairs carrying a heavy-looking cardboard-bound ledger. She delivered it to Gheen.

"Bring me a chair," he said.

The woman found a dusty metal stool that had been tipped on its side by the front wall. She set it where Gheen indicated, directly in front of Lia. Gheen sat upon the stool and balanced the ledger on his lap. Lia had the peculiar feeling that she was back in Romelas, about to take a lesson from one of her tutors.

Gheen flipped though the pages, then paused. "Here we are." He unclipped a ballpoint pen from the binding and poised it over a page. He began writing, speaking slowly as he did so.

"And in the early years of the Age of the Lamb, a girl appeared before the Master, and did declare herself to be the daughter of the temple girl Inge." He looked up. "Correct so far?"

Lia glared at her father, wishing him dead.

Gheen began to write again, reading as he did so. *"The girl, who called herself Lia the Obedient, shared her valuable secrets with the Master, who was her true father, for the greater glory of the Lambs. Her words fell like petals of truth upon the ears of the Master. Filled with joy at her sharing, he blessed Lia the Obedient and allowed her to leave his presence unharmed, absolving her of her many sins."* Gheen smiled, pleased with his work. "You see, this is how the future comes to be. That which is written becomes the future, and those who write it become known as prophets."

"You are delusional, priest." Lia knew her hatred was written on her face; there was no reason to pretend otherwise. "Your words change nothing. I have no secrets to share."

Gheen pushed out his lower lip. "Let us explore an alternate history." He began writing again.

"The whore Inge's daughter's heart, blackened with hatred and bile, did cause her to lie and spew venom before the Master, and did so offend his ears that the Master struck out with great fury,

249

and the whore's daughter did cry out in agony, and when still she would not offer him her secrets, he struck out with righteous anger again and again, until the whore's daughter told all she knew, and the Master ordered her breasts cut off and her entrails ripped from her belly, and her gutted remains were cast lifeless into the nearest Gate."

Gheen looked at Lia and raised his left eyebrow.

"Much better," Lia said. It took all she had to keep her voice from shaking—her heart was beating so hard it sent pulses of pain along her ribs.

Gheen handed the ledger to Emma. He looked at Koan and gestured at the doorway. "Take her outside," he said. "Let her blood moisten the earth."

Koan pointed his rifle at her. "Stand up, Yar."

"I can't," Lia said.

Tamm grabbed her arm and jerked her roughly to her feet. Lia made herself go limp. Tamm made an irritated sound and threw her back onto the floor.

"Untie her feet," he said to Jonas. The acolyte leaned the *arma* against the doorway and came forward to loosen Lia's bonds. Both Tamm and Koan kept their rifles trained on Lia.

Gheen sniffed the air and looked about with a puzzled expression. "What is that *smell?*" he said.

42 CAT

Tucker could smell it too — the fishy, skunky smell of propane gas, flooding the upstairs, drifting down through the stairwell. How long would it be before the embers in the fireplace upstairs ignited it? Not long.

As he watched and listened, Tucker had been quietly feeling around on the floor behind the bench, looking for something he could use as a weapon. His fingers located a pry bar, and a small, heavy object that felt like a one-inch steel socket. Not much against two rifles, but it would have to do.

Jonas finished untying the rope around Lia's ankles and stepped away. Once again, Tamm tried to lift her to her feet. Tucker knew Lia well enough to know that giving her the use of her legs was a mistake. Her booted foot flashed out at Tamm, who jumped back, ready for such a move. At the same moment, Tucker stood up and hurled the socket.

The socket flew flat and true. Koan's eyes flicked toward it, but he had no time to react — it hit him dead center in the mouth. Koan dropped the rifle and fell to his knees, clutching his face. Tucker was already throwing the pry bar at Tamm. The bar hit Tamm in the shoulder, spinning him around, but he held on to his rifle.

Lia was moving too. She threw herself at Tamm, hitting the barrel of his rifle with a scissors kick. The gun went off, punching a hole in the ceiling. Lia landed on her side, her arms still tied behind her back. She spun on her hip and kicked Tamm's legs out from under him.

At the same time, Tucker had grabbed the wooden bench and, holding it like an enormous oblong shield, charged at Gheen, who was fumbling with the shock baton at his belt. The bench crashed into Gheen, sending him reeling back. Out of the corner of his eye, Tucker saw Jonas going for the *arma*. Tucker was on him in two strides — if the *arma* were fired, it would certainly ignite the propane, killing them all. He tackled the acolyte; they skidded across the floor and smashed into the wall. Tucker leaped to his feet and turned just in time to see Gheen coming at him with the baton. He dodged left and slapped the baton aside. Gheen twisted and swiped at him. Tucker jumped back, almost falling into the end disko. Lia and Tamm were rolling on the floor. Tamm had the rifle in one hand, and his other arm wrapped around Lia's neck. Tucker sidestepped another thrust by Gheen, grabbed the stool, and held it up between them. Gheen, panting, jabbed the baton at the stool. The charge from the shock baton shot through the steel stool and up his arms. Tucker dropped the stool and lurched backward, tripping over Koan, who was on his hands and knees, spitting blood from his broken teeth.

The stool had absorbed much of the charge from the baton, but Tucker's arms had gone numb. Tamm and Lia were struggling on the floor a few feet away, and Gheen was coming at Tucker with the baton. Tucker's arms hung from his shoulders like dead things, but his legs worked fine. He backed away from Gheen, shaking out his arms, willing feeling back into them. Gheen lunged. Tucker dodged around the barn post.

Tamm managed to swing the butt of his rifle against Lia's head, stunning her. He jumped up, looking around wildly. His eyes fastened on Tucker. He raised the rifle.

"Tamm, no!" Emma screamed.

Tamm fired. Tucker threw himself to the side the instant he saw Tamm's finger tightening on the trigger. He felt the slug whiz past his left ear. Tamm worked the rifle bolt and aimed again but was distracted by Lia, only half conscious, kicking weakly at his ankles. He snarled and brought the gun around, but before he could fire, Emma slammed the heavy ledger containing *The Book of September* against the side of his head.

Gheen, with serpent speed, jabbed his baton into Emma's side and she went down. Holding the baton like a sword, he advanced on Tucker. Some feeling had returned to Tucker's arms, but not enough. Tamm still had his gun—the blow from the ledger had only slowed him down—while Koan had regained his feet and was staggering toward the *arma*. Lia, dazed and in pain, her hands still tied, was struggling to stand.

Two armless teenagers against three men with weapons. Tamm once again brought the rifle to bear on Tucker. The only thing keeping him from firing was that Tucker was directly between Tamm and Gheen.

"I have him," said Gheen between gritted teeth.

Desperately, with all his strength, Tucker kicked the eight-inch-thick wooden barn post. He had never kicked anything so hard in his life—if it had been a football, the ball would have exploded. The post shattered and tore free from its top, smashing into Gheen's wrist. The baton went spinning off, bouncing off the wall. Tucker dove for the baton as Tamm fired the rifle. Tucker felt the bullet graze his hip. It didn't slow him down. He scooped up the baton and flung it at Tamm, but his arm still wasn't working right. He missed. Smiling, Tamm raised the rifle and took careful aim.

Lia had managed to free her hands. With a scream of rage, she launched herself from the floor, landing three rapid punches to Tamm's nose, jaw, and throat. Tamm reeled back, trying to fend off her attack, but within the space of two seconds, he was on the floor, disarmed and helpless.

For a moment, Tucker thought they had won; then he heard Koan, speaking through broken teeth.

"Enough." Koan had the *arma* and was pointing it at Tucker from fifteen feet away. A single touch of the trigger and he could sweep the blue flame across the room, incinerating both Tucker and Lia. Not that it would matter—the entire barn would likely go up in a propane fireball.

Dazed, holding his wrist, Gheen edged away from Tucker and Lia, getting out of the line of fire.

"If you fire that, we all die," Tucker said, breathing heavily. He could taste the propane in the air with every breath.

Koan shook his head, neither understanding nor believing.

"This building is filling with gas," Tucker said. "You know what propane is?"

Koan looked doubtfully at Gheen.

"That *smell*," Gheen said, understanding at last.

"I'm surprised we haven't blown up already," Tucker said. "There's a fire in the hearth upstairs. It could go any second now."

Gheen's eyes flicked toward the ceiling, then back to Tucker.

"I do not care how you and the Yar die," he growled. "Tamm?"

Tamm had managed to stand up, blood running from his broken lips. Gheen gestured at Emma, who was lying stunned on the floor.

"Take her if you wish."

Tamm grabbed Emma's wrist and dragged her out the doorway. Gheen glanced at the unconscious Jonas. "Leave him." Gheen snatched up the rifle Tamm had dropped and started toward the door. He stopped abruptly and looked back at the row of diskos. The second disko from the left was turning green and emitting a staticky sound.

The disko's surface bulged and crackled. Tucker stepped back. Gheen raised the rifle.

An enormous, black- and orange-spotted nightmare erupted from the disko. The jaguar landed on all fours in the middle of the barn and let out an ear-piercing snarl of rage and fear. Stunned by the cat's size and presence, Tucker froze. He was so close he could feel the heat coming off the jaguar's body. Teeth bared, the big cat swiveled its head, yellow-green eyes taking in its surroundings.

Gheen fired the rifle. The shot went wide. The jaguar saw the open door and leaped. Koan, standing in the doorway, screamed as the big cat's claws ripped through his flesh, sweeping him out of the way. The jaguar was gone. Koan collapsed, blood running copiously from four parallel slashes through his throat.

Tucker, Lia, and Gheen stood paralyzed, unable to take in what had just happened. Gheen recovered first, making a move for the door, but he was blocked by a large, black-clad figure carrying a shotgun.

Kosh.

43 DETONATIONS

MOMENTS BEFORE, KOSH HAD BEEN COMING AROUND the end of the barn, when he saw Tamm dragging Emma toward the SUV. Tamm wrestled her into the passenger seat, ran around the vehicle, and jumped into the other side. A second later, cursing, Tamm got out of the vehicle, only to find Kosh leaning against the back fender, dangling a set of car keys from one finger, holding a shotgun in his other hand.

Tamm held his hands up and took a step back. Kosh put the keys in his pocket. "Don't worry," he said, lowering the weapon. "I'm not gonna shoot you."

Tamm took that as permission to attack. He ran at Kosh, who brought the shotgun up hard. The heavy double-barrel struck Tamm's chin with an audible crack. Tamm went down. Kosh rushed around the SUV and checked on Emma. She was woozy, but she recognized him.

"In the barn . . ." she said, with a weak wave of her hand. Kosh looked at the barn just as a giant orange-and-black cat leaped from the doorway with a horrendous screech and landed a few yards away, between the barn and the SUV.

A leopard? Kosh raised the shotgun. The cat took off toward the trees and melted into the woods. Kosh ran to the barn, where he almost tripped over Koan, who was lying in the doorway. Tucker, Lia, and the priest called Gheen were standing inside, looking as shocked and confused as Kosh felt. Kosh trained the shotgun on Gheen.

"Hey kid," he said to Tucker, "you want to tell me what *that* was?"

"That was a jaguar," Tucker said.

"A jaguar," Kosh repeated. He looked down at Koan. Blood was pumping with alarming speed from Koan's throat. His fading eyes found Kosh, then went still.

"We have to get out of here," Tucker said. "Now!"

Kosh sniffed the air. "Have you been messing with my stove again?" he said. His eyes widened as he realized what a barn full of propane meant.

"Yes!" Tucker said. "Come on!" He grabbed Lia's sleeve and started toward the door.

Gheen, seeing his chance, made a dash for the nearest disko.

"No!" Lia tore free from Tucker's grasp and dove after Gheen. She grabbed the back of his jacket as the disko flashed orange. Lia and Gheen were gone.

Tucker started toward the disko.

"Don't do it, kid," Kosh said.

Tucker hesitated and looked back at Kosh.

Kosh said, "C'mon, Tucker. Let's get out of here."

"You get out," Tucker said. "I'm going after her."

"If you jump into that thing, I'm coming after you."

"What about Emma?" Tucker said. "You can't just leave her here."

He had a point. Tamm might wake up anytime, and Kosh wasn't sure how badly Emma was injured.

"This place is gonna blow any second," Tucker said.

The gas smell was stronger than ever. Kosh knew there was no way he could stop Tucker from jumping into that disko short of shooting him.

"Kosh, behind you!" Tucker said.

Kosh spun around. The youngest Lamb, who had been slumped unconscious against the wall, was on his feet, holding a bound ledger. Clutching the ledger to his chest, he jumped over Koan's body and ran out the door. Kosh let him go.

"Take care of Emma, Kosh."

Kosh nodded. "Good luck, kid."

He had almost reached the SUV when the barn exploded.

Tucker saw and felt it happen as he dove for the disko. Time slowed to a crawl. He felt a pressure in his ears, saw the blue billow of igniting gas plunging from the stairwell. The ceiling above bowed as if pressed down by the weight of a planet. The disko seemed a mile away; he felt suspended in midair. The heat and pressure struck, slamming him to the floor. He bounced once, and then felt nothing.

PART FIVE
REVELATIONS

The rift between Iyl Rayn and the Gnomon leader Chayhim became an embarrassment to the Cluster. Those Klaatu who used the diskos were assumed to be aligned with Iyl Rayn, and found themselves shunned by the Klaatu who agreed with the Gnomon. By the same token, Klaatu who voiced their support for Chayhim were ridiculed by Iyl Rayn and her allies, who regarded them as stodgy and unimaginative. Many Klaatu removed themselves to the outer reaches of the Cluster, where they were insulated from Klaatu politics and the negative flux that accompanied such interactions.

Communications between the factions had been nonexistent for some months when Chayhim received a friendly pulse from Iyl Rayn, requesting a dialogue.

"There is nothing to discuss," Chayhim said. "We are proceeding with the Timesweep program, despite your objections."

Iyl Rayn made a placating gesture and said, "My previous objections may have been overstated."

Chayhim expressed surprise.

Iyl Rayn continued. "Upon reflection, I have become persuaded of the correctness of your actions. I will assist you in dismantling the diskos."

"May I ask what has led you to this epiphany?" Chayhim asked suspiciously.

"I need your help."

Chayhim waited for elucidation.

Iyl Rayn said, "In short, I need the use of one of your Timesweeps."

"For what purpose?"

"It is a small matter," said Iyl Rayn with a shruglike flutter of her extremities. "There are a few minor adjustments I wish to make before the dismantlement begins."

— E^3

44 FEAST

Two days before Christmas, Kosh and Emily sat in Adrian's car, parked just down the road from her house, holding each other.

"I wish we could spend Christmas Eve together," Emily said. "But Greta . . . I think she suspects."

"We'll have to tell her sooner or later."

"I know, but . . . oh Kosh, what have we done? What will we do when Adrian comes back?"

"We'll just tell him," Kosh said, trying to sound confident, even as the thought of confronting Adrian filled him with dread.

Emily sighed and pressed her cheek to his chest. They sat in the car without speaking, letting the windows fog over. After a time, Emily's breathing grew ragged, and Kosh realized she was crying.

"Emily? Are you all right?"

"I'm sorry." She pushed back from him and wiped her eyes with the back of her hand.

"What's the matter?"

Emily shook her head, saying, "Please. Let's not talk." She smiled, but her eyes were wet with tears. "I'm just . . . I just love you so much."

"Me too," he said, his voice husky.

"I have to get home."

"Okay." Kosh was confused. He started the car, turned up the defroster, and wiped the windshield clear with his hand.

Emily sat back in her seat and sighed. "At least we have a little more time. Adrian won't be home for another month."

"I was just thinking that," said Kosh.

The morning of Christmas Eve, with nothing else to do, Kosh decided to cook a turkey, even though it would take him a week to eat the whole thing. He called Frank McDermott, who raised turkeys, and arranged to pick up a fresh bird. By noon, he had the bird stuffed, trussed, larded, and in the oven. He then set about making an apple pie, something he had never before done without Emily's help. He worked carefully, cutting the butter into the flour until the crumbs were like coarse sand, performing every step as if Emily were watching over his shoulder. At moments, he felt as if he could hear her breath, and smell the scent of her hair.

He worked through the afternoon. Mashed potatoes. Green

beans he had grown in his garden and put up four months ago. Squash, biscuits, braised parsnips, cherry preserve, chopped salad, and a noodle hot dish from a recipe left behind by his mother. At five o'clock he took the turkey out of the oven to let it rest, and made giblet gravy from the drippings. He set the table for one and sat looking over the spread. A masterpiece. He searched inside himself for the desire to eat, but could find nothing resembling an appetite.

He had never been so lonely.

At four o'clock on Christmas Eve, Adrian Feye landed at the Minneapolis/St. Paul airport.

Backpack over his shoulder, Adrian walked through the airport, his head whirling with amazement at all that surrounded him. Less than twenty-four hours ago, he had been on his knees in Jerusalem, in the Old City, praying before a stone wall more than twenty-five hundred years old. Now he was surrounded by plastic and metal and glass and hurried, harried people in suits and brightly colored clothing. A few of them were talking into small portable phones, what they called cell phones. It was another world. A godless world. He picked up his pace, almost running. He could hardly wait to get home, to share all he had learned with Emily.

He had planned to stay in Jerusalem another month, but his dreams of Emily had become more frequent, more intense. Convinced that the Lord was calling him home, Adrian had found an early flight back to the states. He would rent a car at the airport, drive straight to Hopewell, and surprise Emily on Christmas Eve.

Emily! How he longed to see her again. His months in the Holy Land had been the most profound experience of his life. He had trod upon the ground where Christ had walked with his disciples. He had stood upon the Temple Mount. He had felt God speaking to him from every stone, every tree, every breath of dry, dusty air. And every night, he had dreamed of Emily, of Hopewell, of the work to be done.

At the car rental counter, it took him several minutes to find his driver's license. The rental agent, a young woman with long blond hair pulled into a ponytail, waited patiently as he fumbled through his overstuffed backpack. Finally, he found his wallet in a pocket that also contained his house keys and a small locket. He handed the license to the agent, then opened the locket with shaking hands. Inside was a photo of Emily, smiling. Adrian blinked and felt tears dribble down his cheeks. He whispered a short prayer.

"Sir?"

He looked up. The agent was regarding him with concern. Adrian's eyes fixed upon her hair. In the Holy Land, blond hair was a rarity. He wiped his eyes with the back of his hand and muttered an apology.

"I'm going home," he told her. The agent smiled.

The rental car was small, with a dashboard that looked nothing like that of his Mustang. He felt as if he had been gone for decades, even though it had been less than six months. He examined the unfamiliar controls, then started the car and backed out of the parking space. As he drove out of the rental facility he saw that it was snowing. Snow was piled alongside the road, and big soft flakes were drifting down. It was beautiful. He felt a broad smile stretch his mouth, his heart beating deep and strong, blood coursing through his veins and arteries. In two hours he would be back in Hopewell.

Emily would be so surprised.

It was snowing again. Kosh climbed into the Mustang and started it, but could not bring himself to put it into gear. He could not stand to be in Adrian's car again. He got out and opened the garage door and looked at his motorcycle. It was a bad idea to ride his bike in the snow on the icy country roads. Stupid. Reckless. He zipped his jacket up to his neck and straddled the bike. Uncomfortable, too—he could feel the cold seat right through his jeans. He turned on the ignition and kicked the starter. He kicked it again. It started on the fourth kick.

All the lights were on at the Ryan house. Kosh sat on his bike, shivering, watching from the road. He saw a shape move past the living-room window. Hamm. He kept watching until he caught a glimpse of Emily, doing something at the kitchen sink. Kosh shuddered, the cold and desire colliding in his chest. After a time, he started the bike and drove off slowly, the image of his uneaten feast overtaking the image of Emily. He imagined the turkey fat congealing on the platter, the mashed potatoes drying, the chopped salad wilting. He turned toward downtown Hopewell.

As he rode up the highway past the interstate, he noticed a compact car, new-looking, come off the exit ramp. Kosh was familiar with most of the cars in Hopewell, but not this one. Somebody from the cities, no doubt, coming to visit a relative. The car flashed by. Kosh concentrated on the road, squinting into the falling snow, watching for icy patches.

Maybe Red was still open. Maybe even on Christmas Eve there was someone there he could talk to.

45 HERR BOGGS

Herr Pincus Boggs and his youngest son, Malachi, followed the tower of smoke up Blank Hill Road. He was glad to be off the highway, cars and trucks whizzing by and stirring up the horses. Kel and Bob were good horses, but they did not like cars. Boggs shook the reins, encouraging the horses to move along a bit faster. The Klaatu had insisted on urgency.

Herr Boggs sighed. He had hoped that here, in this elder time, he would not have to deal with such things. The Klaatu would not even come into existence for another three and a half centuries. It was those blasted diskos. They had been showing up far too often lately.

Malachi thought it a great adventure. Ten years old, and already he was hungry for the World. Well, he would see more than he bargained for here, if what the Klaatu had told him was true.

By the time they turned into the driveway leading to the fire, the smoke had thinned. Boggs could see why. The explosion had flattened the barn, spreading its shards over nearly half an acre. It was a shame — the last time he'd been here, he had thought it a fine barn. Though why it had been painted black was beyond him.

They found the first body on the ground next to a scorched vehicle. A man. A timber from the barn — probably one of the corner posts — had landed across his back, crushing him. Malachi stared wide-eyed at the corpse.

Life ends, thought Herr Boggs. *A lesson the boy will not soon forget.*

They found another man lying facedown on the other side of the SUV, half covered with splintered siding from the barn. He was alive. With Malachi's help, he loaded the unconscious man onto the cart. Inside the vehicle, they found a woman covered with broken glass and ash. At first, Boggs thought her dead, but upon closer examination, he detected a faint pulse. They placed her in the cart next to the man.

Was that all? Herr Boggs told Malachi to wait by the cart. He approached the smoking pile of detritus that had recently been a barn, stepping carefully over smoldering wreckage. Near what must have been the door, he saw a hand. He used his feet to lift away several charred and splintered boards. The arm was attached to a shoulder, which was attached to a head. This man was decidedly gone — his throat was torn open. Herr

Boggs was glad that the boy was not with him to see such a thing.

He moved further into the debris field and saw a series of mangled, twisted metal frames with shreds of charred pink plastic hanging from them. Boggs frowned as he recognized them for what they were—the remains of captive Timesweeps. He shook his head sadly, mourning these people for their hubris, for their recklessness, for their idiocy.

He was about to leave when he noticed something blue poking out from a large section of wooden floor that had fallen from above. He bent over and touched the blue thing, then jumped back as it moved. A toe? He tried to lift the flooring, but it was too heavy. Boggs thought for a moment, then took off his coat and went over to the man whose throat had been torn out and draped the coat over him so that Malachi would not see, then called his son over. The two of them were able to pull the section of flooring aside. Beneath it was another man—or perhaps a boy. It was hard to tell, and even harder to believe he was alive. Boggs rolled him over gently. A boy, he decided, from the smoothness of the few undamaged square centimeters of the boy's face.

Malachi was making choking noises, his face red, his eyes bulging.

"Go," said Herr Boggs. "Be sick, then go wait by the cart. I will take care of this."

Malachi staggered off. He had almost made it to the cart when he dropped to his knees and vomited.

Herr Boggs gazed down at the boy with blue feet. The kindest thing, he thought, would be to let the boy die here. He could cover the boy's crushed and bubbling mouth with his hand and hold it there; in a minute or two it would be over. But the Klaatu had been adamant: *Collect all who are alive.* Herr Boggs slid his arms under the ruined body and lifted it from the wreckage. What were the chances this boy would survive the three-hour ride back to Harmony? *Null,* he thought. The boy would probably die before they reached the end of the driveway. Nevertheless, he carried him back to the cart and laid the mutilated body beside the other two. Malachi looked on with a bloodless face and quivering lips.

Herr Boggs looked down at his blood and soot-stained shirt, then back at the barn.

"Come," he said to his son. He climbed back onto the cart.

"Your coat," said Malachi, jumping down to retrieve his father's coat from where he had draped it over the dead man.

"Leave it," said Herr Boggs. "It is only a scrap of cloth."

46 SEVERS

MAYO TWO, 2313 CE

TUCKER KNEW WHERE HE WAS BEFORE HE OPENED HIS eyes. The smell—or rather, the sterile, characterless *lack* of smell—told him he was in a Medicant hospital.

Again.

"Your readings indicate you are conscious." A woman's voice.

Tucker opened his eyes. The woman looked familiar.

"How long?" he rasped. The way his voice burbled in his throat told him it had been a very long time since he had spoken.

"You arrived in Mayo Two twenty-eight days ago," said the woman.

Days, not years. That was a relief.

"We have met before," the woman said. "Do you remember?"

"You are . . . *Severs* . . . and some number."

"Two-Nine-Four, but I no longer use my numeric designation." Severs looked older. Her hair was the same silver color, but her face was lined, her eyes softer, her lips thinner.

"Am I missing any organs?" he asked.

Severs smiled. The last time he had seen her, she hadn't smiled at all. "In this period, we do not require payment in body parts."

"In this period?"

"The last time we met was more than one hundred years from now. I have . . . transferred, one might say."

"You traveled back in time." Strange how it came out so matter of fact, as if time travel was as common as taking a bus.

"That is correct. This is the year twenty-three thirteen, not so very far in your future. Medically speaking, it is a relatively primitive time. The techs were able to save your life and heal you, but your enhancements—the devices implanted in your bloodstream that made you stronger, faster, and able to heal yourself—have been removed."

"Why?"

"The techs did not recognize the nanotech as beneficial, as that technology has not yet been developed. As I said, these are primitive times. The standard treatment now is to destroy all foreign bodies within a patient, then reintroduce a standard culture of beneficial bacteria. You are now much as you were before your first visit to a Medicant facility."

Tucker lifted his hands and looked at them. "I'm still me?"

"You are more you than ever."

Tucker looked down at his feet. His blue foot coverings were gone. He wiggled his toes. He hadn't seen his feet since the day he had entered the disko on top of his house. They looked very smooth and white.

Severs said, "The foot sheaths represent another technology that has yet to be developed."

"I was getting tired of blue anyway."

Severs laughed. Could this really be the same blank-faced, expressionless Medicant he had met before?

"Do you remember what happened to you?" she asked.

Tucker thought for a moment. Images swirled in his mind: Lia, the Lambs, his mother . . . no, not his mother, but the woman who looked like her. Emma. Lia following Gheen into the disko—where had she gone? He remembered opening the gas jets on the stove. Tucker gasped and sat up.

"The barn!"

"Yes?" Severs put her hand on his arm, steadying him.

"There was an explosion!"

Severs nodded. "I am impressed that you remember what happened to you. Most trauma survivors do not recall the events immediately leading up to their injury, and your injuries were . . . spectacular. If not for the nanotech in your body, you would certainly have died."

"Kosh was there!" Tucker said, remembering more.

"Your uncle survived, as did the woman Emma."

"Are they here?"

"No. They were here for a time. They were not injured so badly as you, and recovered quickly, but three days ago they were both taken by maggots."

Tucker let out a shaky breath.

"By the time we realized our facility had been invaded, it was too late to stop them. Fortunately, we were able to prevent a third maggot from reaching you. In fact, we captured it."

The weight of all that had happened was too much to bear. Kosh, Lia, his parents—all of them, lost in the diskos. As was he. "You should have just let it grab me," he said.

"Why do you say that?" Severs asked.

"Because every place I go, people get hurt. I'm getting dis-koed from one horrible thing to another. I don't know who's doing it, or why."

"Why do you think it is about you?"

"It's not random. Every time I turn around there's a maggot chasing me. I don't know if it's the Klaatu, or the Boggsians, or God, or what, but I'm sick of it."

"I agree that the diskos are not random," Severs said.

Tucker sank back down onto the mattress. "Somebody is playing with us, like it's all a game. I just want it to be over."

"You wish to take yourself out of the game."

Tucker drew a shaky breath. "I can't. Kosh and Lia are still in it, whatever *it* is."

Severs regarded him thoughtfully. "You believe you can change what has happened."

"How can I believe anything else? If everything that

happens—everything we do—is inevitable, then what's the *point*?"

Severs said, "I do not disagree with you. I have witnessed the destruction of Mayo. I have seen Romelas in its bloody decline. I have treated hundreds of people who have been maimed or killed in service to politics, religion, greed. I have visited a distant future where civilization is no more. And now I am here, not even born yet, doing my small part to make the world a better place. Perhaps the point is simply to strive, because if we don't, then it is not worth the trouble to breathe."

Tucker stared at the Medicant. He understood what she was saying, but as she spoke, he realized that none of it mattered.

"I just know I have to go," he said.

Severs nodded and, with a sad smile, said, "You are like your uncle."

"I am?"

"Very much so. We have a captive disko here in the hospital—the one through which you arrived. You are welcome to use it. Your uncle did, when he was treated here the first time. It delivered him to your Hopewell—he told me this on his second visit to our facility. Or, if you wish, you can let the maggot take you. The choice is yours."

"I doubt it makes any difference," Tucker said. "I have a feeling I'll end up wherever the diskos want me to go."

47 HOPEWELL, YET AGAIN

Hopewell, November, 2012 ce

Tucker had a full two seconds to look around as he fell from the sky. By the time he hit, he knew where he was. Hardy Lake. The lake was frozen.

He struck the ice feetfirst, expecting that both legs would be shattered, but the ice was only a fraction-of-an-inch thick. He sliced through, plunging into the water, cold at first, then warmer as he went deeper. Tucker kicked and flailed his arms and broke through to the surface. Treading icy water, he scanned the lakeshore until his eyes fixed upon the leafless branches of the big cottonwood. He swam, breaking through the skim of ice with each stroke. Moments later, he staggered onto the narrow beach, shivering violently. A bitter cold wind from the north cut through his coveralls, blowing hard enough to set the rope swing swaying. The rope had begun to fray. How much time had passed since he had tied it? Months, at least.

He needed shelter. It was nowhere near as cold as the North Pole, but he was soaking wet, and it was plenty cold enough. Below freezing, for sure. He scrambled up the bank, reached the road, and set off at a run toward town.

Downtown Hopewell looked like a ghost town. His father's old church was boarded up, and the sign had been taken down. The hotel was closed—again. The only open business was the Pigeon Drop Inn. Shivering and still damp from his plunge into the lake, Tucker crossed the street to the Drop and pushed through the door.

"Well, well, well. It must be Feye month," Red Grauber said, looking up from his station behind the bar.

Red's only customer was a tall, hefty man, nattily clad in a white dress shirt, red suspenders, and a dotted bow tie, standing at the bar sipping a cup of coffee.

"Feye month?" Tucker said.

"Your uncle stopped by a few weeks back. Borrowed my van and never brought it back."

"Now, Red," said the man with the bow tie, "you got your van back." Tucker did a double take, recognizing Henry Hall. Wearing a *bow tie?* Drinking *coffee? Sober?*

"Yeah, two weeks later," Red said. "Some hunters found it way back in the woods in Wisconsin. They drank all the beer in back before calling it in to the police."

"What about Kosh?" asked Tucker.

"His place burned down the same day I borrowed him my van. Nobody's seen him since."

"The police found two bodies in the wreckage," said Henry Hall. "Neither of them was Kosh."

"The mayor's right," Red said. "Neither of 'em was ugly enough."

Tucker gaped at Henry Hall. *"Mayor?"*

"Hard to believe, ain't it?" Henry Hall thrust out his belly and snapped his suspenders proudly. "Voted in just last Tuesday," he said.

"Strange but true," Red said, with a wink at Tucker. "So what brings you back to Hopewell, son? Have your folks turned up?"

"No, it's just me. When did the hotel close?"

"Couple weeks back." Red sighed. "Nobody comes to Hopewell no more. The pigeons moved on, and that crazy Lamb cult is gone. Can't say I miss 'em. Not that I didn't appreciate the business they brought in."

"The pigeons or the Lambs?"

"Both."

"What about Tom Krause?" Tucker asked.

Red and Henry looked at him with puzzled expressions.

"Who?" Red asked.

"Tom Krause. You know, the Krause's oldest? Wasn't he. . . . Didn't something happen to him?"

"You know any Krauses?" Red asked Henry.

Henry shook his head. "Didn't see any Krauses on the voting rolls."

A chill ran through Tucker's body. *Everybody* knew the Krauses; they'd lived in Hopewell for three generations.

"These Krauses, whoever they are, sure aren't patronizing my fine establishment," Red said.

"We'll get you some customers," Henry Hall said, reaching across the bar and patting Red's hand. "I have big plans for Hopewell."

"Yeah, like what?"

"You know Elwin Frahlen?"

"Sure I do."

"Well, Elwin's been making a ball of twine for the past seventeen years. Another six months, he says it'll be bigger than the one in Darwin, Minnesota. We'll cart that thing downtown and build a gazebo and get the Guinness Records folks out here to certify it. Biggest twine ball in the world. That'll bring folks to Hopewell, you better believe it!"

Red rolled his eyes. "Henry, you made more sense when you was a drunk."

"Well, I darn sure don't hear anybody else coming up with any ideas," Henry said petulantly.

"How about you get them pigeons to come back?"

"How about you give me a refill on this coffee?"

Tucker backed away, leaving the two men to their bickering, and went back outside. It had started snowing, fine crystals coming down hard, at a slant. *Now what?* he thought in despair. *If I go home I'll find an empty house. If I go to the Krauses, I'll*

probably find an empty field, or a house occupied by another family.
If I head for Kosh's place, I'll find a field of snow-covered wreckage.

His only choice, it seemed, was to throw himself into yet
another disko, and keep doing it until luck or fate brought him
to wherever Lia and Kosh had gone. The nearest disko he knew
of was on top of the hotel. He crossed the street to the sidewalk
in front of the entrance. He was trying to decide whether to
break a window or force open the door when he heard a clop-
ping sound from down the street. Squinting into the wind, he
saw a dark shape emerge from the snow: a horse, followed by a
two-wheeled cart driven by a man wearing a broad-brimmed
black hat. The man stopped the cart at the curb in front of the
hotel, said something to the horse, and climbed heavily to the
ground. He walked past Tucker and up the steps to the front
door, removed a key chain from his pocket, inserted a key into
the lock, and opened the door.

Turning, he said to Tucker, "Well? Are you coming or not?"

The Boggsian was in a terrible mood, muttering irritably to
himself as he led Tucker down the hallway and up the carpeted
stairs. When they reached the fourth floor, he turned to Tucker
and said, "You will please tell that Klaatu that I no longer wish
to be her *shklaf.*"

"What's a *shklaf*?"

"It is a slave. I am not a slave."

"Who are you?" Tucker asked.

"I am Herr Pincus Boggs, and you are keeping me from my dinner."

"How do you have the keys to the hotel?" Tucker asked.

"Should I not have keys to my own property?"

"You own the hotel?"

"I regret to say yes, to my financial ruination. Hopewell House, bah! I open, I close, I lose money at every turn."

"Why are you here now?"

"I am paying for foolishness. Never make a bargain with a Klaatu. They are relentless."

"A Klaatu told you to come here?"

"Why else should I be out in this *verlaten* weather?"

"I don't know," Tucker said.

"Yes, you know nothing. Come, I will take you to the disko."

"The disko on the roof?"

"Where else?"

"Where does it go?"

"I should know this? Bah, I am as ignorant as you. I do as I am told." He opened the door at the end of the hall to reveal the steel steps leading up to the roof. "Go. I am done here."

48 THE BROKEN BLADE I

The Terminus

The disko delivered him to another forest. Tucker stepped away and took in his surroundings. He was in a small open glade, surrounded by white three-petaled flowers. Trilliums, his mother's favorite. The forest smelled like spring—a mushroomy, green aroma, quite different from the richer, compostlike odor of late summer, or the dry dark tang of autumn. The trees surrounding the glade were a mixture of conifers and birch.

The disko sputtered, faded, then swam back into view.

If this was the Terminus, some version of Awn might be waiting for him. Unless this was after her time. Only one way to find out. He began to walk, moving slowly, his eyes and ears keen for any sight or sound. Before long he came upon a faint path. He followed it to the right. The trail led past several other diskos, some nearly obscured by tall grasses and brush, giving them a forlorn, neglected appearance.

It was not until he came upon the disko that had once led him to Golgotha that he got his bearings. He kicked at the leaves surrounding the disko until he unearthed the rust-caked hilt of a broken sword. It had not been so rusty before. Nearby, he found a chunk of squirrel-gnawed wood that might once have been a wooden troll. This was a later time, then. Months, or perhaps years, after Awn's death.

Awn's cabin would be another half mile away, over a piney hill, along the creek, and across the grassy meadow where the priests had killed her. He continued, taking his time, watching and listening. The piney hill was as he remembered it—tall, straight trunks rising from a mushroom-studded bed of needles. The creek was running high. He walked along it for several minutes before he found a place to cross. Tucker climbed the far bank and headed through an area dense with poplar and scrubby spruce, and then fought his way through a ragged patch of buckthorn. He had taken several steps into the meadow before he realized that he had arrived.

The forest was taking over the meadow, its edges were blurred with growths of hazelnut, buckthorn, and sumac. Tufts of grasses stood waist high, and the center of the field had been invaded by patches of thistle and buttonweed. He heard the buzzing and chirping of insects, the distant call of a wood-pecker, the breeze tickling the tops of the grasses.

He approached the cabin cautiously, stopping every few feet to watch and listen. About halfway across, skirting a patch of nettles, he saw that the front door was ajar. He stopped and watched the door for a long time. No one appeared.

"Hello!" he called out, ready to dash back into the forest if a priest — or worse — came out to greet him.

There was no response.

He climbed onto the porch and pushed the door open. Inside, the cabin looked exactly as it had the last time he was here. The trestle table was there, and the wooden chairs. The floor was swept, the ceramic dishes neatly stacked on open shelves, a heavy iron pot on the stove. Tucker lifted the lid. Bean stew, still warm. He looked in the bedroom. Instead of one bed, there were now two, both of them neatly made.

Was it possible Awn was still alive? He had seen her scorched and bisected body, and this couldn't be an earlier time period — the rusted sword hilt proved that. But . . . could an earlier version of Awn have used the diskos to travel here, to the future? Maybe she had made the bean stew and left it for him. But that would mean that Awn had known of her own death, and known that he'd be back here on this particular day. It seemed unlikely.

He went back to the stove and scooped up some warm beans with his fingers and tasted them. Spicy, like Mexican-style beans. Awn's food had always been tasty, but bland. Tucker replaced the lid and went back outside. The smart thing to do would be to hide in the trees and wait for whoever it was to come back. He was just stepping off the porch when he heard a scream.

The sound came from the woods, a long ways off. He listened, but the sound was not repeated. Could it have been an animal? He didn't think so — it had sounded distinctly human.

It had sounded a lot like Lia.

Tucker ran. He followed a path toward where he thought the scream had come from, passing several diskos. He reached the creek, slowed, stopped, and listened. Nothing but forest sounds. He crossed the creek and climbed onto a ridge, walking silently, listening for any unusual noises. Nothing. He stopped at the intersection of two paths, and he noticed something odd about the bird sounds. He could hear their peeps and chirps and calls in the woods to his right and directly ahead. Behind him, where he had just walked, the birds were silent. And they were silent to his left.

He followed the path that led to where the birds were not singing. A few minutes later, as he reached the base of a long, low hill, he heard voices.

49 PAIN

LIA HEARD HERSELF SCREAM AS SHE FELL FROM THE disko. Twisting in midair, she had only a second to orient herself. She glimpsed the rocky, fern-covered hillside an instant before she hit. She heard her right ankle snap—a sickening pain rocketing up her leg—then she was tumbling down the steep slope, the whispery softness of the ferns punctuated by harsh jolts from the rocks. She felt as if every bone in her body were splintering. Then she hit the water.

The water was ice-cold, but only a few feet deep. She fought her way to her feet, the shock of the cold water momentarily suppressing the agony in her ankle, her shoulder, her left hand. Gasping, she splashed toward shore, ignoring the silent shrieks of protest from her ankle, then threw herself onto the bank. She lay facedown on the muddy bank for several heartbeats, taking inventory. Ankle probably broken. Shoulder injured, but working. Something was wrong with her hand. She raised her left hand and looked at it. The nails of two of her fingers had been peeled back. Lia shuddered and looked away.

Master Gheen! They had come through the disko together. Where was he? She rose painfully to her knees and looked up the steep hillside but saw only a confusion of foliage. He had to be nearby. She listened and heard a groan from the slope above her, then the rustling, crunching, of feet shuffling through leaves.

Gheen was alive, and he was moving.

Moments ago, in the barn, she had been ready to kill him. Now she just wanted to get away, to curl up someplace safe.

She tried to stand but her ankle would not support her. She crawled upstream along the bank, gritting her teeth to keep herself from crying out. Her shoulder hurt, but she could use it. She continued up the creek, stopping every few moments to listen. She couldn't hear Gheen anymore, only the burbling of the creek and the occasional rattling admonishment of a squirrel.

Shortly, she came upon a deer trail leading up the slope, away from the creek. She stopped there and once again examined herself. The sharp, stabbing pain in her ankle had become a dull, throbbing pressure. The sharpest pain was from her ruined fingernails.

Once, when Lia had been hurting after a particularly vigorous dojo session, Yar Song had taught her a trick. *Pain is a coward; it cannot stand in the face of your scrutiny. Find it and face it, and you control it.* Lia closed her eyes and focused on her hand, the fingers, the raw, stinging, bleeding nailbeds.

As Yar Song had promised, the moment she located the source of the pain, it slipped away, up her arm to her shoulder, yet another source of torment. Lia refocused on the new point of discomfort. Again, the pain slid away. *Cowardly pain,* she thought. *Face me! Declare yourself!*

It declared itself in her ankle, her neck, and her belly, where Master Gheen had kicked her. The pain was slippery, elusive, persistent. She could shift it, but she could not make it go away.

She heard splashing from downstream, and a muttered curse. Gheen was close. Pain forgotten for the moment, Lia turned away from the creek and crawled uphill along the deer trail for a few yards. She concealed herself in a stand of tall ferns. Through the fronds, she caught a glimpse of Gheen as he passed by, following the creek. He was walking slowly, dragging one leg, using a broken branch as a cane. Lia enjoyed a moment of satisfaction that he had been injured too, although he didn't look as bad off as she felt. She waited until she could no longer hear him, then dragged herself farther up the path, out of sight of the creek.

I can't just keep crawling through the woods, she thought.

What would Yar Song do? She remembered one afternoon when she had been going through her dojo routine automatically, moving from position to position while her mind wandered. Song, watching expressionlessly from the edge of the mat, had suddenly stood up, grabbed Lia's hair, and rapped her on the forehead with one incredibly hard knuckle. *"Think!"* Song had said in her crisp, penetrating voice. With that, Song left the dojo, and the day's lesson was over. Lia had looked at that bruise on her forehead for a hand of days before it faded.

She had to *think*. What did she have to work with? One good leg. Two arms. One good shoulder. Eight fingernails. Her clothing. Rocks, sticks, and leaves. She eased off her right boot. Her ankle was visibly swollen, showing purple streaks. She found a piece of broken rock with one sharp edge and used it to cut roughly through her trouser leg, just above the knee. The fabric was tough, but after a few minutes, she had cut it free and dragged the pant leg down over her ankle. She tore the cloth into long strips and wrapped one around her damaged fingertips. They hurt less when she didn't have to look at them. The other strips she used to bind her ankle tightly. She tried to stand. The pain was not as bad as before, but it still hurt too much to walk. She tried to pull her boot back on over the wrappings. It was too tight. It hurt. Gritting her teeth, she pulled harder. The boot popped on. The pain almost caused her to pass out; the forest spun around her. She focused on her breathing. After a few seconds, the spinning stopped. Her ankle was still a knot of agony, but the wrapping and the tight boot would keep it stable.

Seeing a fallen tree a few yards away, she crawled over to it and used the sharp rock to hack off a branch. She fashioned the branch into a crude crutch. With the crutch, she was able to walk upright in a sort of hopping, foot-dragging fashion, similar to the way she had seen Gheen moving along the creek.

Now she could put some distance between her and Master

Gheen, and give herself time to figure out what to do next. Continuing up the deer path, she arrived at the crest of the hill, upon which stood a Gate.

As she approached the Gate, it began to hum and glow green. Lia backed away from it, holding her breath. The Gate emitted a waft of reddish mist, then settled back to gray. The pine needles beneath the Gate were sprinkled with red dust.

I have been here before, she thought. This was the Gate that Awn had told her led to a genocide.

There would be more Gates. Awn might be here too. The strange woman had helped her before. Maybe she would do so again.

"Yar Lia."

Lia whirled, automatically assuming a defense posture despite the pangs from her damaged body. A few yards away, almost invisible in his camouflage garb, Master Gheen was sitting on a fallen tree, watching her.

50 THE BROKEN BLADE II

"Do not be afraid," Master Gheen said.

Afraid? Fear was not what she was feeling. It was more like rage.

Gheen held up one hand, palm forward. "I mean you no harm." He reached behind the log, came up with the blaze-orange hunting cap, and placed it on his head. Using his stick like a cane, he stood up and took two unsteady steps toward her, dragging his left leg. "Look at me. I am no threat. I can hardly walk."

"Best you stay still, then," Lia said.

Gheen's mouth stretched into a smile intended to be friendly and reassuring. It looked to Lia like a leering devil mask.

"We are both injured," he said in a soothing voice. "Let us set aside our differences. We can help each other."

"I do not need your help."

"Of course you do. You are crippled."

"As are you."

"This is my point. Do you know where we are?"

"The future," Lia said.

Gheen nodded. "The future." He pointed off to his left with his stick. "The Cydonian Pyramid is only a few minutes walk in that direction. It is now, of course, a ruin, even more decayed and sunken than it was the last time I was here. The Gate that once hovered above it is gone."

"There are many Gates," Lia said. She pointed at the Gate that had produced the red dust. "Why don't you use that one?"

Gheen looked at the Gate and sniffed dismissively. "I think not."

"Then choose another."

"I do not trust these Gates. In any case, it seems I have little to go back to. You and your friends have destroyed us."

Lia did not reply. Gheen shrugged. Using his stick as an aid, Gheen walked back to the fallen tree and sat down heavily.

"I am not a bad person," he said. "You are angry with me for the things I have done. I accept your anger. We do what we are meant to do, as the winds of time blow us hither and thither. I wonder sometimes if even God, in all his magnificence, has any real choices."

"You are saying you are not responsible for what you have done?"

"I am just a man."

"An evil man."

"What is evil? I once thought the Yars to be evil. Apostates such as yourself. Now I understand that we are all victims. You may never call me a friend, but I am your father, as you know."

"I would just as soon forget it," Lia said.

"Be that as it may, we are connected. I come to you now asking your forgiveness."

Lia considered the man sitting before her. Was it possible he was sincere? If so, did it matter? He had tried to kill her more than once—her and Tucker both. Could such a man change so quickly? She did not think so.

"You think me insincere," said Gheen, as if reading her thoughts.

"I think you a liar," Lia said.

With obvious effort, Gheen held on to his smile. "I have lied in the past," he said. "This is the future."

"Not for you."

"What would you have me do?"

Lia pointed at the Gate. "Leave."

"As I told you, I am done with the Gates. *This* is where the Lord wishes us to be. The Lah Sept we once knew are gone—the Lord found them wanting. But we are here. We have been blessed with the chance to begin anew, to rebuild without repeating the mistakes of the past."

"You want to start the Lah Sept all over again?"

"And why not? I do not believe we are alone here. There must be others—lost souls who need guidance. It is my hope that you will join me. You are, after all, my daughter."

Lia laughed. She was startled by the sound that came from her throat—a laugh harsh with bitterness and bile, pain and fury. It resembled the snarl of a jaguar more than any sound from a human throat.

"I am building nothing with you, old man," Lia said.

Gheen's face darkened. He lifted his improvised cane as if to strike her.

Please try, Lia thought.

Gheen lowered the stick. "Come, now," he said in a syrupy voice. "There is a cabin nearby to provide us with food and shelter. Come with me, and there we will talk some more. In time you will understand."

Lia gave him a look of disgust and loathing. "I understand that I am done with you." She turned her back and began to hobble back down the hill. She had gone only a few steps when she heard a movement and turned.

Gheen was limping after her, teeth clenched, raising his stick.

Yes, she thought, *this is the father I know.*

Gheen swung the stick. Lia hopped back on one leg, raising her crutch to deflect the blow. Gheen's stick, larger and heavier, snapped Lia's slender branch in half. Lia fell, landing on her back. Gheen raised his stick. Lia hurled the broken branch at him. The short length of wood struck Gheen's bad leg; he collapsed with a cry.

Lia crawled rapidly up the hill toward the Gate, gaining the higher ground, then climbed onto one leg to face him again.

Gheen approached, more cautious now. He was breathing hard, his face red with anger and frustration.

Let your opponent's emotion devour him, Yar Song had said.

"I come to you with arms open," he said, "and you reject me. I should have known — once a Yar always a Yar."

Lia felt weirdly calm. She had faced this version of Master Gheen before; she was on familiar ground. She let him come closer. He made a tentative jab at her with the stick; Lia batted it aside. Gheen reached into his jacket pocket with his free hand and pulled out something wrapped in a black cloth. The cloth fluttered to the ground. In his hand was the obsidian dagger, the same blade that had once sliced open her face.

Lia stopped breathing. The sight of the dagger sent a quiver of fear through her.

Your fear is powerful. Use it.

Lia set her jaw and willed strength into her limbs. It was just a piece of sharpened stone. A rock in the hands of an angry old priest.

Holding the stick in one hand and the dagger in the other, dragging his leg, Gheen backed her toward the Gate. Lia could hear its excited buzzing. When she felt the emanation from the Gate stir the hairs on the back of her neck, she stopped and assumed the pose that, at Yar Song's insistence, had consumed many of Lia's hours in the dojo.

"Why is this called the warrior pose?" Lia had asked Song, as they each balanced on one leg, bodies parallel to the mat, arms thrust back. "It is a poor defense posture."

"It is the worst *defense pose*," *Song agreed,* "which is why you *must know it. It is a lesson in gravity, balance, focus.*"

"*That makes no sense*," *Lia said, whereupon Song had kicked her in the ribs.*

Gheen, bemused by her odd stance, hesitated. "More Yarish tricks?" he said.

Lia smiled.

Gheen lunged, faking a jab with the stick as he slashed at her with the knife. Lia thrust her leg back and spun her body in midair, dropping to the ground on her back. The blade sliced though the air inches above her face. Her hand shot out and grabbed his wrist as it passed. She brought her good leg up, planted her boot in his belly, and catapulted him into the Gate.

The Gate flared orange. Gheen's hunting cap fell to the ground. The stone knife struck a rock and shattered. The Gate's surface pulsed and faded to gray.

Master Gheen was gone.

Lia lay on her back, heart pounding, her chest shuddering with each breath. She rolled over and, on her hands and knees, crawled away from the buzzing Gate. She pulled herself up onto the log where Master Gheen had recently sat. She stared at the Gate, looked down at the red dust scattered before it, at the broken black blade, at the bright orange cap.

It had really happened. Awn had told her that all who passed through this Gate would die. Master Gheen — her *father* — was gone. She searched inside herself for feelings of triumph or regret, but found neither. The Gate sputtered; its swirling gray surface began to break apart, its edges growing indistinct.

Lia looked up at the rustle of footsteps on leaves. A head appeared over the brow of the hill—long tousled hair, blue eyes. . . .

"Hello, Tucker Feye," Lia said.

Tucker looked from Lia's face to the fading Gate, then down at the blaze-orange cap on the ground beneath it. He took a deep breath and let it out shakily.

"I thought you might be in trouble," he said.

"I'm okay." Lia smiled. "Except for my ankle."

Tucker sat beside her and put his arm around her shoulder. Lia winced.

"And my shoulder."

"Sorry."

She held out her bandaged fingers. "And a few other things."

"You're alive," Tucker said.

"That is something."

Together they sat and watched the Gate fade slowly out of existence, leaving behind only the cap, the blade, and a few grains of reddish sand.

51 GENOCIDE

MARS, 1976

A THIN WIND, INHUMANLY COLD AND DRY, SWEPT across the Chryse Planitia. Powdery grains of sand moved near the surface, tumbling over one another as they had for uncounted millennia. The scant Martian atmosphere transmitted the soft hiss of colliding silica crystals, though there was no one there to hear it. The sun, small and distant, teased at frozen fragments of water and carbon dioxide, but not enough to coax them from their solid state.

Time passed.

Three meters above the surface, an anomaly appeared. A spark of orange became a miniature orb, then flattened to become a shimmering disc the size of a manhole cover. The disc continued to grow until it was 1.3333 meters in diameter, and the thickness of a hydrogen atom. For the next three rotations of the red planet, the disko hovered patiently above the rock-strewn sands.

A new star mounted the horizon, rose high over the plain, then separated into two lesser objects. One continued in its orbit; the other entered the atmosphere. A parachute blossomed, slowing its descent.

Three intensely bright points of light erupted from the bottom of the object. The parachute broke free and drifted off as the craft continued its descent toward the surface. The three points of light resolved into spikes of blue flame supporting a complicated-looking metallic construction. Slowly, the spacecraft sank through the thin atmosphere. As it neared the surface, three gangly legs unfolded from its belly, giving it the appearance of an arachnid amputee.

The disko, almost directly beneath the descending spacecraft, awakened. Its gray surface became mottled, turned sickly green, then flared bright emerald and spat out a Klaatu. The Klaatu was followed by several others. Their numbers grew to become a crowd of several dozen hovering, ghostlike figures, all looking up at the approaching craft, now clearly recognizable as the Viking 1 lander.

At first, it looked as if the lander would collide with the disko and the waiting crowd of Klaatu, but it missed them by several meters. The touchdown was abrupt; the legs struck the surface, flexed, sprang back. Dust exploded from beneath the rockets and billowed out, creating a huge torus of particulates that quickly distorted and was swept away by the thin wind. The jets sputtered and winked out, the lander settled, the dilute roar of its arrival gave way to the near silence that had persisted for millennia.

Six hundred seconds later, the quiet was interrupted by a buzzing sound. A dish-shaped antenna unfolded from the top of the lander and rotated several degrees until it was pointed at Earth. The Klaatu watched. More buzzing and clicking came from another part of the lander as the camera began to record and transmit images of the rocky plain. From time to time, the sounds would cease, then start up again.

The Klaatu became bored. One by one, they floated back to the disko and were drawn inside, until none were left. The disko remained. The lander continued to perform its various functions. The wind blew. The planet rotated as it continued its long, ponderous journey around the sun.

For several Martian years, the Viking lander continued to transmit information back to Earth, although the clicking and buzzing occurred less frequently. On the 2,248th Martian day after its arrival on Mars, the lander emitted its last click, then fell silent.

Time passed. The disko remained dormant. Dust built up around the legs of the lander and filled its crevasses and openings, making it look less like an alien presence and more like a native thing that had emerged from the sand and stone of Mars.

On the 2,522nd day after the landing of the Viking, the disko awakened, flashed green, and spat out a man wearing a camouflage hunting jacket.

The man landed on his back. The impact drove his last

breath from his lungs—a cloud of moist, oxygen-rich air crystalized, then fell like snow to the arid surface. Master Gheen staggered to his feet, gasping for air that was not there, looking around wildly as the surface of his eyeballs froze. He clawed at his chest and staggered toward the lander, but he made it only a few steps before falling to his knees, then pitching forward to bury his contorted face in the red earth of Mars.

Cell by cell, the process of freeze-drying began. Plasma membranes burst, spilling cytoplasm, mitochondria, nuclei. Proteins, prions, and other complex, carbon-based substances flaked from the frozen corpse to violate the delicate Martian ecosystem.

The thin wind blew.

Flecks of silica collided with the alien particles.

The sun rose and fell.

The planet began to die.

52 PROMISES

This has got to be the weirdest Christmas Eve ever, Kosh thought.

He had been trying to talk Red into serving him a beer when this kid walked in off the street—a kid with longish sandy hair and the fuzzy beginnings of a beard. Strangers were rare in Hopewell, especially at Red's Roost, especially on Christmas Eve. But what made this kid *beyond* strange was that Kosh felt as if he knew him. At the same time, he was sure they'd never met before.

The kid walked closer to the bar. He was dressed in gray coveralls, like a janitor, and what looked like bright blue plastic socks. He was saying something to Red, but Kosh was too astonished by the kid's face to hear what they were saying. Except for his hair color, the kid looked like what Kosh saw every morning in the mirror.

"Do I know you?" Kosh asked.

The kid looked at him. One corner of his mouth turned up in a smile.

"Not yet," the kid said.

Before Kosh could ask what he meant by that, the door banged open and Adrian strode into the bar.

"Adrian," Kosh said, his heart pounding.

Adrian Feye had changed during his months in the Holy Land. He was thinner, his features more crisply defined, his skin dark from the Middle Eastern sun. But what Kosh saw most clearly was the anger and pain in his brother's eyes.

Adrian *knew*.

Kosh didn't know what else to do, so he walked to Adrian and held out his arms and said, "Welcome back, bro."

He never saw the punch coming. Adrian's fist took him on the point of his jaw, snapping his head back. Kosh staggered into the bar, his elbow knocking Henry Hall's beer into his lap.

"What was *that* for?" he asked, even though he knew *exactly* what it was for — and he knew he deserved it. Adrian was coming at him again, yelling something about his car. Kosh dodged Adrian's second swing and tripped over a chair. He scrambled to his feet just as Red came around the bar and grabbed Adrian.

"Take it outside, boys." Red marched Adrian to the door and shoved him outside. "You too, Curtis. Out!"

Kosh followed his brother out onto the sidewalk. *Maybe I can explain,* he thought.

There was no explaining. The moment the door closed behind him, Adrian attacked.

Kosh had been in fights before. Too many fights. Every time, there was a point when a sort of berserker rage took over—it didn't matter who he was fighting, or why. He would feel it first as a numbness in his spine that rose up through his neck and filled his head. At that point, he stopped feeling the punches, and all that remained was an animal part of his mind telling him to lash out, destroy, defend.

The first time Adrian hit him, it hurt. The second blow felt like a distant explosion. After that, Kosh felt nothing but the satisfying crunch of his fists crashing into Adrian's face, chest, shoulders, head. They were on the ground, on the sidewalk—Kosh didn't know how they'd gotten there. It didn't matter.

A sound from Adrian penetrated his rage. A sob. In a moment of clarity, Kosh saw himself rolling around on the sidewalk, hitting his brother, the man who had raised him, the man he had betrayed. He thrust Adrian away and jumped to his feet. Adrian dove at him and wrapped his arms around Kosh's leg. Kosh punched him on the forehead, jerked his leg free, and staggered over to his bike.

"I'm sorry, bro," he said in a choked voice.

Adrian, blood running down his face, climbed to his feet and lurched unsteadily toward him. Kosh kicked the engine to life and took off.

Emily Ryan, wearing a parka and moon boots, sat on the porch swing in the dark, watching the snow drift across the tracks Adrian's car had left in the driveway. Inside the house, Greta cleaned the kitchen, Hamm smoked his pipe, and a pile of wrapped gifts sat neglected beneath the Christmas tree.

She felt sick to her core. Her world had come to an end.

An hour ago, when the doorbell rang and she had seen Adrian standing on the porch, she had, for the first time in her life, wished herself dead.

She had told him everything. A cavernous future gaped open, promising a lifetime of regret for all of them. Adrian had stormed off in a righteous fury. She could not blame him. She could not blame him for anything.

The door opened. Greta stepped out onto the porch.

"Honey? Why don't you come inside. It's cold out here."

"I'm okay," Emily said.

"Are you sure? Adrian seemed upset. We could hear him shouting from all the way inside. Do you want to talk about it?"

"Not now, Mom."

"Well . . . don't stay out here too long."

"I won't."

Greta closed the door. Emily hugged herself, but took no comfort in her own embrace. The pain within her breast was beyond physical. She could not hug it away, or cry it away.

She sat in the cold, dry-eyed and waiting.

Kosh loved his brother. From the day their father had died, Adrian had raised him, doing his best to be both brother and surrogate father. Kosh respected Adrian, but he had never understood him. He loved his brother, but he did not like him.

He suspected that Adrian had never liked him, either. Their mother had died giving birth to Kosh. Did Adrian hold him responsible? How could he not? Kosh held *himself* responsible for killing the mother he had never known.

Still, all that was nothing compared to the betrayal by Kosh, stealing away Adrian's fiancée. He deserved to be punched, and more. Years of rage—from both of them—had erupted on the sidewalk in front of Red's. Now it was over.

Kosh slowed his bike and rolled through another drift. The wind whipping across the flat farmland between downtown Hopewell and the Ryan farm created snaky snowdrifts across the highway, some of them several inches deep. Insane to be out here on his bike. He didn't care. As bad as he felt about what he had done to Adrian, the worst of it was over. He and Emily would have to leave town, but at least they would be together.

All the lights were on at the Ryan house. As he parked his bike he could see the Christmas tree through the window, and a curl of smoke from Hamm's pipe coming up over the back of his easy chair. Kosh stepped up onto the porch and reached for the doorbell.

"Kosh?"

Startled, Kosh looked over at the porch swing and saw Emily sitting there.

"Why are you out here?" Kosh asked.

"I knew you would come," Emily said. Her voice sounded small and distant.

Kosh sat on the swing beside her.

"I saw Adrian," he said.

"He was here. I knew he went looking for you." She was staring straight ahead. Kosh felt a seep of fear behind his breastbone.

"He found me at Red's. We had a fight."

Emily closed her eyes. Kosh sat beside her on the swing.

"He knows about us," Kosh said.

Emily nodded slowly. "I told him." She turned her head to face him. "Kosh, I am so sorry." Her face looked dead-white, her lips were pinched, and the pupils of her eyes looked like pinpricks in the middle of opaque green irises.

Kosh moved to put his arm around her.

"Don't," she said.

His heart was pounding and he could hardly breathe; his stomach was filled with icy sludge.

"We can go away," he said desperately. "Tonight. I have money. My inheritance."

"Kosh. . . ." She placed her gloved hand on his forearm. It weighed a thousand pounds. "I'm going to marry Adrian, as I promised him."

"No," he said. It came out like a gasp.

"I'm sorry."

"Stop *saying* that! What about *our* plans? What about *me*?"

He hated how whiny he sounded but he couldn't stop himself. "You don't *love* him. You *told* me so!"

"Please, Kosh. I hate myself enough already. Please don't make this any harder."

"What did he say to you? What did he do?"

"Nothing, Kosh. He did nothing. I'm sorry."

Kosh stood up abruptly. The porch was spinning. He grabbed the railing and descended the three steps from the porch to the ground, and dropped to his knees. He willed himself to throw up, but the pool of sludge in his gut refused to move. He staggered to his feet and walked unsteadily to his motorcycle.

"Kosh." Emily was standing on the steps, her face hollow, drawn, and excruciatingly beautiful. He looked back at her without saying anything. "Please, Kosh. Be careful."

Careful? Kosh swung a leg over the bike and kicked it to life. *Careful?* Why should he be careful when he'd just lost everything he had ever cared about. He grabbed his helmet and threw it on the ground, dropped the bike in gear, spun it around, fishtailed up the short driveway and onto the road, winding out every gear, not caring if he lived or died.

53 THE WALK

The Terminus

"Awn's cabin is about a quarter mile from here," Tucker said. "There's food, and shelter."

"Awn is here?"

"Maybe. Somebody is, but I don't know who."

Lia looked at the blaze-orange cap. "At least we know it's not *him*."

"Can you walk?"

"I can hobble. Except my crutch is broken."

"I'll carry you."

"Really?" Lia looked doubtful.

"I think I can." He wasn't sure. "Piggyback," he said.

"I don't know what that is."

Tucker showed her, and moments later they were headed down the hillside toward Awn's cabin with Lia's legs gripping his hips, her arms wrapped around his neck. They made it about a hundred yards before Tucker had to stop to rest. Clearly, his Medicant enhancements were no longer working.

"You're heavier than you look," he said, breathing heavily.

"Thanks a lot!"

"We'll get there. Just give me a minute."

Lia said. "We can make a crutch, then I can walk partway at least."

"No!" Tucker said. "I'm going to carry you."

"It hurts my shoulder."

"Okay, let's try it this way." He scooped her up in his arms and began walking again. He liked that better—he could see her face. "How does this feel?"

"Like we're about to fall over," Lia said.

"We won't."

They made it only about twenty yards before she made him stop.

"I feel like you're going to drop me. I'd rather walk."

"You can't."

"Yes, I can."

The improvised crutch, made from the forked branch of a balsam tree, enabled Lia to hop along at approximately the speed of a turtle. Every so often she allowed Tucker to help her over a deadfall, or up a steep hillside, but most of the way she managed by herself. Tucker could tell she was in pain, but she was determined to hobble along on her own.

They stopped frequently to rest. Once, they sat on a pile of rocks near a disko.

"I wonder where that one goes." Tucker said.

"Chances are, it goes to someplace horrible," Lia said.

The disko sputtered and faded away.

"That's the third one I've seen do that," Tucker said. "The diskos are disappearing."

Lia gave Tucker a searching look. "What happened after I went into that maggot in Kosh's barn?"

"Well . . ." Tucker laughed. "As soon as you left, the barn exploded."

"Is Kosh . . . ?"

"He's okay. Emma, too. They were at a Medicant hospital, and so was I, but a maggot took them and I don't know where they are. I was hoping they'd be here. Oh, and I met a friend of yours at the hospital. Severs."

"Severs!" Lia said. "Was she okay?"

"Yes. She was really nice. She asked about you."

"What did you tell her?"

"That you were amazing."

They reached the meadow at dusk. There was a light in the window, and a steady plume of smoke rising from the chimney.

"You'd better wait here while I check it out," Tucker said. He set off across the field. After a few paces he looked back. Lia was limping after him. Tucker started to object, but then saw from her face that she was determined not to be left behind. Together, they made their way slowly across the overgrown meadow to the cabin. They were almost there when a woman stepped out onto the porch.

"Hello," she said. "We have been waiting for you."

The woman had reddish hair pulled back in a loose ponytail. She wore a dark green shirt tucked into loose, earth-colored trousers, and appeared to be in her forties or early fifties: slightly thick around the middle, wide mouth framed by deep but not unattractive lines, streaks of gray showing in her red hair. Her eyes were green, a lighter green than her shirt. She looked like an older version of Emma. But more than that, she looked like Tucker's mother.

54 REVELATIONS I

"Mom?" The word came from Tucker's mouth in a high-pitched little-boy voice.

Lia looked at him in surprise, then at the woman. This was Tucker's mother?

"I am not your mother." The woman smiled. "I am Emily Three. You may call me Emelyn."

Tucker stared at her, speechless.

"You look like the temple girl, Emma," Lia said.

Emelyn's smile broadened. "Emma is my sister. Would you like to come inside?"

Tucker helped Lia onto the porch. They followed the woman into the cabin. The stew pot was bubbling on the woodstove.

"You are injured," said Emelyn to Lia, as she pulled one of the wooden chairs from the table. Lia sat down. The woman knelt before her and tried to remove her right boot. Lia cried out; her ankle was so swollen there was no way the boot could be pulled off.

"I'm afraid your footwear will not survive this operation," Emelyn said. Using sharp shears, she cut through the sides of the boot and peeled it away, then carefully unwrapped the strips of cloth. Lia's ankle was grotesquely swollen and purple streaked with yellow and red. Lia turned her head, looking as if she might be sick.

"That does not look good," said the woman. "Let me see your hand."

Lia held out her hand, and the woman unraveled the makeshift bandage to reveal the two nailless, bloody fingertips.

"Oh, that must have stung."

"It did," Lia said.

"Let's see what we can do to get you fixed up."

Tucker felt as if he were swimming through a dream. The woman calling herself Emelyn not only looked like his mom, she talked like her, and moved like her. *Let's see what we can do to get you fixed up.* How many times had he come home with a cut, a scraped knee, a bee sting, and been sat down in a kitchen chair by his mother and heard her say exactly those words? How many times had she knelt before him and soothed his pain and calmed his fears?

Emelyn opened a cabinet beside the stove and brought out a small plastic object. She pressed the device to Lia's swollen ankle. Lia's shoulders slumped, and some of the tension went out of her face. Tucker hadn't realized how much she'd been hurting. Emelyn applied the device to Lia's hand, to her shoulder, to her neck. Each time, Lia relaxed a little more, and the hardness in her eyes faded.

"Can you carry her?" Emelyn asked.

"She doesn't like being carried."

"Look at her. She's about to fall off that chair." Lia's face was slack, and she was wavering. "I'm sure she won't object if you carry her a few steps."

Lia fell asleep moments after Tucker lowered her to the bed. He returned to the main room. Emelyn was sitting at the table, reading the small screen on the Medicant device.

"She has a fracture of the distal fibula, a minor shoulder separation, and a number of contusions. These are things I am able to treat. She will recover."

"Are you a Medicant?" Tucker asked.

"Me?" Emelyn laughed and placed the device on the table. "Hardly, although this is one of their instruments, as I'm sure you know."

"Then what *are* you?"

"I am a historian."

That was about the last thing Tucker had expected her to say. She might as well have claimed to be a lion tamer, or a taxi driver.

He said, "When we first walked in, you said, '*We've* been waiting for you.' Who is *we?*"

Emelyn pointed at the ceiling. Hovering in the rafters was a Klaatu.

"Tucker, this is Iyl Rayn."

"I think we've met."

"More times than you know," said Emelyn. "She has much to share with you."

Tucker regarded the gauzy figure suspiciously. "Is she the one that's been doing all this? Sending us all over the place?"

"Yes and no. It is complicated."

"You sound like Awn."

"Awn is my sister, too. To answer your question, Iyl Rayn designed the diskos, but her ability to manipulate them is limited. The Gnomon have been attempting to manipulate them as well, with limited success. Much of what you have experienced was the result of being caught in the web of their conflicting efforts."

"I thought the Boggsians made the diskos."

"Yes, at Iyl Rayn's behest. Later, the Gnomon commissioned the Boggsians to build the disko-bearing automata known as Timesweeps, or maggots. These conflicting efforts resulted in a number of paradoxes. Iyl Rayn and the Gnomon are now working to resolve matters."

"Is there a way for me to talk to her?" Tucker asked, looking up at the Klaatu.

"Tomorrow we will go to Harmony, where there is a device that will allow her to speak with us directly, and we will rejoin Kosh and my sister Emma."

"Kosh? He's here?"

"He has been for some weeks. He'll be glad to see you. Are you hungry?"

"Yes." Tucker couldn't remember when he had last eaten.

"Eat then. I must do some repairs to Lia's injuries. Tonight, we will rest. Tomorrow, we have a long walk ahead of us."

55 REVELATIONS II

"Help me out here, Clyde," Kosh said. "I got no idea what I'm doing."

The horse did not reply. Kosh glowered helplessly at the tangle of leather straps and buckles he was holding in his arms.

Emma, perched nearby on a wooden fence rail, said, "I don't think you're speaking his language."

Kosh fumbled with the harness. "This part looks like maybe it goes over his head. Hold still, Clyde." He tried to drape the strap over the horse's neck. The horse backed up, shook its head, snorted, and stamped its foot, narrowly missing Kosh's toes.

"Whoa!" Kosh said, jumping back.

Emma convulsed with laughter.

"I don't think I'm cut out to be a farmer." Kosh threw the harness to the ground and joined Emma on the fence rail.

"Maybe Emelyn can give us some pointers."

"You think she knows how to harness a draft horse?"

Emma shrugged. "She couldn't possibly know less than you."

"Sitting here dressed like a couple of Amish farmers and we can't even hitch up a plow," Kosh grumbled. They were wearing clothing the Boggsians had left behind—Kosh in bib overalls and a straw hat, Emma in a dark blue long-sleeved dress.

Two weeks ago, they had been snatched from the Medicant hospital by maggots. The maggots had delivered them here, through the disko in the barn. A woman who looked like she could be Emma's mother had been waiting for them. She had introduced herself as Emelyn.

"This is Harmony," Emelyn told them. "It was once a thriving Boggsian settlement, but the last of the Boggsians are gone. You are welcome to anything you find while you wait."

"What are we supposed to be waiting for?" Kosh asked.

"For Tucker Feye."

"Who *are* you?" Kosh asked.

"As I told you, my name is Emelyn." She smiled at Emma. "I am your sister."

"But—"

Emelyn held up a hand. "Be patient. You must wait. Feed yourselves. Rest. Know that you are safe. All will be explained in time."

With that, she disappeared into the disko.

They had found food in one of the houses—stocks of canned vegetables, flour, hard cheeses, squashes, potatoes, and a barrel of slightly wrinkled apples. The Boggsians had not been gone long. In the sheds beside the house, they discovered several bags of seed grains and legumes stored in drums, and an abundance of tools. A half-acre vegetable patch behind the house was green with spring onions, lettuce, chard, radishes, and carrots. The draft horse—Emma had immediately named him Clyde—had shown up the next day, strolling through Harmony as if he owned the place.

They had everything they needed to run a farm—except the knowledge of how to harness a horse.

"I feel like a monkey trying to rebuild a carburetor," he said.

Emma wrapped her hands around his arm and leaned close. "We'll figure things out." She gave him a kiss on the cheek.

Kosh glared down at the tangled harness, but he was smiling.

Lia awakened to the aroma of fresh-baked bread. She opened her eyes. A few feet away, Tucker was sprawled on the other bed, snoring lightly. Lia tipped her head up and looked at her feet. Her right ankle and foot were encased in a plastic sheath. She sat up. Aside from some stiffness, she felt good. Putting her feet on the floor, she tried to stand. Her ankle bore her weight with only mild discomfort. Placing her feet carefully, she walked into the main room of the cabin.

Emelyn was sitting at the table, writing by hand on a large paper tablet. Next to the tablet was a basket of sliced bread and several jars of condiments. She looked up and smiled.

"You are awake," she said. "Are you hungry?"

Lia nodded and sat down. Emelyn pushed a plate across the table.

"We have hazelnut butter, blueberry preserves, and jam made from thimbleberries."

Wordlessly, Lia spread a slice of bread with the preserves and ate. Emelyn watched her for a moment, then returned to her writing. Lia ate the entire piece of bread. It was delicious. She helped herself to another slice, put a small dab of the hazelnut butter on it, and tasted it.

"I prefer the blueberries," she said.

"Ah! She speaks at last!" Emelyn said. "You should try the jam."

"I do not know what thimbleberries are," Lia said, irritated by the woman's brusque good cheer.

"You will never know if you do not taste them."

Lia spread a small amount of the pinkish jam on her bread and took a bite. She chewed thoughtfully, swallowed, then said, "I prefer the blueberries."

Emelyn laughed. Lia scowled.

Emelyn sobered and said, "How is your ankle?"

"It is better. Thank you."

"You may need to wear the brace for a week or two, but you should be able to get around on it. Now, I imagine you have some questions for me?"

Lia spread more blueberry preserves on her bread and ate. When she had finished her second slice, she said, "What are you writing?"

"I am recording a history."

"Of what?"

"Of you, among other things."

"Why?"

"It is what I do."

"Why?"

"We must all do something."

"I have done all I care to do."

"Do you think so?"

"I have met my mother and killed my father. I am done with doing things."

"I hope not. You are young."

"I do not feel young." In fact, now that her hunger was sated, Lia felt very little at all. She thought of Tucker sleeping in the next room. A boy she hardly knew. What did she feel for him? She tried to recall the affection, the respect, the fierce attraction she had once felt, but it was like trying to feel for a needle with thick woolen mittens. What was *wrong* with her?

"You have had a shock, both in your body and in your mind," said Emelyn. "It will get better."

Lia stared at Emelyn, watched her features blur and quiver. She blinked; tears coursed down her cheeks.

"That's a start," said Emelyn.

Tucker, blinking sleepily, appeared in the bedroom doorway.

"What's going on?" he said.

Lia stood and walked to him. She put her arms around him and buried her face in his chest and sobbed. Tucker looked past her at Emelyn, his face a study in utter bewilderment.

"She's doing much better," Emelyn said.

56 REVELATIONS III

As HE HAD BEEN DOING EVERY DAY SINCE ARRIVING IN Harmony, Kosh visited the disko at the back of the barn. He stood before it, careful not to get too close, and stared into the swirling gray disk. Facing the disko made him feel alive and in control, like jumping on a motorcycle or standing at the edge of a cliff. Anytime he wanted, he could step forward into another life.

A large waist-high table stood next to the disko. It was not an ordinary table. The top was made of glass, or some similar substance, and it was warm. Occasionally the table clicked and hummed, as if it contained active electronics. There were no apparent knobs or other controls. Kosh left it alone.

One day Emma came into the barn and found him gazing into the disko.

"Kosh?"

He looked back at her and smiled. "Just thinking," he said.

"Thinking about leaving?"

He shook his head. "No. Besides, we have to wait for Tucker."

"I like it here," Emma said.

"So do I." Kosh was surprised to hear himself say it. He *did* like it, although he could see it would get lonely in time. But for now, just being with Emma was enough. He had resisted his attraction to her at first—it had seemed wrong. Was he falling in love with her, or did he feel that way only because she looked so much like the Emily he remembered? But as the days passed, he came to realize that Emma did not resemble Emily as much as he had thought. She was her own person. Her physical appearance came to matter less and less.

"Look," Emma said. The disko was changing from gray to green. Kosh grabbed Emma by the hand and they backed away as the disk bulged. A blob of mist oozed from its surface. The blob morphed into a roughly humanoid shape, drifted over to the table, and hovered there.

"A Klaatu," Emma said.

"You've seen them before?"

"The Klaatu are said to be the spirits of our ancestors."

"You think it can hear us?"

The figure waved a blobby hand.

Emelyn's voice came from behind them. "She hears you."

Kosh and Emma turned. Emelyn was standing in the doorway. Behind her were Tucker and Lia.

"Look who's here," Kosh said. "The kid who blew up my barn."

"Sorry," Tucker said, grinning. "It seemed like a good idea at the time."

Kosh walked up to Tucker and held out his hand for a fist bump, then changed his mind and wrapped his arms around his nephew and squeezed, lifting him off his feet.

"*Oof,*" Tucker said. Kosh put him down and looked at Lia.

"Please do not do that to me," she said. "I am injured."

"I see that," said Kosh, noting the sheath encasing her ankle.

"It's good to see you," Lia said.

"Likewise." Kosh turned to Emelyn. "Thank you."

"I don't deserve your thanks," said Emelyn. She crossed over to the table, reached beneath it, and activated a switch. The table's surface emitted a bluish glow, and the Klaatu came into focus.

"Greetings," said the Klaatu, its voice emanating from the table. "I am Iyl Rayn, and I beg your forgiveness."

The image of Iyl Rayn was that of a woman, but it had a blobby, unfinished appearance. Most of the fine detail was missing. Her hair was an orangish cloud, her features a blurry approximation of a face, and the spotted dress she wore seemed fused to her pale flesh. Her voice, coming from speakers concealed within the table, sounded flat and artificial as well, but there was something familiar about it.

"I know you have many questions, not all of which I will be able to answer to your satisfaction. I am a Klaatu, as you know, but I was not always so. I was once a living biological person like you. I was a Pure Girl in Romelas, a teenager in Hopewell, a lover, a mother, and a madwoman.

"My name, at the time of my transcendence, was Emily Feye."

57 THE FIVE EMILYS

THE KLAATU'S WORDS STRUCK TUCKER'S EARS AND SKIT-
tered off. He stood there blinking stupidly. He knew something
important had just happened, but he didn't know what. Lia and
Emelyn were staring at him. Kosh was gaping at the Klaatu.
The air felt thick as it moved in and out of Tucker's lungs, and
the floor was very far away.

Had the Klaatu just said something about his mom?

He said, "What?" His heart was pounding in his ears and
the walls seemed to be tilting. Lia grabbed his arm.

"I am sorry to tell you this way," said the Klaatu. "I know it
must be difficult."

Tucker said, "Wait. What did you say?" He looked around
frantically. His eyes landed on Emelyn. "What did she say?"

Emelyn said, "Tucker, your mother was very ill. Do you
remember when she went away?"

"Of course I remember!" He jerked his arm free from Lia's
grasp. "That's how all this got started."

"Yes. Your father took your mother to a Medicant hospital."

"I know! He told me she *died*! Why are you *telling* me this?"

"I did not die," said the Klaatu. "I was transcended."

This time, her words registered. Tucker stared at her, his mouth working silently. No words would come.

"By the time I was delivered to the Medicants there was little left of my mind. Irreparable fissures had opened in my brain. The Medicants could not help me, so I was given to a Boggsian, who made me into a Klaatu."

"You're my mom's *ghost*?" Tucker said.

"I am not a ghost. I live, though not as a biological being. Once I was freed from my physical body, my thinking once again became clear. My memories, however, remained fragmented. It was my efforts to regain my memories and make myself whole that led me to create the diskos. I hoped to use them to observe historical events—specifically, my own lost past. I was successful, in a sense. I have watched you grow up. I have—" Her voice caught, and the image turned to face Kosh. "I have found echoes of longing, and regrets."

Why is she looking at Kosh? Tucker wondered.

"So, you're like a ghost with memories and feelings," Tucker said.

"No, I am your mother." Iyl Rayn turned back to him. "Do you not recognize me?"

"You're sort of blurry," Tucker said.

The table emitted an electronic sound that may have been a sigh. "My body memory is fading," she said. "As for feelings . . .

I have feelings. For you I feel love, joy, and pride. But my feelings do not carry the power they once did. Transcendence saved me from who I was, but it also took away something elemental. This is why I cloned myself."

Tucker looked at Emelyn and Emma with sudden understanding. Emma was gripping Kosh's hand so hard her knuckles were white. Her face was even whiter. Kosh, gaping at the Klaatu, did not seem to know Emma was there.

Emelyn was looking intently at Tucker. "It is true," she said. "We are clones of your mother."

"There are five Emilys," Iyl Rayn continued. "The original Emily was a Pure Girl of the Lah Sept, who as a young child was abducted from the temple and taken through a disko to Hopewell. She was adopted by Hamm and Greta Ryan.

"I commissioned the Boggsians to create three clones from a sample of my original DNA, which they obtained from the young Emily Ryan. The first clone, Emily One, was flawed— her DNA degraded during gestation. The clone did not physically resemble the original Emily, and was able to absorb only a few fragments of Emily's already fragmented memory, including the numerophobia—a fear of numbers—impressed upon her as a child by the Lah Sept. That clone was augmented with new eyes and enhanced musculoskeletal features. She was also fitted with an experimental telomere regenerator to extend her useful lifespan. She became, in essence, a cybernetic organism, and was sent to the Terminus, where she lived a very long life as the custodian of the diskos. You knew her as Awn.

331

"The second clone, Emily Two, was physically identical to the original Emily, but the memory transfer was again unsuccessful. She was sent to replace the original Emily, Lah Emma, in Romelas. This cruelty was necessary to deceive the Gnomon, who might otherwise have removed the original Emily from Hopewell. Emily Two was raised as a Pure Girl until shortly before her blood moon, when she was taken by the priests to serve them in the temple. She became the woman you now know as Emma.

"The third clone, Emily Three, received a full set of my fragmented memories. She was further educated based on the observations I later made of my corporeal life by using the diskos. She is as close to the Emily Feye you grew up with as was possible. She is what I might have become, had I remained corporeal without becoming ill. In some ways, she is more the me I once was than I am. You know her now as Emelyn."

"I share most of your mother's memories, and all of her DNA," Emelyn said.

"But you're *not* her?" Tucker said, a part of him wanting her to disagree.

Emelyn smiled his mother's smile. "Iyl Rayn is the continuation of your mother — the main trunk, you might say — while I, and Emma, and the woman you knew as Awn, are limbs."

Tucker looked back at Iyl Rayn. "You said there were *five* Emilys."

"I am the fifth Emily," said Iyl Rayn. "I am your mother's imago, her ultimate manifestation."

"A Boggsian once told me that Klaatu are nothing but information."

"As are you."

"I'm not just information," Tucker said.

"I once believed that of myself," said Iyl Rayn. "Is there such a thing as a soul? I still do not know, though I have had millennia to think about it."

"How old *are* you?"

"Today, according to the calendar system with which you are familiar, is the third day of June, in the year ninety-nine ninety-eight."

Tucker thought for a moment. "You mean it's my eight thousandth birthday?"

"There are many ways to compute that. Subjectively, you have lived five thousand nine hundred sixty-three days. That is, by your reckoning, precisely sixteen years, one hundred nineteen days. But yes, according to your ancient calendar, today is the anniversary of your birth."

"Wait a second," Kosh interrupted. "June third is your birthday?"

"Yeah," Tucker said, startled by the fierce expression on Kosh's face.

Kosh wheeled on Iyl Rayn. "You were *pregnant*? And you *knew* it?"

"That is true."

"Why didn't you tell me? I would never have left!"

"You were not ready to be a father, Kosh."

"I could've been! If you had told me. I *loved* you!"

"As I loved you. But you were only seventeen."

"And you were only nineteen!"

"I had no choice for myself. But I could make the right choice for you."

Kosh glared at her. "It was not yours to make."

Emma, who had been standing by with a bewildered and stricken expression, suddenly turned and ran out of the barn.

"Perhaps not," said Iyl Rayn, "but it is done, and now you have choices of your own to make. You have a woman who may love you as I once did. And you have a son."

Kosh clenched and unclenched his fists, then closed his eyes and took a deep, shuddering breath. When he opened his eyes, he was looking at Tucker Feye.

58 KNOWING

TUCKER DIDN'T THINK THAT ANYTHING COULD SHOCK him more than finding out his mother was a Klaatu, but he was wrong. Kosh was his *father?*

Neither of them knew what to do. All Tucker could think was, *My mother is a ghost. My uncle is my father.*

Still, looking at Kosh's bright blue eyes, at his long, stubbly chin, Tucker realized that deep inside he had sensed for a long time that Kosh was more like him than his father—than the man he had *thought* was his father.

Kosh, looking as stupefied as Tucker felt, slowly reached out and placed his hand on Tucker's cheek, as if to make sure he was real.

"Kosh . . ." Emelyn touched Kosh's sleeve, then inclined her head toward the barn door. "What about Emma?"

"Where did she go?" Kosh asked, looking around confusedly. He hadn't noticed her leave.

"I think you should find out," Emelyn said.

Kosh looked from Emelyn to Tucker, then at the image of Iyl Rayn, then back at Tucker. "I still can't believe you blew up my barn."

"That was long ago," said Iyl Rayn. "Emma is here now."

Kosh stared at her, drew a shuddering breath, then ran out after Emma.

"Kosh is not very smart sometimes," Lia said.

"Yes he is," Tucker said, leaping to Kosh's defense.

"That's not the kind of smart I meant," Lia said.

"Kosh is more tender and thoughtful than you know," said Iyl Rayn. "He will make Emma happy."

"Yes, but first he will make her cry," Lia said.

Emelyn laughed.

"Kosh and Emma will have to make an important decision soon," said Iyl Rayn. "As will you all. We are at the Terminus, as you know—the forward edge of the existence of the diskos. I have made a pact with the Gnomon. The diskos are being dismantled even as we speak. Soon, the disko you see before you will be the only remaining portal to the past. One day it, too, will be gone."

"Why do the Gnomon want to destroy the diskos?" Lia asked.

"The Gnomon fear being caught in a loop," said Iyl Rayn. "They were unduly disturbed by your cat-with-no-beginning-or-end, and by the time stub in which Tom Krause found himself."

"Tom?" Tucker heard himself say.

"What is a time stub?" Lia asked.

"Tom Krause returned to a Hopewell in which neither of you ever existed. In fact, his continued existence in that time stub is uncertain."

Tucker recalled his visit to Hopewell when Red Grauber and Henry Hall had claimed to have never heard of the Krauses. Had that been a time stub too?

"How is that possible?" he asked.

"This is precisely what concerns the Gnomon. They fear that which they do not understand. It may be that we live many lives, that we each contain within us multitudes. And if each tic and quaver of the timestream creates a new reality, what of it? Consider the lepidopteran as it moves through the stages of its short life: ovum, larva, pupa, imago. Egg, caterpillar, chrysalis, butterfly. Ovum, larva, pupa, imago . . . over and over again, for millennia upon millennia. Is each turn of the wheel unique and special? To the butterfly, perhaps. The universe remains indifferent.

"The Boggsians, for example, are content to relive their lives again and again. They have retreated into the past. They work their farms, raise their children, and live their lives as they always have. They have created their own time stub. That choice is available to you as well. So long as this disko remains functional, the past remains open to you."

"I can think of places I would prefer not to revisit," Lia said.

"Me too," Tucker said. He thought for a moment, then asked, "What happened to Dad? I mean—"

"You mean the man who loved you and raised you as his son," Iyl Rayn said.

Tucker swallowed, surprised to feel his eyes well with tears.

"He did love you," said Iyl Rayn, "He lost his way; but never doubt that he loved you."

"He tried to kill me."

"Had it come to that, he could not have brought himself to do so. Master Gheen would have wielded the blade, as he did with your friend Tom."

"But what happened to him?"

"Adrian was visited by a Timesweep in his prison cell in Hopewell. He was transported to Romelas, at the time of the Yar Rebellion, where he ended his days preaching the word of Christ, as he set out to do as a young man."

"It's true," Lia said. "I saw him there, in a church. A Christian church. He recognized me."

"But Romelas is gone," Tucker said. "Are there any Christians left at all?"

"The world is large — I am sure there are some, possibly the descendants of those whom Adrian reached with his message. What about you?"

"I don't know what I am anymore," Tucker said.

"You have time to think about it." Iyl Rayn's indistinct features swam, then coalesced into a smile, and for the first time, Tucker saw in her his mother's face.

"Will you stay here with us?" he asked.

"For a while, although eventually, without the support of the Cluster, I will dissipate."

"The Cluster?"

"That is what we Klaatu call our society."

"So the Klaatu are gone? Except you?"

"The Cluster is moving on."

"Does that make you afraid?"

"I have lived a very long time, and I am more curious than afraid. Will I persevere, or become bits of energy scattered across the universe? I may one day discover the answer, or all may go to black. But before I go, there is one last task I must ask you to perform."

59 PURE GIRLS

ROMELAS, *ca.* 2800 CE

TUCKER LANDED LIGHTLY ATOP THE FRUSTUM. IT WAS dark and cool, with no moon in the sky. The zocalo was empty. Tucker made his way quickly down the side of the pyramid. He stood at the base for a few moments and looked around. He was dressed as a Lah Sept acolyte, in a loosely woven, colorless robe, and rope sandals. There was no reason for anyone to notice him — just another shadow in the night.

In his mind, he again reviewed the map that Lia had drawn for him. Her crude sketches became real as he strolled around the perimeter of the zocalo: the convent of the Yars, the temple of the priests, the colonnade. He slowed as he approached the Palace of the Pure Girls and glanced around again to make sure he was not being observed. No one was watching. He approached the front gate. He reached through the bars of the portcullis and rapped on the door. Time passed; there was no response. He rapped harder. A minute later, the door opened a crack.

"What is it?" A woman's voice, in the language of the Lah Sept.

"The Pure Girl Emma," said Tucker in the same language. "She is required."

"By whom?"

"Master Gheen."

The woman made a sputtering sound with her lips and closed the door.

Tucker waited nervously. A few minutes later, the door opened. A thin dour-faced woman stepped out and unlocked the portcullis. Behind her stood a sleepy-looking red-haired girl, perhaps four years old, clutching a doll made of cloth. The woman unlocked the portcullis, muttering a complaint that Tucker could not understand—Lia had taught him only a few words in her native language. She swung the gate open just far enough to push the girl through. She took the doll from the girl as she did so.

"Pepe!" the girl whined, grabbing for the doll. The woman held the doll out of reach and closed the gate. Tucker took the girl by the hand. She looked at him with wide eyes.

"It's okay," Tucker said as he led her away from the palace and across the zocalo to the pyramid.

"Where are we going?" the girl asked.

"I'm taking you home," he said.

"Who are you?"

Tucker knelt down and looked into the girl's blue-green eyes. *She will remember nothing of this,* he told himself. His heart filled his chest. He could feel tears welling in his eyes. He looked away. He did not want to frighten her.

"My name is Tucker," he said. He lifted her in his arms and carried her up the steps of the pyramid.

At dawn, as the sun touched the top of the pyramid, the citizens of Romelas began to wander onto the zocalo, buying bread and other foodstuffs from the numerous vendors. The smell of roasting garlic, peppers, corn, and meat drifted up the sides of the pyramid.

The disko known as Heid flickered to life, taking on a faint greenish hue. A moment later it flared bright green and expelled a small figure. A pale, red-haired girl wearing a light silver shift dropped to the frustum. She fell to her hands and knees with a cry, then climbed to her feet and looked around. She was alone. She walked uncertainly to the edge of the frustum and looked down upon a large plaza. She knew, somehow, that the plaza was called the zocalo. People were moving around below. They looked tiny. There were several carts, some mounded with what looked like piles of fruit, others were emitting swirls of smoke. People were visiting the carts and putting things in their mouths. Eating. The light breeze shifted, and she smelled something delicious. The girl felt a twinge in her belly that she recognized as hunger. She climbed down onto the next tier, and the next, until she reached the bottom.

Following her nose, she was drawn to a brightly painted two-wheeled cart that was giving off a particularly nice smell. A woman with dark sun-dried skin stood beside it, tending to a smoking metal box. Several brown twisted things hung from strings along the side of the cart. The girl recognized them as fish. Smoked fish. She knew the words for things when she saw them, but she could not remember ever having seen them before.

The woman noticed her and smiled. She was missing a tooth, but it was a friendly smile.

"Hello, little one."

Looking at the string of fish, the girl said, "Hello." It was the first word she could remember ever having spoken aloud.

"And who might you be?"

The girl shook her head. She still did not know her name. She pointed at one of the fish, the smallest one.

"Are you hungry?" the woman asked.

The girl nodded.

The fish vendor, whose name was Pilar, considered the small child standing before her. The girl could not have lived even a hand of summers, and with that red hair and pale skin . . . Pilar looked toward the Palace of the Pure Girls.

"I think you are lost, little one," she said. Clearly, this was a Pure Girl who had wandered off. Pilar had no love for the priests and their ways. It occurred to her, briefly, that she might give the girl a bit of smoked fish. It was good fish. But the Pure Girls, she knew, were forbidden from eating flesh. If she were seen feeding the child fish, things would not go well for either of them. On the other hand, if she were to return the girl to the palace, there might even be some small reward in it for her.

"What is your name?"

"I do not know," said the girl.

"You don't know your own name?"

The girl shook her head.

Pilar frowned. Perhaps the girl had hit her head, or been otherwise injured. In any case, it was none of her concern. She squatted down next to the girl and pointed across the zocalo toward the Palace of the Pure Girls.

"Do you see that lovely building? The one with the orange trees in front?"

"I like oranges," said the girl, though she could not remember ever having eaten one.

"That is where you live. I will take you there."

The girl took a step back. "I'm afraid," she said.

The fish vendor smiled. "There is no need. Come. They will feed you persimmons and dates, and you will be adored." She took the girl's small hand and walked her across the plaza. They entered the shade of the orangery, and approached the palace gate. Pilar rang the brass bell attached to the portcullis. A few seconds later, the door behind the gate opened and a Sister looked out. Her eyes landed on the girl and she let out a startled exclamation.

"Lah Emma!"

"I found her wandering on the zocalo," said Pilar.

The Sister darted her a suspicious look.

Pilar spread her hands. "I brought her here immediately," she said.

"It is well that you did," said the Sister. She opened the gate and pulled the girl through.

"I had hoped for some small emolument," Pilar said, irritated to boldness by the Sister's haughty manner.

"Emolument? You will not be whipped. That is emolument enough."

Pilar bristled at the suggestion that she should be punished for doing nothing wrong, but she knew to hold her tongue. The Sister's threat was not empty. Others had been punished for less.

The Sister backed into the palace, dragging the girl with her. As the door closed, Pilar heard the girl's tiny voice say, "My name is Emma?"

HOPEWELL, 1982 CE

Tucker looked out over downtown Hopewell from the roof of the old hotel. Standing beside him, holding his hand, was the girl who would one day become his mother.

"What is this place?" the girl asked.

"Your new home," Tucker told her.

"Is it nice?"

"It is very nice." Tucker smiled sadly. "You will have many friends. You will meet a man named Kosh, and you will have a son named Tucker."

"Tucker?" She looked up at him. "But that is your name!"

Tucker laughed. "I guess it is."

"I like it," said the girl.

Tucker took the girl down through the hotel, jimmied a window at the back, and helped her climb out. He led her around to the side of the building where there were several large, overgrown lilac bushes.

"I'm going to leave you here for a bit while I go back inside," he said. "Can you wait right here?"

The girl looked frightened. Tucker knelt down before her and took both her hands in his. "Please don't be afraid."

The girl's eyes were filling with tears. "I can't help it."

Tucker wiped his own eyes with the back of his hand. He wished he could take her with him back to Harmony, to the Terminus.

"Very soon, a nice man will come and take you home with him," he said in a choked voice. "His name is Hamm."

"I want to go back," the girl said.

"Perhaps one day you will."

A minute later, Tucker was back on the roof, looking down over the parapet at the red-haired girl sitting behind the lilac bushes. He could hear her faint sobbing. He felt horrible. Looking toward the street, he saw Hamm Ryan come out of Janky's barbershop. Hamm crossed the street to where his pickup truck was parked. As Hamm opened the truck door, he looked toward the hotel with a puzzled expression. He walked over and peered though the lilacs.

Tucker waited until Hamm had led the girl back to his truck and helped her inside. He watched them drive off, then he crossed the pebbled roof to the disko. He was about to enter it when he noticed a small gray cat sitting on the parapet, staring at him.

"Hello," he said.

The cat said, "Mreep?"

60 THE ROPE

The cottonwood arched over Hardy Lake, its rough gray trunk rising forty feet before the first great limb branched out over the waters. Tom Krause, lying on his back on the narrow beach, thought, *That tree must be two hundred years old, maybe older. It might have been growing before the first European settlers arrived in Hopewell. It must be the biggest tree in the county. Maybe in the state.*

Tom imagined himself climbing out that long branch and looking down on himself. The thought brought a tingle of fear and excitement. How high was it? Eighty, a hundred feet? He blinked, and for a moment he saw a dark, sinuous line trailing down from the branch, like a long rope. He blinked again and it was gone.

Clearly, there was nothing there . . . but he had seen something. He stared hard at the branch, wondering what he had seen. He closed his eyes and opened them. Nothing. He tried looking away from the branch, then back, and there . . . no, it was gone. If he looked off to the side, just far enough so that the branch was at the very edge of his vision, he could see something hanging. A rope. It definitely looked like a rope. But as soon as he tried to look straight at it, the rope was gone.

It was the same with his family. Lately, the more he looked at them, the less real they seemed. And it was the same for them. Some days they didn't recognize him at all. Every morning when he woke up, Will asked him the same question: "Who are you?"

When his teachers had started referring to him as "the new boy," he had stopped going to school. Nobody noticed him missing. He felt the world receding, rejecting him, turning him into a wraith.

I do not belong here.

He spent as much time as he could at Hardy Lake, where he sometimes remembered things he had forgotten. It was warmer now that spring had arrived, but the memories came less often.

Despite the fact that he could not look at it directly, the rope *felt* real. More real than home, than his family. Maybe it *was* real, like a different reality in a different universe that was almost exactly the same as this one, only with a rope hanging from that branch. Like maybe another version of Tom Krause had climbed up a different version of that cottonwood and made a rope swing.

A rope swing! Now *that* was an idea. A giant rope swing. He could swing from the top of the bank out over the water and dive right in. All he needed was a rope.

Tom imagined himself inching his way out that branch, dragging behind him a hundred feet of rope. His stomach swam; he didn't think he could do it.

Tom let his mind drift into a fantasy he'd had ever since he could remember. A friend who lived just down the road. A kid who wasn't afraid to try stuff. Somebody he could ride bikes with, and explore the river caves. A kid who would recognize him, and remember his name.

Once again, Tom let his focus drift off to the side. The rope reappeared.

It would be really great to have a friend like that. A friend crazy enough to climb out along that branch and tie a rope to it.

A green flash caught his eye. He sat up and looked out over the lake just as something bright pink popped into existence, dropped into the water, and disappeared beneath the surface. Tom stood up and walked to the water's edge. A bird? Something falling from a passing plane? A meteorite?

Half a minute later, a few yards from shore, the water heaved and bubbled. The pink thing broke the surface and crawled up onto the beach. It looked like a fat, pink, smooth-skinned caterpillar the size of a hog.

Tom stood rooted to the spot. The thing stopped about ten feet away and seemed to be looking at him, although it had no eyes.

Okay, Tom thought, *now I know I'm insane. This can't be real.* He wondered why he wasn't afraid.

A small opening appeared at the thing's front end, like a mouth. The mouth slowly expanded until it was about a yard across, but instead of a hole, it was a flat, gray, perfectly circular panel. Tom had seen such a disk before, but where? He searched his memories, and a name appeared.

Tucker Feye.

He hadn't thought about Tucker Feye in a very long time. Suddenly, he remembered the rope swing, remembered Tucker tying the rope, and jumping into the lake. How could he have forgotten? He looked up at the tree. There was no rope swing. He remembered that bizarre night in Hopewell, the Hopewell of the past, when he had last seen Tucker. And before that, the futuristic hospital, where he had been sent through a disk that looked exactly like this.

The pink thing was not moving. The disk pulsed and swam. Tom took a step toward it. The pink thing quivered, as if in anticipation. Tom thought about turning his back on it and walking home. Would there be a place for him at the table? Would his mother recognize him? Would Will?

He took another step toward the disk. If none of this was real, what did it matter?

He could feel the disk tugging at him, urging him forward.

Why not? he thought.

61 IN THE BEGINNING

ADRIAN FEYE STOOD BESIDE HIS WIFE'S BED, GAZING IN awe at the miracle she held in her arms. A new soul had come into the world. If ever he needed proof of God's existence, he would always have this moment.

His wife had given birth to a boy.

Emily, smiling dazedly, cradled the newborn.

"Isn't he beautiful?" she said.

"He is," Adrian agreed. "We will christen him Matthew."

"Matthew?" Emily looked puzzled. "But his name is Tucker!"

"Tucker? What sort of name is that?"

"It is *his* name. I've told you many times that I wanted a son named Tucker."

"You have?" Adrian loved his wife, despite all, but he did not always listen when she talked. "I was thinking of something more . . . biblical."

"His name is *Tucker*," Emily said.

Neither of them spoke for several seconds, then Adrian nodded.

"I suppose it is nothing to do with me," he said.

"He is your son, if you will have him," Emily said. "Would you like to hold him?"

Adrian lifted the child and held him, clumsily. The boy began to cry. Adrian rocked him back and forth, but the child would not be comforted.

"He seems rather small," he said.

"Five pounds eight ounces," Emily said with a defensive note in her voice. "The doctor said that was perfectly normal."

"The low end of normal, perhaps." Adrian handed the squalling infant back to its mother. "He will be the first child baptized in my new church," he said.

62 IN THE END

THE TERMINUS

"HEY, TUCKER!"

Tucker looked up from the fence post he was setting. Tom Krause, who had been digging another hole a few yards away, was holding up what looked like a green plastic bottle. They had been finding a lot of odd bits of trash, mostly plastic and glass.

"I think it's a Mountain Dew bottle," Tom said.

"Anything left?"

Tom shook the bottle and peered through the clouded plastic. "Nope. How old do you think it is?"

"About as old as we are," Tucker said. "Who knows? You might've drunk out of it. Eight thousand years ago."

Tom laughed and tossed the bottle back into the hole. "Maybe in another eight thousand years somebody else will dig it up." He measured off three paces along the edge of the field and started on another hole.

He's doing better, Tucker thought. Physically, Tom was still only fourteen, but the past few weeks in Harmony had been good for him. When Tom had first arrived, Tucker had feared for his friend's sanity. Tom had kept asking him about the rope swing. Tucker assured Tom that the rope swing had been real.

"How do I know *you're* real?" Tom asked.

Iyl Rayn told them Tom was suffering from the after-effects of being caught in a time stub. Emelyn agreed. "He is also grieving for his lost family, but he will recover. Keep him busy; it will help."

It seemed to be working. There was plenty to do on the farm: planting, weeding, harvesting, cooking, cleaning. . . . The list was endless. Tom had grown up on a farm and knew more about it than all the rest of them put together. He had been the one to suggest building the fence around the cornfield to keep the wild hogs out.

Lia, to Tucker's surprise, had befriended the horse, Clyde. She was the only one who could ride him and the only one he would permit to harness him to a plow.

Emma had embraced most of the household tasks; she preferred working indoors. She and Kosh had grown closer than ever. Kosh was teaching her to cook. Privately, Tucker thought she was better at it. In his spare time, Kosh had made several trips to the ruins of Romelas to collect scrap metal. He said he was going to build a motorcycle from scratch.

Severs had arrived through the disko a few days after Tom. She came well equipped with Medicant devices and supplies.

Her arrival was perfectly timed. Only hours before, Tucker had nearly cut off his foot while splitting firewood.

"I grew weary of living with the shadow of Mayo's destruction looming over me," she told Tucker as she cleaned his wound. "I much prefer an unknown future."

"How did you find your way here?" Tucker asked.

"I am not certain. I entered the disko in the hospital and found myself here. I expect the Klaatu had something to do with it. Hold still." She applied a thin bead of adhesive to the cut on Tucker's ankle. "I recommend that you not injure yourself in the future. My supplies are limited."

After Severs had finished treating his wound, Tucker limped out to the barn to speak with Iyl Rayn.

"Severs is correct," said Iyl Rayn. "Your injury required treatment, and I believed Severs was unhappy in Mayo, so I convinced the Gnomon to assist me in bringing her here, as I did earlier with Tom Krause. My agreement with the Gnomon allowed me to interfere in other ways as well. I sent the Boggsian to guide you out of the time stub in Hopewell, and to rescue Kosh after he had been shot. I sent the same Boggsian after you, Kosh, and Emma were injured in the barn explosion. And I was responsible for sending the jaguar—a dangerous move, but it was the only means at hand to prevent you from being killed. There were other times when I used the diskos to alter events . . . not all of which worked as I had hoped. My influence with the Gnomon is waning, however. This disko will very soon be nonfunctional."

"So that's it? It's just us here?"

"You are not alone."

It was true. They had met others. A band of folk known as the Fishers lived along the banks of the wide, slow-flowing river once known as the Mississippi. They traded in sturgeon, carp, mollusks, and jewelry made from polished otoliths. Another group, an extended family of traveling merchants calling themselves the Honest Folk, traveled up and down the rivers on long, brightly colored barges, trading artifacts they excavated from the ruins of ancient cities, and small livestock such as chickens and rabbits. On the endless plains to the west were scattered several small farming settlements, possibly related to the Boggsians. They called themselves the Ya Mish.

Far more numerous than people were the passenger pigeons, their enormous flocks darkening the sky at times. Killing the pigeons was everywhere taboo, though few people remembered why.

Tucker and Tom labored on the fence all afternoon. It was hard work, but Tucker enjoyed it—something about setting a solid post in the earth was immensely satisfying. Tomorrow they would string the posts with wire they had found in one of the barns.

"This fence might keep the pigs out, but not the pigeons," Tom said, wiping his brow with his shirtsleeve.

"That's okay," Tucker said. "Pigeons have to eat, too." He saw Clyde coming up over the rise with Lia's slim figure perched on his back, the Harmony sky vast and blue behind her. Emma had no doubt sent her to call them to supper. Tucker rested the point of his shovel in the earth and cupped his hands over the handle and watched as Clyde's unhurried gait carried her toward him through the rows of bright green corn plants. Evening sunlight reflected from her hair, bleached to the palest imaginable yellow by the long summer days. As she drew closer, he raised a hand. She waved back, and he could see the white of her smile.

EPILOGUE
AFTER ALL

With the departure of the last Boggsians from Harmony, transcendence technology has become unavailable in the regions surrounding the dead city of Romelas. Those who remain behind tend to congregate in family groups, and to eschew technologies beyond that of the lever and the wheel.

Tucker Feye, Kosh Feye, the former Pure Girls Emma and Lia, the Medicant Severs, and Tom Krause remain in the old Boggsian settlement known as Harmony, farming the land and occasionally trading with the Fishers and the Honest Folk.

The Klaatu Iyl Rayn visited Harmony often, until the viewing table that allowed her to communicate with them failed. After that, she was present only as a ghostly, floating presence. On the day Tucker and Lia's first child was born, Iyl Rayn faded to a wisp of fog, and since that day she has not been seen.

I live out my quiet days in my sister Awn's cabin a few miles to the west. I visit Harmony from time to time, but most of my days are spent writing these histories. It is a good life, and I would have no other.

— E³ (EMELYN)

From the *La Crosse Courier Herald,* November 30, 2012:

Endangered Cat Killed by Deer Hunter North of La Crosse

A La Crosse–area deer hunter received an unusual surprise last Saturday.

"I was hunkered down in my tree stand over by Van Loon Lake," said Greg Rondecker, age 24. "Not much deer action, so I was thinking about hanging it up for the day. Then I hear something. It's moving fast, so the second it comes into view I shoot. Thought I'd bagged myself a spotted deer. Only it turns out it's this big pussycat."

The "big pussycat," according to State Zoologist Harding Kremer, was a full-grown male jaguar, a species known in the United States only from southern Arizona.

"No one has ever seen a jaguar this far north," Kremer said. "I can only guess that it escaped from some private zoo."

Jaguars are protected in the United States under the Endangered Species Act. They are the largest native American cat, and can weigh up to 350 pounds.

Law enforcement officials have said they will not press charges against Rondecker. Robert Wilcox, an officer with the Wisconsin DNR, said that the 280-pound cat had "no business here in Wisconsin." He went on to say that the jaguar might have posed a significant threat to public safety.

"Probably just as well he shot it," Wilcox said. "I'd hate to see what a cat that size could do to a man."